Black Inferno

BY KIM LUKE

BOOK II OF A SERIES

CIRCLE OF SUN

BLACK INFERNO

For information:
kimjluke59@gmail.com or kimlukeauthor.com

Published April 2015 by Kim Luke
ISBN-13:
978-1508936237

ISBN-10:
1508936234

To Keli, Nicholas and Mikaela: Being your mother has been my life's joy, my greatest contribution to the world. From you I receive an endless ocean of inspiration and passion. You three have always been my reason to persevere, overcome and thrive.

To my parents Jerry and Judy: The life lessons learned from your examples of faith and family created a sturdy bedrock to build a beautiful life. In my world every flower blooms from these roots.

Other Books by Kim Luke:

Circle of Sun

Prologue

Quinn can't sleep. She takes in the view of the rolling Missouri hills from her window at Royce Estate. At first glance she could be any woman, but Quinn Clarke Royce is no ordinary woman, not any more.

Since discovering her family and being chosen as the new Polaris to the Circle of Sun, there is little remaining of her former life. Quinn and those she loves navigate in a new world as Guardians. The lack of sleep is a fraction of the price she will pay while growing into a leadership role that defies reality. Few days remain before the announcement of the Quest. A selected Guardian must accept before knowing any details about the Quest, and only Quinn knows a Quest can take them to a place untouched by the passage of time.

Her past days of collecting and selling books, merchandizing and marketing, are replaced by a crash course in the angelic realms. She's learned the various ranks of Guardians, Sleepers, Pathfinders and Knights and the existence of Living Stones and how they are used to measure the balance of goodness. Like opening the cover of a book and reading a fantastic tale of the battle between light and dark, her journey now spans the ages.

Quinn's homeland, identified in the angelic realm as Nadellawick is peaceful this night, but only a short time ago the battle raged, destroying the evil Petulah and her River People. The victory over the darkness and recovery of a missing Fidesorb in Nadellawick was celebrated by everyone except one. A storm brews and bubbles and a thick fog moves in from the river.

Chapter One

White Oak, Missouri
Present Day

There is nothing good about a bad dream, except waking up. His new reality is a walking nightmare. The initial shock faded but his hopelessness remains. The emptiness is constant, his existence black like this moonless night.

The windshield wipers cannot compete with the driving storm. Wheels careen around a sharp curve high on the bluff. The lost soul pushes harder on the accelerator, inching closer to the white line. Air fills his lungs as he inhales for the last time. A loud and deafening crack of lightening jolts the senses of this broken man and illuminates the road and a figure before him. Thud! A sudden impact thrusts the car into a spin, ripping a path into the opposite ditch. He lies motionless, sprawled across the seat. Regardless of his intent, consciousness returns in fuzzy lined scenes. The engine is dead, but he is not. Headlights show nothing but pellets of rain cutting through the darkness. For a moment he forgets the incident that put him there. Nothing happens when he turns the key. The driver side door can't be opened so he slides to the passenger side for exit. With the vehicle at a steep angle, the weight of the door flies open and dumps him into the saturated roadside.

Attempts to stand are thwarted by the relentless wind. Not wearing boots his shoes fill with water as he sloshes through the tall grasses. Relieved when his feet reach pavement, he scans the perimeter for a victim. The gusts whip drops that sting, making the search difficult. A flickering light between boulders at the bluffs edge captures his attention. Could it be a signal for help? The massive rock is slippery, but his second attempt finds a small foothold to boost himself up. The boulder places him even higher above the dangerous rim. Unsteady against the punishing winds he crouches down. The source of the mysterious flashing illuminates his wide-eyed gaze and nature muffles his terrified gasp. The empty man searches for signs of life amidst the blood and bits of fur. Motionless, he stands as the familiar moves and reveals itself to him. On this night, seconds before his life should have ended, he finds the reason to go on.

Chapter Two

London, England - 1666

The persecution of Catholics is allowed by King Charles II to appease his subjects, even though his wife is Catholic. Popularity is good, he thinks. Loyal subjects vie for influence. Ambitious men understand the advantages of being on his good side. Eldon Fischer, the Lord Mayor of London, befriended the monarch to gain influence and favor, but made little progress again. Frustration follows him the rest of the day.

Annabeth Chatfield keeps time by tapping her foot to the music while awaiting Fischer's arrival. From elsewhere in the house, the melody played by a fledgling musician echoes throughout the grand home of this powerful man. The parlor offers relief from a hot afternoon sun. The lady is no longer worried her sugary confections might melt. White linen conceals the contents of the delivery basket on her lap. Fair- skinned Annabeth wears a fitted white satin bodice with panned sleeves lined in powder blue and matching petticoat. Some of her blonde tendrils fall from under her hat. From the lobes of her ears hang delicate pearl eardrops and upon her creamy smooth décolleté', she wears a pearl necklace.

Rushing into the room, Fischer asks, "My dear Madame Chatfield if you do not accept my deepest regrets for your wait, whatever shall I do?"

He accepts her extended hand, raising it to his lips. Eldon Fischer is of average height. The copper hair is thinning and lies straggly around his face. White breeches and a short charcoal waistcoat of fine velvet bolster his image of an aristocrat.

"Oh, I am more than pleased to be in your company again, Lord Mayor. The occasional tardiness of a busy man does not offend me," she says.

"With your popularity rising, you might be busier than I." With childlike enthusiasm he claps his hands. "I can't wait any longer."

"Of course!" she says.

A gathered knapsack lies under the linen coverlet.

"Your order included a pound and a quarter," she says. She plucks the cloth knapsack adorned with a pink bow and places it on the table.

"Ah, the toast of London!" he says. A tug releases the package, and all four corners drop, revealing the source of his enthusiasm; dark and light swirls of chocolate fashioned into the shape of clamshells. "Yes, these will do fine," he says. "Tomorrow night, we are hosting Horace Milner and his wife. These treasures will create the finale to an important dinner. A mark of distinction will bolster my reputation when I present something so unique."

Collecting one corner of the knapsack at a time, she begins to wrap them away, but he stops her. The sweets tempt him.

"Just one small edible to sample?" he asks, but changes his mind. "No, I shall refrain for now."

A blush comes to her cheeks and she lowers her eyes. "A simple pleasure," she says.

"Oh, my dear, your little creations have added spice to our stale society. Yesterday your name and these chocolates were mentioned twice on Lombard Street alone. How will you keep up with the demand Madame?"

"The reception pleases me."

"Soon there will be no time for baking, only these. How did the concoction originate?" he asks. Frustration from his day turns to relaxation as he pours hot tea and slips closer to her.

"After father died, the bakery struggled to profit. I remembered his important principle of reaching outside of your circumstance. Perhaps adding a new and different product would be my answer. The finer citizens of London enjoy their cocoa drinks. After observing how the French make chocolate solid, I created my own recipe. Most of my results came through trial and error, my father watching over me."

"Well, I am mesmerized by your story. Your visit is a sweet respite from the remainder of my day. I endured a boring finance meeting with dull people and a few who get under my skin, and now dread my evening duties at the Blackfriar's. Oh, what I wouldn't do to get out of that!" Slumping in his chair, he sighs. He ultimately succumbs to the temptation by selecting and sinking his teeth into a treat, exposing the almond crème center. With his eyes closed he allows the delicacy to melt in his mouth and a smile bends the corner of his lips upward.

"Your finales will be gone before tomorrow evening!" she says.

The Lord Mayor eats the other half of the seashell.

Content, she sips from the cup, allowing him his pleasure.

"Ah, delicious they must be savored. I think I can handle the rest of my day!"

Annabeth puts her hands together in satisfaction.

"Gratitude fills my heart, sir. Why does the remainder of your schedule trouble you? Being in your position would be a fine life."

"Well, one would think so. But our monarch is interested only in his popularity and merry making. So I join in, abandoning any agenda I hoped to advance."

"Remember how we discussed this before, alliances not enemies? When you heed this advice, I predict fewer roadblocks from the monarchy. Perhaps your time spent in court will further your relationship with him."

"The Archbishops of Canterbury and York have great influence with His Majesty. Their causes are carried without questions and requests always honored."

"What issues do you bring to him?" she asks.

"I want him to favor me before I bring any real issues to him. The climate of discord is stormy within the government. Heed the call of neutrality is my motto. Don't rock the boat."

"So you stand for nothing?" Annabeth asks.

"Keeping my position and my head is cause enough."

"Unlike you, I will not underestimate your aptitude for leadership and influence," she says.

The conversation begins to sour the Lord Mayor's disposition again.

Annabeth reacts to his reaching for another confection by swatting his hand.

"Stop your foolishness!"

The politician takes the opportunity to capture her hand, pulling her from her seat and twirling her around the room.

"My wife travels and ours is such a sweet interlude."

The small statured woman breaks free, but he pursues and reaches for her once more, only able to grasp the shoulder of her dress. The sleeve rips from its seams. Stunned at his behavior her anger supersedes her fear.

"What is wrong with you?" Annabeth holds her shoulder, covering her exposed skin.

"I beg your forgiveness, I behave poorly at times."

"Please behave as Bishop Larson, Francis Sandborne and the others, complete gentlemen. Your future behavior from this moment forward remains pure and genuine or you may go back to mixing your chocolate and drinking it!" Annabeth says heatedly. Her petticoat layers rustle as she hurries to the door. "My kind nature is put to the test, Sir! No deliveries unless I am given an apology and a promise of respect and honor. In fact I will require Lady Fischer to join us when I call next time!"

"Oh, don't make me include the dragon!" he whines following her brisk walk towards the door. "I'm afraid I rely on your dose of common sense in my approaches to politics. Do not deny me."

But Annabeth is out the door, his voice to trailing as she departs with her basket and opens the gate.

"Perhaps not," she replies while walking away, "but will expect an increase in endorsements within a few days' time. Good day Sir Eldon Fischer!"

Chapter Three

Attempts at influencing the Lord Mayor are getting tedious for Annabeth. Before reaching Dr. Culpeper's she walks her frustration out and regains her composure. The doctor serves as an apothecary as well, and she chooses her usual herbs and supplies from the rows of jars and hanging botanicals. From behind the counter he crushes a substance with his pestle and offers a kind smile to one of his regular patrons.

"How are you today Miss Chatfield?" he asks.

"Quite well now, most of my day is behind me."

"Didn't you say your niece comes for a visit soon? Perhaps she can help with your growing workload; I know you employ only one kitchen helper."

"You are right. She could be helpful indeed." Annabeth studies her list, paying little attention to him.

The doctor notices the shredded edges of her torn sleeve.

"What on earth has happened, Miss Chatfield?"

"Eldon Fischer behaved foolishly."

"The Lord Mayor? I thought him a fine gentleman."

"A gentleman he is not," she says, plucking and examining a box from the shelf. With little regard for his concern, she places the items in her satchel.

"Are you hurt? A woman must take care conducting business throughout the city unescorted. Maybe when your niece is here she could go along with you," he suggests.

Distracted, she stands motionless, her eyes fixed ahead. After a moment she offers a stone-faced reply.

"Nothing shall I fear."

Dr. Culpeper scratches his head during the awkward exchange. The lack of emotion and odd response are puzzling. Without so much as a nod, she leaves the shop.

The streets of London are bustling and Miss Chatfield navigates her way past many shops and vendors on her way to Pudding Lane. She checks her mental list of tasks yet to complete for the day. A young woman approaches her.

"Excuse me madam, Miss Butters is me name. Would ya' be the proprietor of the Bake House? I beg ya' to forgive me forward nature. Nothin' will come of my dreamin', everyone in the bleedin' royal staff told me so. The senior cook knows all about your sweets and my suggestion to make them for his majesty. Would ya teach it to me? I don't wanna be an apprentice forever, ya' know?"

Miss Chatfield refrains from spouting the first thoughts that come to her mind. The eager apprentice stops for a breath, and Annabeth manages to squeeze in her response.

"Your request is granted. I plan to start straightaway. Mattie prepared everything for the next batch. The honor would be all mine if the King were to endorse me."

With her head held high, she walks down Pudding Lane and raises her white glove, bidding her to follow.

The bakeshop is empty, except for the assistant. Without the courtesy of an introduction she is handed the satchel of supplies to put away.

"How Londoner's love their cocoa! I developed a way to make England's best loved indulgence solid, and I may be the first in England to do so. The cocoa beans must be ground to a fine powder like this. The finer the grind, the smoother the finished product. Butter is added to form a paste, and heavy cream and sugar."

After the mixture is poured in a caldron, Annabeth stirs with care. From the back room a commotion ensues. Annabeth eyes the curtain concealing the back room. She glances at Miss Butters, then disappears behind the curtain. Believing the batch may burn, Miss Butters takes to stirring when she's interrupted by the sound of falling crates and a disturbing shriek. Riveted by the drama, she leans to hear more. A final clashing of bake tins and thumps jolts Miss Butters. The scolding comes next, and she's thankful it's for someone else. Miss Chatfield's voice is stinging, but she hears nothing from Mattie.

"Fine with me! Show yourself out the back door… but return before sunrise tomorrow." Miss Chatfield emerges with a forced smile, shaking her head in disapproval. "Mattie belongs on a farm, not in a kitchen, clumsy girl!"

The sight of the young lady stirring her chocolate elicits an objection.

"Kindly move away from the pot!" Annabeth snaps. The wooden spoon is snatched from the surprised apprentice and Annabeth stirs with enough force to splash some of the contents on the fire. The flames rise in response. The frightened young lady steps backward.

"What happened? Lordy, I was only tryin' to help ya'!" she explains.

The chocolate maker calms herself and slows her stirring.

"My apologies, Miss Butters, I am quite private about who may assist."

"Are ya' worried folks will steal your recipe?"

"Heavens no! But I do consider the mastery of making the confections an art. Not everyone will be able to produce them." Annabeth checks her skirt. "Looks like I've been sloppy," she says. A clean apron hangs from a hook and she ties it on. "Never mind, Mattie. A simple spider sent her running for cover. Sometimes she is of no assistance at all!" Annabeth takes the cauldron to the counter of readied clamshells. "Please fetch the bowl of small stones by the oven."

"Stones, what in creation are they for?"

"You will learn, soon enough."

With Miss Chatfield occupied, Miss Butters lingers near the curtain, curious about the commotion causing Mattie to leave for the day. But she ignores her curiosity and fetches the bowl.

"Here you are ma'am."

Miss Butters is mesmerized, shaking her head in amazement as the stones are buttered and placed inside each mold.

"Lordy, what are ya doin'?"

"This is the secret," she says. Annabeth pours a thin stream of the liquid and fills the shells then leaves them to harden while mixing a honey almond crème.

"I like secrets," Miss Butters says.

"Secrets are to be kept, not shared," Annabeth says with the last stir of the crème.

The point of a knife is used to loosen and remove the stones, leaving a small well in each shell. Every well is filled with the white colored crème, before shell top is placed and they are pressed together.

"The crème mixture is the gooey bind sealing the confections. They will become more firm but can be sampled now. Would you like to sample one?" With tongs she selects one to offer her.

"I don't 'ave money, Miss Chatfield."

"Please take it and enjoy."

The entire piece goes in her mouth. When she can make words audible through the sticky sweet chocolate she says with enthusiasm. "Blimey! Oh me goodness! This is sinful!" Her response makes Annabeth smile.

"There you go, your confection making lesson is concluded."

Other shoppers arrive at the bake house.

"Mercy, I'll take all me knowledge back to ol' Mrs. Henry. There is a promotion in me future! Thank ya', Madame!"

Annabeth greets the new patrons as Miss Butters leaves.

"Welcome to Chatfield's Bake House, how may I assist you?"

The young apprentice sits on the bench under the shop awning to make a few mental notes. Using her fingers she references each step in the chocolate making process. A preoccupied and unaware Miss Butters does not notice how an early evening shower washes the streets clean, as well as the fresh blood from the soles of her shoes.

Chapter Four

Surrounded by stacks of files, paper coffee cups, his laptop and a half-eaten breakfast sandwich, Ace Kennedy answers the ringing desk phone.

"Kennedy."

"Why aren't you answering your cell?" asks a voice on the other end of the line.

"Good morning to you too, Tracie," he says.

Kennedy's coworker rolls his eyes.

"We're friends, right?" Tracie Glenn asks.

"Sure, we're friends. Hey, I'm pretty tied up. What can I do for you today?" he asks.

"Will you be my escort next week to the Sheena McNeil concert at Kaufmann?"

"Well, I am covering the symphony event for the paper. But we can go together, sure," he says. Ace grimaces toward his coworker Craig.

"Good. You'll be connected to the right people soon enough," she says.

"I appreciate it... I guess."

"Are you kidding? In journalism or any other field, it's who you know!"

"Right," Ace says, only half listening.

"Now, what are you doing for lunch? My week is demanding and I am ready for a good stiff drink. Meet me at the Plaza?"

"Sorry Tracie, some documents with my late uncle's estate need signatures, so I'm driving to White Oak."

"Well, a drive in the country sounds delightful."

"I'm surprised your office can afford your absence," Ace says.

"They will contact me a dozen times, I'm sure. Text when you leave and I will be down in front of my building." She hangs up, not giving him a chance to object to her plans.

Craig shakes his head.

"A friend, or a leech?" he asks.

"A leech, but a powerful leech. She wants a friend with influence in the media."

"Did she notice your recent bylines for the St. Vincent's Chili Cook-off couldn't be found on the front page?" Craig asks, and snickers at his own gibe.

Ace throws his empty paper cup at him.

"They will be putting me in the mix soon," he says.

"That's precisely what she is waiting for! After her epic fumble she needs good press. Like a piranha, she went after that innocent young couple, hoping to showcase her skills. Instead, the charges are dropped and her reputation damaged. You could be the source of the good press. That's my hunch," he says.

"I'm well aware of what happened. I followed the whole story before I moved down here. But regardless of how much squeeze she puts on me trying to get to the Governor's mansion, I stand by my ethics. I plan to use the relationship to get what I need. A woman with her passion for power steps on plenty of people along the way, and I own a ringside seat."

A chic Tracie Glenn in dark glasses and scarf waits for Ace. She drops her half smoked cigarette, smothering it under the toe of her designer pumps when the old beat up Mustang convertible comes to the curb. She tosses her purse in the back seat and hops in. After twenty minutes of traffic the Mustang carries them to the Missouri countryside where her wind-whipped scarf dances and twirls behind her. The sun can't burn through the thick morning fog. The light blue Mustang is invisible, concealed within the dense haze of a valley as they travel along the Little Blue River.

"You are quiet this morning, Tracie."

"Am I?"

"By now you are grilling me about everything I know," Ace says.

"Is that how you think of me, Ace?"

"Yup!"

She winks over her lowered sunglasses.

"Well, you are right," she says. Tracie removes her sunglasses and uses the end to point at the horizon. "That tower on the ridge, rising above the fog line is the estate of the Royce estate. I can't figure them out. They guard their privacy like most well-to-do people, but they don't even run with their own kind."

"Still trying to get him to like you?" Ace teases her.

"Someday I will win them over. What I could do with Royce support! No matter what kind of digging, I'm not able to find out where their wealth comes from. But who cares? The endorsement alone is huge. It makes no difference how weird they are."

The sun is all but lost now in the heavy mist. The old Mustang engine stutters as they pass the estate. Tracie notices the concern on Ace's face. The classic car rolls to a standstill on a bridge spanning the Little Blue River. Ace turns the key to restart the engine. The car sputters and when it doesn't start after a couple of attempts, he thumps the steering wheel hard with his palms.

"Great!" he says with sarcasm as he leaves the car and opens the hood. Tracie joins him.

"What's the problem?" she asks.

"The Mustang is old, that's the problem."

"I'll call a tow." She walks to the end of the bridge, cell phone to her ear. "No signal!" she raises her phone in protest.

"Wait, I'm connected," he yells out to her.

Tracie explores the banks of the murky river. Dense fog prevents her from seeing Ace or the car any longer. The soupy air is suffocating, and she inhales without thought. She finds the sound of the moving water peaceful and spies a rock for sitting while waiting for the tow. Attempting to brush the surface clean, she draws her hands away instantly.

"Ouch! Ace, come down here. This rock is hot I burned my hand! Look at this thing!"

She crouches down at the water's edge and soothes her fingers in the cool water. Movement on the opposite side of the river grabs her attention and she strains for clarity in the gloomy mist. A blurred figure walks along the shoreline. She reaches to raise her sunglasses, but finds them already on her head. Then a jolt sends her toppling over. Her glasses fly into the water. They float and bob away in the swift flowing river.

"What the hell? Excuse me!" she says.

The man does not respond; he keeps walking. Within moments the figures fade into the fog. After searching the shoreline, she climbs back to the bridge.

"People walking! One ran right into me! He never said a word."

"Are you ok?" Ace asks.

"Well I did burn my fingers on a rock, but… they don't hurt… anymore."

"Burned? What are you talking about?" he asks.

"Follow me, this is bizarre." She leads him down from the bridge to the rock. "Right here it is. I barely touched the surface. It burned me!"

"The rock is not hot, feel for yourself."

Tracie Glenn inches her hand toward the rock's surface.

"I swear my fingers were burned."

"How are they now?" Ace asks.

"Once I put them in the water, the pain evaporated. This man walked along the shoreline over there, another one bowled me over and kept right on walking!"

"Fishermen with poor manners, I'm sure."

Tracie plops down on the rock in frustration.

"Those men wore suits, and were not fisherman! And the rock was flaming hot! I want to know what is going on!"

Crossing his arms, Ace takes a stab at reasoning with her.

"Calm down. Are you suggesting aliens and lava rock?"

An idling truck cuts the conversation short and Ace leaves to meet the tow service.

Tracie stands and shifts her weight from side to side, then waves with drama.

"Sure, go on, leave me and this possibly juicy headline." Realizing she's alone again, she hustles to catch Ace. "Wait, don't leave me here alone."

It takes less than five minutes for a diagnosis. The tow driver tells Ace he's out of gas. After putting a few gallons in the tank for him, the driver makes sure the car starts.

"The gauge is broken, so I am never quite sure," Ace says with a shrug.

Tracie huffs past him on her way to the Mustang.

He hopes the beauty of the surroundings will calm her drama down a few notches.

Chapter Five

The white dogwoods lining Main Street give a formal welcome to those visiting the tiny riverside village of White Oak. Branches of honeysuckle droop over white fences, its scent heady and sweet. German immigrants brought family vines from home, preserving their heritage and spreading the art of wine making. A dozen wineries with acres of vineyards make their home among the rolling hills and valleys along the Missouri River. Tourism bolstered growth in the form of restaurants, coffee shops, bed and breakfasts and unique storefronts filled with local art and old world delicacies.

The restored McCracken House, home to the Chamber of Commerce, sits across the street from Lena's German Bakery. The aromas of baking savory onion pie and buttery strudel fill the morning air for joggers or dog walkers. The post office, City Hall and a refurbished old theater stand next to Marmaduke's European Confections.

The richness of the roasting coffee beans lead many to the door of Mocha Joe's and Fireside Books. Although no visible damage remains after the flooding only a few months earlier, nothing is the same in White Oak. Professor Gunderson Enderlee appears dapper in his bow tie and apron as he serves coffee to his first customers of the day. His blue eyes and kind smile welcome strangers like friends, and his small town charm brings most of them back.

"Glad you stopped in. The name is Enderlee I am the proprietor here. Are you first time visitors to our area?"

Tracie cups her steaming mug and lowers her eyes as the young man answers Professor Enderlee.

"Kennedy. . . Ace Kennedy . . .journalist with the Kansas City Star." He offers his card and the professor reads each line. "I'm in town to handle some paperwork concerning my late Uncle Elliott. My friend joined me for the drive."

Besides his obvious youthfulness, he is the opposite of the narrow-nosed, beady-eyed but inquisitive late Elliott Kennadie. Unkempt wavy red hair frames a rounder face. Professor Enderlee extends his hand. Ace pushes his glasses higher on his nose and accepts the handshake. The professor carefully chooses his words.

"Don't spell your surname like your Uncle, huh?"

"Reads better in a byline," Ace says.

"He did a… fine job for the newspaper here in White Oak," the Professor says.

"Thanks. May I introduce Tracie Glenn, county prosecutor for Jackson County?"

Tracie seems less than pleased with the introduction, and gives a slight smile and quick handshake. The professor senses her impatience and leaves them to their coffee. As soon as the Professor is out of earshot her sarcasm surfaces.

"You fit right in here, Ace. I don't need to meet everyone in this county."

"Aren't you the voice for the people?"

"Funny, Ace! I thought you understood, I'm not the baby kissing kind. Let's get out of here."

Ace holds her arm stopping her from sliding out.

"Wait Tracie, take a breather. Kissing babies and shaking hands is the journey of the politically motivated. Why not take time to smell the roses along the way? Take five and enjoy your coffee. Besides, I hold the keys."

"I got this far kissing as few babies as possible. The most effective way to win is through contributions. I agreed to take a ride in the country with you for mutual gain. What's going on in the city and how can your journalistic skills help me get positive media?"

"Plenty of scandal and tragedy goes down daily," Ace pauses and drinks his coffee. "Sadly, I am not assigned those stories, and you already know more than I do about what is happening in society. I'm covering the symphony event next week, escorted by you. Remember Tracie, if I end up providing you with media exposure it will be through fair and unbiased reporting. I want bylines, but I am not in such a race that I'll cut corners to get them."

Tracie's eyes narrow and she sits back and crosses her arms.

"The Sheena McNeil concert will bring them all out. Millions of dollars are represented at a symphony gathering; precisely why I'll be present. Rubbing shoulders with wealth is my version of kissing babies. And, for the record, our association benefits you more than me." Tracie Glenn nodded at Ace before sipping her coffee.

"Will you be rubbing shoulders with the Royces?" Ace asks.

"Don't make me repeat myself. Romulus Royce declines to support anything to do with my political aspirations. I would like nothing more than to upstage Mr. Royce by quietly adding his circle of influence among my supporters. He'll look foolish for not putting his money on a winning horse."

"Romulus Royce doesn't run with a pack. I'm not sure your vendetta will affect him too much."

"Perhaps not, but when I can count on a majority of support within the arts, his lack of endorsement won't hold as much weight. I don't let the voice of others dictate my future, and I won't start now. I find the whole family quite odd."

"Odd because you can't win them over?"

"And because of the reports of strange lights near the estate last year. The same time as the dead birds and the city water problem. Your uncle covered some of those stories," Tracie said.

"You are adding the hot rock and the fisherman to this file, since their property is nearby?" Ace asked.

"They weren't fisherman. Very unusual experience," she says.

"Yes, like a twilight zone. I am not dismissing what you think you saw, but I don't think the county prosecutor should be repeating it, if she is interested in a career in politics," Ace says.

The five extra minutes are the extent of her patience and she slides out of the booth at Mocha Joe's. Professor Enderlee waves to Ace Kennedy and to the back of Tracie Glenn, who is already out the door.

Professor Enderlee reads a text from Keefe about arriving early to the Royce Estate tomorrow for a gathering of the Circle of Sun. The view from Mocha Joe's is peaceful now. But it wasn't long ago, chaos and pandemonium gulped the town whole. The River people and their Cesar used fear and doubt to gather more undecided into their fold. He shakes his head remembering how close the darkness came to taking his life and the lives of his friends. The meeting tomorrow will provide more answers. Quinn is like a daughter and Circle of Sun is his new family, filling his emptiness. The Professor brings coffee through to Fireside Books for Chamous and Tera.

The newest shipment of merchandise is being unpacked by Chamous, while Tera, with head phones on, is busy at counter. Expressive dark eyes are beautiful, even behind reading glasses, her pencil stuck in her bushy bun of brown hair.

"Good morning!" the professor says.

Chamous greets him, and Tera removes her earbuds, noticing his presence.

"Hello Professor," she says, "I was lost in my music."

An embrace is their standard greeting with him, and today is no different.

"Seeing you two makes my day," he says.

"Do those earbuds work any better?" Chamous asks.

"Yes, thanks for picking them up," Tera says, touching Chamous' arm. "The others were defective. My music sounded…scratchy, Chamous picked me up some new ones."

"Easier than convincing her otherwise," he says. He smiles and winks her direction.

Fireside Books is lit up and ready for business. Colorful flowers stand in vases and roses float inside crystal bowls on dark oak shelving. Windows are opened wide, letting the morning sunshine fill the shop. Delicate lavender Verbena with trailing vines spills over the window box to the sidewalk outside.

Chamous stands with his arms around Tera.

"How are you doing, Professor?" he asks.

"Today is a blue-ribbon day. Brought you both a sample of my new blend I call 'Missouri Morn', what do you think?"

All three sit as the coffee is sampled.

"This rich dark roast is delicious," Chamous says.

Fireside Book's resident feline, Thomasina, curls up next to Tera and purrs.

"Quinn isn't here daily, she misses her."

"Missouri Morn's been served twice today. Ace Kennedy, Elliott's nephew, stopped in for coffee. He's in town on business and brought his friend, Tracie Glenn"

Chamous says, “I suppose she is working on her image after the fiasco last year. Keefe served on a task force with her once, making it clear he dislikes her company. Not the wording he used though.”

“Well … her visit was brief,” the Professor says.

“I hope they at least enjoyed the coffee,” says Tera.

“They didn’t stay long enough for comment,” the professor tells them. “Are you still enjoying the bookstore?”

“Tera loves running it. It was smart putting us here, close to the heart of the community and privy to any rumors about the former community leaders lost in the…bus accident.” Chamous says.

Tera responds, “While touring the devastation…made a plausible…explanation.”

Professor Enderlee crosses his arms and agrees.

“The transition has been easier because of you two. What about your church, Chamous?”

“Yes, we are growing again. The Barn is buzzing with activity daily.”

“That’s first-rate news,” says the professor.

“Polaris to the Circle of Sun, the announcement about our Quinn was shocking. Not sure how she’s adjusting,” Tera says and removes her reading glasses. “What thoughts went through her mind?”

The trio sat for a few moments in silence.

“I witnessed her strength of character after the climbing accident. Quinn’s faith was her rock, as the ashes of her life lay at her feet,” Tera says, shaking her head.

“And along with her new role as Polaris, she found her family, so she has support she never had before,” Chamous says.

“We will offer our support at the Senate meeting tomorrow night. I really miss seeing her every day,” Tera says.

Chapter Six

Sapphire holds the shirt up by the shoulders. The hem waves in the afternoon breeze on the campus green with spring.

"How do you like your new shirt, Pony?" Sapphire asks.

"Hey, UMKC! You've been shopping at the bookstore!" Pony says with delight. "I was wanting one, Sapphire."

"Well, if you're going to be part of the school, you need the right gear. Leave it to the girlfriend to think of that," she says, poking fun at herself.

Pony says, "Let's get you one."

"Done!" Sapphire laughs as she pulls another shirt from the bag. She sits on the grass next to Pony, her chestnut curls catching a gentle wind.

"Thank you for the shirt." Pony leans in and kisses her cheek. He takes a small wrapped gift from his backpack.

"I have something for you too."

"What is this?" Sapphire asks. The small pink bow falls away, then the white paper, all landing in her lap. She lifts a simple silver ring from the box.

"It was my mom's. You are my world and this symbol is your reminder."

Sapphire slips the ring on. It fits her perfectly.

"And you are mine, thank you. I love you Pony."

Another kiss is exchanged.

Sapphire smiles, laughing under her breath. "And you only got a tee shirt!"

"That was thoughtful, Sapphire. I'm reminded why I like you so much."

She frowns and nudges him.

"Hey, you forgot why you like me? Wait, give it back!" Pony chuckles as she grasps for the shirt he holds beyond her reach.

"Ok, but when all the females on this campus see you in the shirt, remember I was the one who gave it to you."

They share a laugh.

"Whatever," he says.

She gathers volumes of curls into a hair tie, while smiling back at him.

"Original, one of the qualities I love about you, Pony."

"Original meant different and growing up, I wanted to be like everyone else."

Sapphire says, "That's understandable, but I am learning differences are a good thing."

"Diversity makes the world colorful, or so I've been told," Pony says.

"I want to be more open to people who are different. Ok… embracing diversity is my new focus. Join me?" she asks.

"Sure, why not?"

Sapphire says, "With this new chapter in our lives, let's try to accept differences, compassion for all souls."

The opportunity to embrace diversity will arrive sooner rather later. The afternoon sun is warm on Sapphire's face. She lies on her back observing the blue skies while Pony studies. Butterflies chase, fluttering in circles, and Sapphire sits to see one land on her shoe. Across the way a group is gathered, a woman in the center signing autographs.

"That is the vocalist Jexis booked to perform with the symphony." She waits until only a few fans remain before approaching her.

"I'd like to introduce myself. My name is Sapphire Royce. Are you Sheena McNeil?"

"Yes, I am," she replies.

"I know about you from my sister Jexis." Sapphire extends her hand.

The petite woman in faded jeans and long white tunic pauses when she hears the name Royce, then her eyes light up and she smiles back. Dark, smooth long hair lies in direct contrast to her ivory skin and delicate features. Wispy lashes surround innocent looking blue eyes. Multiple bracelets jangle when she shakes Sapphire's hand.

"Yes, I'm Sheena, so nice to meet you Sapphire. May I introduce my traveling companions and friends from Romania? This is Finnegan."

The taller of the two is attractive with a flirtatious smile. He wears a simple oxford button-down shirt, slim indigo denim and boots. Strands of hair from a loose ponytail frame his classic features. Stepping forward, he uses two hands when shaking Sapphire's hand. Instead of retreating to his space, he confines himself in hers.

She wishes he would step back, but notices a sweet scent of cedar and tobacco.

Sheena ends the awkwardness.

"This is Albert."

The lettering on Albert's black tee shirt is foreign to her but his denim and boots are similar to Finnegan's. Dark hair stands in a styled wave above his forehead, but trimmed over his ears. The whisker stubble and tired eyes are out of place with this group. Some deep scratches on his throat compete for her attention as she tries her best to avoid staring.

He nods to her.

Could that be some bruising on his left cheek, she wonders.

"Good afternoon," he says.

"I am pleased to meet you, Albert." But Albert offers no response. His gaze becomes fixed beyond her. What is he staring at, she asks herself. Sapphire glances quickly behind her but finds no source for his distraction. His behavior provides a second awkward moment.

"My boyfriend would enjoy meeting you too," says Sapphire.

"Our pleasure," Sheena says.

Sapphire leads them over to Pony. From the corner of her eye she confirms Finnegan's fix on her as they walk.

"This is Sheena McNeil, the vocalist who is performing with the symphony. This is Finnegan and Albert."

"Nice meeting you," Pony says.

Finnegan is only interested in Sapphire. Pony senses her uneasiness and puts his arm around her.

Sheena picks up on it too.

"Our social customs are different than yours and they are new to the English language." Her simple explanation interrupts Finnegan's fixation. She touches his shoulder compassionately and continues. "I will love meeting Jexis. She coordinated my appearance with the symphony. Are you both students at the University?"

Albert walks off mumbling and Sheena glares Finnegan's way; the latter excuses himself and follows Albert.

"Pony is enrolled here. Not sure yet if college is for me," says Sapphire.

"I know it can be a challenge to choose a path at this age," Sheena says as she watches over her two friends.

"I'm looking forward to your performance with the symphony. Your voice is remarkable," says Sapphire.

"Thank you, that is very kind. I'm excited about our show here and seeing the rest of your family. I understand the Kauffman Performing Arts Center is a magnificent piece of Kansas City architecture. Are you aware of my performance at the Missouri Repertory Wednesday evening? I can offer you tickets if you want to come," she says.

"Tickets would be awesome. Is Albert ok?"

Pale faced Albert sits at the base of a tree.

Finnegan leans against the same tree, watching Sapphire.

Albert manages a weak wave in their direction.

"Albert's been… under the weather since we arrived. Finnegan is always too eager," she says.

"Eager?" Pony asks.

"Eager to . . . embrace new cultures and make friends. I am so happy we ran into each other. Two tickets will be reserved under Royce for you at the Rep." Sheena says.

"Thank you," Pony says. He gathers his books.

"Break a leg," Sapphire says.

The trio walks away, heading off campus.

"Weird!" Pony says.

"Was Albert in a fight or just sick? And Finnegan . . . so strange!" Sapphire says.

"He's mesmerized by you."

"Besides their cultural differences, I sensed another difference… not sure. But diversity is colorful … right?"

They share a laugh.

"I'm starving, how about Pizza 51?" he asks.

"Sounds good to me!"

The couple walks to the popular campus eatery, holding hands.

"Pony…is that you?" a voice from behind calls out.

A young woman with an arm full of books hurries to catch up, her small dog trotting beside her.

"I thought so," she says.

She is breathless and pauses for a moment. His expression tells her Pony doesn't remember her.

"Astronomy with Fitzel...we're new study partners....Lucy Toffet?"

"Oh, sorry Lucy! How are you?" a surprised Pony says.

Her dog yanks on the leash, and her books fall out of her arms. Loose papers catch a breeze and cartwheel across the grass.

Pony chases and retrieves them for her. He stoops with her to collect the other dropped items.

Lucy giggles.

"I am such a klutz."

Sapphire pets the happy puppy.

"This one is so cute, what's her name?"

Pony blushes still not recognizing the girl, and forgets to introduce Sapphire. He blunders through the introductions.

"Sorry, this is my girlfriend, Sapphire. Sapphire this is Lucy... Toffet. She is in my astronomy class."

Lucy's full bangs sit above the rim of her large black glasses. Her plaid skirt and white oxford shirt are more like a uniform.

"My dog's name is Lucytoo," she says.

Lucy giggles more.

"Hi Sapphire . . . and, don't forget, we are also study partners Pony!" Lucy says, showing more enthusiasm than Pony would care to see. Her wide smile reveals perfect white teeth surrounded by bright red lips.

"That's right, Fitzel assigned those just today," he says as he nods to Sapphire with emphasis. He feels slight discomfort at Lucy's obvious infatuation.

"I am pleased to meet you, Lucy," Sapphire says with sincerity.

"Was Sheena McNeil on campus? I am a big fan, counting the days till her performance!"

"Yes, just a few minutes ago," Sapphire tells her.

The little dog pulls hard at the leash, ending the conversation. Lucy yells back over her shoulder as she leaves them.

"Well, I guess I'll see you in class, Pony. Nice meeting you, Sapphire."

Both of them wave as Lucy and her loaded arms and rambunctious dog cut across campus.

"Lucytoo, how strange! Who names their pets after themselves?" she asks.

"Diversity is colorful, right?" Pony teases her.

"Didn't tell me about a study partner, now did you Pony?" Sapphire raises her eyebrows, teasing him right back.

"She's part of an assigned study group with four others, so you know," Pony says, putting the encounter in the right light.

Sapphire waves off his concern and puts her arm around his waist as they walk through campus.

They wait for soft drinks and pizza in their favorite booth. A man towards the front of the shop sits at a table reading.

Sapphire says, "I don't think anyone should eat by themselves."

"Some people like eating alone. They can study or mess with their phones, which is what he is doing."

"True, but what if we made his day better by inviting him to share a dinner table with a couple of happy people like us? I'm going to ask him if he wants to join us," Sapphire says.

Before he can object, Sapphire is already sliding out of their booth. Pony hopes embracing diversity isn't going to be like this. Pony checks his phone for messages.

The scream cuts through the restaurant, raising every set of eyes towards Sapphire.

"Call 911, he's bleeding everywhere!" she says. Sapphire frantically reaches for napkins and sends a glass of soda and ice flying everywhere.

"Pony, hurry help us!"

Pony bolts from his seat.

The man pushes Sapphire away.

"Get off me! What's wrong with you?" the man says. He jumps

up with enough force to topple his chair and upset the table.

"The bleeding must be stopped! He needs help!" Sapphire pleads.

Pony grabs her flailing arms and brings them down and holds them.

"What's the matter? What are you doing?" he asks.

The stranger backs away from Sapphire and joins onlookers. With a clenched hand full of napkins Sapphire's eyes lock on Pony's. For an instant she is paralyzed. Her eyes travel to the man and back again to Pony who puts his arms around her.

"Sapphire, what's happening?" he asks.

With every set of eyes on her she quietly responds, "He is bleeding."

All eyes return to the man.

"Keep your crazy girlfriend away from me! She's nuts, man!" he says with as much confusion as she feels.

Sapphire's eyes fill with tears.

Without breaking eye contact with her, Pony announces in a calm voice, "911 won't be needed."

Confusion gives way to embarrassment, and Sapphire runs out of the pizza shop. Pony gathers their things and follows her. When he catches her, she throws her arms around him. Pony drops everything and holds his trembling girlfriend. She buries her face in his chest.

"What happened, Sapphire?" Pony says and lifts her chin.

"When I asked the stranger to join us his face was raw and bleeding! Blood oozed from missing fingers. His injuries were horrific. I can't get the scene out of my mind! What's wrong with everyone?"

"Sapphire, the man was all right, no blood, no injury. I don't know what you saw. But I do know you are the only one who did."

Chapter Seven

Nestled among massive oak trees, Bordeaux's is lit up and ready for business. After the demise of Carolynn and Adam Langford, the restaurant and winery closed down for a while before being purchased by a corporate team that hired locals to run it. Limestone walls surround spacious smooth wood booths and bistro tables covered in crisp white linen cloths. Each glowed with a stout candle, inviting patrons to relax and enjoy their wine tasting or their dining. Tera waits for Chamous to arrive and later Pony and Sapphire. Tera stretches her legs out and listens to music through her new earbuds. Her eyes close and she drifts off. Tera is startled by the server.

"Miss, I am sorry to disturb you," she says. She sets a glass of wine in front of Tera, who gently tugs her earbuds out.

"Please don't apologize; I didn't intend to doze off."

The full bodied Chambourcin is as smooth as the jazz and Tera goes back to her music, savoring both.

A whisper brings her upright again. She glances around expecting the server again. Tera examines the earbuds and listens again. Audible whispering in the music! Again and again she restarts the song to listen and still, the same soft murmuring. She's jotting in her notebook when a hand touches her shoulder and she jumps.

"Hi lovey," Chamous says. He leans in and kisses her.

"You scared me!"

"You're a little jumpy. I may have to cut the evening short and return to the church, its movie night at for the teens at The Barn," he says.

"No problem, I will go with you. What's going on there tonight?"

"Movie night, full house," Chamous says.

Tera says, "Would you listen to this song?" Tera hands Chamous the earbuds.

"Static again? Those the new earbuds I picked up for you?" Chamous asks her.

"Just listen."

Chamous listens, while Tera waits for the song to end.

Chamous removes the earbuds.

"Did you hear anything?" Tera asks.

"Nope, the music sounds perfect. Perhaps an appointment with an audiologist?" he suggests, moving some hair from her face.

Tera would like to tell Chamous she is hearing more than static in the music, but she can't be certain of what she is hearing. It's all so outlandish.

"How was the meeting?" she asks.

"Productive, but I need to head back over there later."

Tera says, "No problem, I'll come and help. I thought Quinn might join us tonight but she's tied up."

"You thought living on the grounds would mean more time together?"

Tera sips her wine.

"I still think it will, but perhaps not until after the Senate meeting tomorrow."

"It gives me more time to spend with you," Chamous says, knowing Tera has missed the time with Quinn.

She lays her head on his shoulder.

"Keefe asked us to be early to the estate to help with preparations," Chamous says. "The suggestion for additional transits may be discussed and, of course, the important announcement of the Quest."

"Quinn's limited time must be difficult on Keefe too," Tera says.

"He is as busy as she is. Romulus aluded to changes coming for some of us. I guess we will find out tomorrow at the meeting."

Chamous and Tera slide out of the booth when they see Sapphire and Pony talking to the server.

Sapphire lingers when she embraces Tera.

"What's wrong Sapphire?" Tera asks.

After Pony and Sapphire are seated, she recounts the bizarre experience with the man at the pizza shop. The recounting of the scene upsets her. Pony hears detail for the first time.

Sapphire says, "I don't understand. It's not like the visions in my dreams. I was terrified, humiliated. Anyone witnessing thought I was crazy."

Pony tries to comfort her by putting his arm around her. The server delivers iced tea for Pony and Sapphire and the Chambourcin for Chamous, along with appetizers.

"I will feel better after I talk to Father."

"It may be like the commission Keefe has. In some instances, Keefe can foresee things to come, and warn or help," Tera says.

"If so, I …did nothing to help him," Sapphire says in a whisper, her green eyes tearing up.

Pony shakes his head, wondering how he can help her.

Tera says, "Sapphire, look at me. We will find out everything we can from your Father. We are all struggling to learn what being part of the Circle of Sun means. I do not pretend to understand the horror you witnessed, but I am sure all of our questions will soon be answered."

Sapphire manages a half smile.

"I'm leaning on that faith, Tera."

Pony squeezes her hand and offers a new subject.

"I am taking an astronomy class I find pretty interesting."

"Yes, Lucy is a study partner." Sapphire says. She's relieved when the subject changes and she can put the unpleasant aside.

Pony clarifies, "We're assigned study groups and Lucy is in my group. We ran into her on campus."

"And don't forget Lucytoo," Sapphire says with a hint of sarcasm.

"Right, she has a little dog," he says rolling his eyes.

"How do you like UMKC, Pony?" Chamous asks.

"It's great! We're going to The Missouri Repertory this week to see Sheena McNeil perform."

Chamous says, "Jexis talked of her talent and bringing her to Kansas City."

Sapphire relaxes her shoulders and samples some of the appetizers.

"By the way, Rita Ordell gave me those books she bought for you when she was abroad I will bring them with me to the bookstore," says Sapphire.

"I'll be anxious to see them. Chamous and I are also going to Sheena's performance this week. We've heard great things about her," Tera says.

Pony tells them, "We met her two travel companions, also from Romania."

"We sure did," Sapphire adds, "Finnegan and Albert, two odd fellows for sure. Albert suffered from jet lag or something. He had scratches and some bruises. And Finnegan was… creepy."

"He almost devoured Sapphire with his eyes," says Pony.

"Yes, he stared, stood too close…just a weird guy. But one should be tolerant with others who are different than ourselves, right, Pony?" says Sapphire.

"Yup, we have a motto: Diversity is… colorful!" Pony says.

Sapphire goes back to picking at her food, her eyes lowered.

"Sapphire, are you sure you are ok?" Tera asks

Sapphire pauses and then takes a deep breath and says, "I think I'm just tired."

Chamous reads a text from his buzzing phone.

"Tera and I have to run over to The Barn to help, but you two stay and finish the appetizer. We can be back here by 8:30 or 9. Sound good?" Chamous asks.

"Sure, no problem. Don't worry about me, Tera," says Sapphire.

"Yeah, great. We are going to take the winery tour so we'll see you later tonight," Pony says.

After Tera and Chamous leave, Pony leads Sapphire to the back of Bordeaux's to catch the last wine tour of the night.

"Sapphire, you got quiet, what's wrong?" Pony asks.

"I can't control the things I am seeing. I'm all right, now that I am away from the dining room. I am ready to have some fun," she says.

"Do you want to talk about it?"

"No, I want to talk to Father. He will help me understand. Aww, we missed it. Tours are over for tonight…maybe next time," Sapphire says.

Pony glances around and lifts the theater rope closing off the stairwell for Sapphire to duck under.

"Time for some adventure," Pony says, guiding his girlfriend and taking a lighted lantern for tours from its hook.

A staircase leads them to Bordeaux's lower level and a drop in temperature. Sapphire puts on sweater she had tied around her shoulders. The lantern illuminates a line of oak barrels resting against the stone wall of the cavern.

"I had no idea this many barrels were here," says Sapphire running her hand over the smooth oak.

"Whoa, those two on the end are huge," Pony says, pointing.

In steel forged cradle racks sat two massive barrels, each nine feet wide and nearly the same in height. A black and white photo above shows a man standing inside one of the barrels and identifying them as historic examples of German craftsmanship original to the winery.

"Let's get our picture inside one!"

Pony puts his hands on the second giant barrel and forces an opening.

"Pony, I don't think that's a good idea," says Sapphire.

"Yeah, this isn't part of any tour." Pony uses the lantern to light up the dark empty space and crawls inside.

"This is cool! Come on Sapphire, I want to be able to say that I was inside one of these bad boys."

Before she can respond, the dim cavern goes black.

"Hurry, get in here, staff turning off lights!" Pony says laughing.

"We're going to get busted!" she says, stepping in quickly. Pony closes the door behind her.

"Shhhh, whisper!"

"Ok. My goodness, look at the size of this thing!" Sapphire says in hushed tones.

Pony says, "We'll wait five minutes and head out."

Sapphire snaps a picture of Pony. She shows it to him.

"That is awesome!" says Pony.

He uses his free hand to draw Sapphire closer to him. With his face only inches from hers, he looks into her green eyes and kisses her. She lays her head upon his chest, unpleasant experiences worlds away.

"I'm glad you're not afraid of me. I might scare some guys away," she says, making light of her valid concern.

"I am afraid of you, spooky girl," Pony says teasing her.

"Hey!" she says playfully, punching his shoulder in objection.

Pony often wonders how he ever got a beautiful girl like Sapphire.

"I'm in love with you, Sapphire. I will always take care of you."

"I love you too. With all that has happened, I sometimes wish

I could get away from here. It could really help me to process everything."

"Go somewhere without me?" Pony says, making a sad face.

"Only for a couple of days, but the timing isn't good right now."

"I understand. You need time alone to sort things out to listen to only one voice...your own. But I am glad you are not going right now." Pony kisses her forehead.

"Look Pony," Sapphire says pointing to the opposite end of the massive barrel, "is that another door?"

"Sweet!" Pony says. He hands the lantern off and pushes hard against the oak barrel. "It's not budging."

Sapphire says, "There's a good reason for that, the barrels sits against the stone."

"Got it!" Pony says with growing excitement.

"What, are you serious?" Sapphire asks.

Pony and Sapphire both know what the other is thinking. Without any discussion, Pony crawls out the slightly smaller opening and takes the lantern from her so she can follow.

"Oh my goodness, what is this place?" Sapphire asks. She accepts Pony's hand and climbs down to the stone floor.

Pony holds the lantern up.

"A passageway, a tunnel!" Pony exclaims.

Both stand in awe of their discovery.

"I, for one, would like to discover where it leads," he says.

"I'm not so sure that's a good idea, Pony. Remember the Langfords? They were the former winery owners and we all remember . . . which team they were on."

Pony says, "That's reason to investigate. I don't think we could be in any danger. Curiosity is a good thing and besides, I am liking this adventure."

The couple holds hands as they walk down the tunnel, too intrigued to turn back. With only the lantern light to illuminate the complete blackness, they walk for several minutes in silence, except for the rhythmic squeak from the swinging lantern. Without warning, Sapphire shrieks, flailing her arms wildly. Pony raises the lantern. Sapphire is covered in spider web residue.

"Relax, spider webs won't hurt you," he says laughing.

"Many webs mean many spiders. I dislike spiders," she tells Pony after she is free of all the strands.

"Wait, there is light up ahead," Pony says.

The stone floor begins a gradual incline as they approach the source of the light. They finally reach the end of the tunnel and a wooden ladder leading up to the light.

"It's a ladder leading to the surface. I can see the stars," says Pony. He emerges and helps Sapphire out to the cool spring air.

"We're in the vineyard, how beautiful by the light of the moon," she says.

A gentle breeze swishes through the vines and crickets chirp.

"We actually discovered a secret passage out of the winery. This would give you an option if you didn't want to be seen leaving or entering the winery. Wait here," he says.

Pony walks to the end of the row and back.

"We are east of Bordeaux's."

Sapphire says, "We should be headed back, Pony."

"Yup, this was adequate adventure for one night," Pony says, happy with himself.

The walk is quicker when they are descending and soon they arrive at the level part of the tunnel.

"Not much further now," he says.

Their light begins to grow dim and abruptly flickers and fades to black. The two stand in total darkness.

"Oh boy, enhanced adventure," Sapphire says in jest, before using her phone to replace their lost light. But, with a low battery they are soon in the dark again.

"Pony, use your phone."

"Ok, wait here while I run to my car and get it."

"Very funny," says Sapphire.

"Ok...take hold of my hand and I will let the wall guide us back. That way it will be me that runs into any lurking spiders and webs."

"Chivalry lives!" she says squeezing his hand.

"We can't be too far from where we entered," Pony says, speculating and then unexpectedly stopping in his tracks. "Wait!"

"What? You're scaring me!"

"I can't feel the wall!" he says.

"What?"

"Oh, hold on…ok, here it is. We are… turning a corner," says Pony.

"A corner? We didn't turn any corner before," she says.

"We just didn't realize, I guess."

"Pony we had the lantern and would notice a corner. This is not right. I don't think we should go off course. Let me find . . . where the wall continues." She breaks her grasp from Pony and tries to reach out for the wall.

"It's like there is nothing but space. I can't feel the wall! I can't even see my hand in front of my face! What if there is a drop-off? I would totally fall right in… Pony I'm scared! I'm coming back to you." Sapphire turns her direction and shuffles back, hands in front of her. "Pony, Pony where are you?" Her question echoes. "Pony! Pony, this is not funny!" Her heart begins to beat faster. Still, no response from him. "I am staying calm. I might be talking out loud to myself, but I am remaining calm. I will clear away my fear and deal with this matter at hand. I will not panic."

"This isn't funny at all. I'm getting mad. If you are trying to scare me… it's working! Pony, come on!"

She is surrounded in darkness and now, a strong, distinctive scent surrounds her. Finally, his hand grasps hers and pulls her along. Relief washes over her.

"Don't ever do that again! Why didn't you answer me? Pony! There's a light up ahead!"

In the same instance Pony pulls her in the opposite direction of the light.

"Wait, Pony. It's lit up the other way."

Sapphire looks back over her shoulder. Her eyes focus on a figure slouched against the glowing tunnel wall. She stops abruptly. It becomes clear now, it's Pony. Her breath is literally stolen from her body as she pulls her hand away from the hand she's grasping. Sapphire screams. The hand grabs her arm. She breaks free and runs to Pony.

"Pony, Pony! Are you ok?" she says, rushing to his side, still fearful of the aggressor.

"I think so," he says in a daze.

"My goodness, what happened? How did you get this far down the tunnel? Did you pass out?" Sapphire asks in desperation.

"I don't know what happened. I don't remember anything." Pony arches his back suddenly getting away from the wall. "I can't lean against it, it's hot."

"What do you mean?" Sapphire asks. Her test of the wall surface proves his statement. "Yes it's hot. What does it mean? Pony, someone was leading me. I thought it was you. It wasn't you! He tried to lead me away from you! We're not alone down here."

Still groggy, Pony rises slowly with her help.

"It smells weird down here," Pony says.

She glances nervously around.

Pony puts his arms around her.

"Don't freak out. Keep a cool head. Come on Sapphire. You are ok. I'm here. Let's get out of here!"

"That's the kind of glow we've seen in the Madowent!" Sapphire says.

Pony plucks a small glowing stone from the floor and puts it in his pocket. He leads Sapphire once again through the tunnel.

"This is not the way we came. I don't know where we are going to come out," she says.

"I don't care. I just want to be out of this maze."

The glowing wall casts enough light for a short time, but they are once again in darkness when Pony stops.

"Why are you stopping?" Sapphire asks anxiously.

"We are at the end. I'm not sure, but this feels like it could be the barrel."

With effort, he is able to pop the door open on the historic old barrel and they crawl through it.

"I can't believe this. I don't know how we ended up here but I don't care. I just want out," Sapphire says.

Walking quickly, they round the corner to the flight of stairs leading them back up to Bordeaux's when they run right into Father

Mopsi.

"Pony! Sapphire!" he says with surprise.

"Father Mopsi! We are lagging behind from the tour," Pony explains.

"Terra contacted me when she couldn't reach you, Sapphire. She wants Pony to drive you to The Barn."

"Ok, thank you, Father," Sapphire says. The two quickly climb the staircase.

"Right behind you," Father Mopsi yells out to them, moving slower.

With a somber expression, Sapphire slows her pace as she walks past the lingering patrons of Bordeaux's. They drive the short distance to The Barn through the rain. Pony texts Tera so she knows they are out front. Sapphire fidgets with her ring, rotating it round and round as she sits staring ahead. The rain droplets stream down and Sapphire watches their fall across the windshield glass.

"Quinn will need to know what we have seen under Bordeaux's. I don't think we should tell anyone else until then." Sapphire says quietly.

"That tunnel was dark, in the evil sense of the word. I assume the tunnel was used by the River People."

"Doesn't seem to be . . . dormant," she says.

"I know."

"Someone was down there with us!" Sapphire says.

"You think I was dragged away and then he went back for you?"

"He was going to bring me to the glowing area?" she continues.

"The glowing area…it was hot and that scent, patchouli or something." Pony says.

"Whoever was down there was caught off guard by us."

When Pony sees Tera come out of The Barn, he kisses his girlfriend's forehead.

"Get some sleep. I will see you tomorrow. I love you Sapphire."

She forces a smile and kisses him back before getting in the car with Tera for the drive back to the estate.

"Sorry, that took longer than I thought. I tried to reach you," Tera says.

"I had to charge my phone. I'm sorry I worried you," Sapphire says softly.

Tera says, "It's alright. Well, I am glad the winery and our town are getting back to normal again. They had a good turnout."

Sapphire sits quietly with no response.

"What is it? Is everything ok, Sapphire?"

Finally she responds in barely a whisper.

"The server at Bordeaux's had only one hand. The man at the bistro table next to us had a broken neck. That woman back there in the parking lot was missing her left eye. No, I don't think everything is ok."

Chapter Eight

Professor Enderlee soaks up the beauty while riding with Pony and Chamous to the Royce Estate. Pony is worried about Sapphire and wants to get there earlier than they had originally planned. The air is crisp this bright spring morning and rows of vineyards glisten with dew. Most of the journey to the Royce Estate runs parallel to the Missouri River. Fog rises over the water concealing it completely. After turning south, the road travels alongside the Little Blue River, a small tributary that feeds into the Missouri. Beneath his Gatsby hat, the Professor's eyes follow the same kind of misty opaque trail leading all the way to the Estate. Professor Enderlee breaks the silence.

"A scene from the movies, the way the condensation sits on the water."

Pony answers, "A ground cloud…cool!"

"On the days the fog is present, I've driven to the north side of White Oak and parked by the river's edge, wondering if I would see them," the professor says.

"Ever spotted any?" Pony asks.

"No…would they look different than us?" the professor wonders aloud.

Chamous says, "Their physical bodies are unchanged while traveling through the Shrouded Pass. But the spiritual importance of their journey to the Madowent renders a semi-conscious state, with no speaking either. They make the trek in absolute silence."

"Freaky," Pony says.

Chamous continues, "Time is suspended. Their absence and return is not noticed. Each victory, no matter the size, is carried through the Shrouded Pass by a Pathfinder to the Madowent."

"How bizarre is that? Just zombie-like guys walking along the river. Victory? What exactly does that mean?" Pony asks.

"Victories… as in a good deeds, making good choices or acts impacting society positively. Each of those victories is called a Living Stone. The Pathfinders carry the Living Stones they collect and deliver to the Madowent through the Shrouded Pass. That is actually quite difficult…to grasp," the professor adds.

"It's hard to imagine I was getting guidance from Pathfinders all along. I am constantly running through my life experiences, wondering how many Pathfinders impacted me," says Pony.

"Pathfinders are the one rank of Guardians always with us. We all have those people in our lives that saw the best in us and encouraged us. Hard to forget those influences," Professor Enderlee says.

"With the mess in my family, it is pretty easy to look back and identify the Pathfinders. My journey was as wobbly as a kid on training wheels," remarks Pony. He remembers how slim his chances were to have a good life.

"That is true for most people. The Pathfinders help us to steady the ride. You eventually began making good choices and look how far you've come," Professor Enderlee notes.

"But my parents, they had Pathfinders to guide them too. There was no happy ending for them," Pony says.

Chamous explains, "The right of choice is still up to each individual soul. The best Pathfinder still can only throw so many successes in your path. Ultimately we choose our own way to live."

"It would be a tough job. I wouldn't want to be a Pathfinder," says Pony.

"But remember, they are also responsible for selecting the special ones. Think about the gratification of plucking the exceptional from the folds. How exciting, recommending ones to be considered for elevation!" Professor Enderlee exclaims.

"Knighthood: It sounds ridiculous and awesome, all in the same sentence. Having experienced the battle to save Nadellawick, I saw firsthand the power and importance of Knights. Still, Pathfinders have the most challenging duties of the Guardians within the Circle of Sun," Pony says.

"That's because we don't know everything about Knights yet. We will learn," says Chamous.

Towering piers with round finials mark the entrance to Royce Estate. The elaborate, wrought iron gate opens, allowing their car to pass. They travel beneath a natural arch formed from the connecting branches of the budding sugar maples that line each side of the lane.

Once the hill is crested, the grandeur of the Royce Estate lies in full view. Towers of limestone flank the gothic style country manor surrounded by a dense forest of Northern Red Oak. Manicured grounds consist of formal gardens, Orangery, lodges, a Dutch barn, stables and a lake. Chamous pulls the car under the carriage structure instead of parking near the North Lodge where Tera now resides.

The Royce estate only retained one of its staff members from before the battle and defeat of the Caesar. Beef was given the choice to remain or leave after learning about the Circle of Sun. There was never any doubt in his mind. He would be staying with the Royces. Ever loyal, Beef hand-selected household staff from Guardians who make service to others their life's work. As usual, Beef runs the Royce estate with complete professionalism and attention to detail. He shows the trio to the sitting room where they are joined by Keefe Remington.

Chapter Nine

As soon as dawn breaks, an overwhelmed Sapphire leaves Royce Estate. Pony will be disappointed to find her gone when he arrives. Longing for solitude, she remembers Quinn found sanctuary at Langford Inn after her house fire. The Inn has yet to reopen under the new management. She even remembers where the hidden room key is kept.

Cold air fills the little suite. She lights a small fire in the fireplace and curls up on the sofa with a quilt. The dry logs crackle and the flames mesmerize and relax her.

Sapphire will see her father before the senate meeting. Her father's love is the constant she can rely on. Her father served as Polaris, and now as member of the Senate and a governing Knight, but he had her adoration and respect long before she learned of the secret hierarchy. Shock and then instant jubilation; those were her emotions when it was revealed Quinn would be replacing her father as Polaris to the Circle of Sun. Then came the discovery of Quinn as her half-sister.

Her father has been through so much, losing his wife and child all those years ago in the flood waters, only to discover Quinn survived and that the tragedy was no accident. Only after his father remarried Petulah and moved to the United States from England was Romulus blessed with a little girl to fill the void left by the loss of his firstborn. Jexis came first and then a son, Cashton. Their mother was never happy in her new country and pined for her homeland. Romulus built the estate as an exact replica of their home in England, but she was never pleased. She was a demanding mother and an ungrateful wife. Years of discord gave way to the disaster that shook Nadellawick and the Circle of Sun to its core.

And now Sapphire is part of a whole new world. Today she just wants to understand her role. All Guardians protect innocent souls, but upper ranks are warriors. In rare instances, all Guardians may be needed to defend in times of crisis, which was the case with the recent battle. That experience was frightening but empowering, and since then Sapphire discovered only Knights, those elevated elite, are warriors. Perhaps her upsetting visions are part of a specific power she possesses. Who would want that, she wonders. All Knights possess a specific commission or gift, making them unique, like Keefe's ability to foresee violence in some cases. Sapphire has always had visions in dreams. She remembers the shock Quinn had when viewing one of her paintings. The scene was the base of the cliff that took Alec's life and almost ended Quinn's in the climbing accident. Sapphire and Quinn didn't know each other when she painted it.

It is still early morning and Sapphire falls asleep, wrapped in the warm quilt. She dreams.

Her spirit flies high above the grounds of Royce Estate. With powerful wings spread, she glides through blue skies. Each downward thrust lifts her higher. She leaves her fears struggling for breath on earth and soars up to a lofty crystal arch atop pillows of clouds. Without hesitation, Sapphire steps upon the fluffy white and enters a new dimension. The crystal structure towering above her glistens in the golden sun, sending shimmering droplets exploding delicately around her. With infinity for a ceiling she enters the fortress called the Tower of Living Stones. At the far end of a massive great hall lies a marble staircase of magnitude that rises to a throne. A regal lion stands watch over the rooms of the tower. His eyes follow Sapphire's every move. Faint, angelic harmonies carried on gentle breezes kiss her face and flow through her hair. In the first room stands a golden urn filled with pearl-like stones rising far into the heavens. The other six rooms hold the same kind of urns, four of which are abundant like the first, three of which contain little. Sapphire gingerly takes the first step of the gold encrusted staircase leading to the watchful lion. She grips the bannister, rising closer to the magnificent animal. She addresses him when she reaches the top.

"This is the Tower of Living Stones," she says aloud.

The lion speaks.

"Yes."

"I am..."

"I know who you are," he interrupts.

"How?" she asks.

"It is of no consequence, Sapphire. As long as three of the Fidesorbs remain missing, there will always be a shortage of Living Stones. The Fidesorbs must be recovered and returned to the Archangels guard. Come closer and bow," the lion says.

Sapphire bows before the Lion. He places a necklace with a ball-shaped pendant around her neck.

The lion says, "You will save a life, thereby saving your own. That is all. You must go."

"But I don't understand. I..."

The lion says, "Warrior for the King. This may be your calling someday; only time will tell. Your capacity for mercy produces your power. Look beyond the surface, claim what is yours alone."

The lion closes his eyes and Sapphire opens hers to the familiar surroundings of the Inn.

The dream is filled with such beauty and peace she savors the drowsy state before it dissipates, leaving her once again searching for answers. She wonders what she is. She knows she's not a Knight, or a Pathfinder. She assumes she is a Sleeper. When Quinn helped Tera from the river, she performed the duty of Guardianship, but as a Sleeper she had no recollection of it. Sleepers make up the majority of Guardians. It is a vast testing ground, like a giant sieve producing a harvest of potential candidates for Knighthood.

She makes the decision to accept these visions as part of who she will become. She chooses the city square in White Oak to face her fears. Seeing people who are hurt, injured or maimed is frightening to her, but not understanding why scares her even more. Sapphire sits on a park bench and is soon joined by a middle-aged woman with her morning coffee. The fingers clutching the paper cup are deeply scratched and dirty, her nails broken and jagged. Before leaving, the woman checks the time on her wristwatch. Sapphire notices her arm dark with bruises. A city worker, clipboard in hand, inspects around a building. Horrifically, blood trickles from fresh stitches spanning from ear to ear. A woman puts her shopping bags in her car, her center hollow, invisible. There are no signs of pain. Sapphire remembers the words of the lion from her dream.

"See beyond the surface."

She wonders how that would be possible. The scenes frighten her. Feeling defeat, she closes her eyes and offers her simple prayer.

"Lord, what am I to do with the views shown to me? Please cover me with calm peace and fortify me with wisdom and understanding . . . and courage."

"May I join you?" a man asks. His heart lies bloody and beating outside of his chest. "Sapphire, are you alright?"

"Father!" She falls into his embrace.

"What's wrong, why are you here?" he asks, filled with concern.

"Father, I am seeing injuries, afflictions others do not. The young boy walking his dog over there, do you see him Father? Where are his ears?"

Romulus cannot see what Sapphire is seeing.

"Try again, Sapphire," he says.

The horrible scenes evaporate.

Romulus says, "You didn't recognize me when I sat next to you."

"Your heart was… outside of your chest. It was mangled and damaged and bloody." Sapphire covers her eyes as she recalls the vision.

"Darling, I don't know what you were seeing. I am fine," he says.

"I just want to keep my eyes closed. I just want this to end. I feel like I need to get away from here for a while."

"Running away from this won't make it go away. You don't see the devastated bodies any longer do you? I appear normal, don't I?" he asks.

"You do now," she replies.

"Maybe it's not their future you see but their past. People smile, but one can never truly know what others have endured. Maybe that's what you are seeing. A compassionate soul may have special insight others don't have."

"Yes that could be it." She says. "But what about your heart, Father?"

"I have had my share of heartache. The accident that claimed my family, the betrayal of your mother. Many battles have left me with wounds and scars, my heart wrenched and broken…but I am healed.

The good Lord willing, we can heal from devastating heartbreak, trauma and illness."

"I understand," Sapphire says. Once more Sapphire sees the young boy and his wounds from life's battles. A warmth flows from her heart for the pain the young boy has endured, and it surrounds her entire being. Sapphire is filled with compassion and hope for the boy. Once again, he appears to her as a normal boy, walking and playing with his dog.

Romulus says, "As we go through our day we pass dozens of people, never knowing the battles they fought, what they've endured. But challenges and adversities do make a lasting impact on our lives. Like fine steel, our spirits are forged by fire and made stronger. You, Sapphire, would see the price that was paid. I can't think of anything more merciful in our earthly experience," Romulus smiles at her, his pride beaming. "I believe this is your commission, sweet daughter."

Sapphire's eyes return his love.

"I think you are right, Father." She stands with new confidence and accepts the new perspective of the now bustling main street of White Oak. "I had a dream I was at the Tower of Living Stones. A lion that guards the seven rooms told me that my capacity for mercy would be my power. That it's mine alone and I should claim it. So, I claim it, faithful that it will be for the good of the Circle of Sun."

He rises and holds her close, regretting the trauma his daughter has had to experience. Romulus knows it's not the time to tell her the lion has a name.

Chapter Ten

Tera enjoys a morning run along the Little Blue River. The usual Missouri humidity is absent and the air is light and crisp. She is serenaded by birds of the morning and an occasional croaking bullfrog. Warmed up and ready to hit her stride, she pops in her earbuds, pacing to the beat of each song. The senate meeting and the Quest top everyone's mind. Tera can't imagine what a Quest would be like. After seeing the destruction and the battle with the River People and the Caesar with her own eyes, she can assume it wouldn't be like anything she knows. To think Romulus's own wife could deceive and destroy her family haunts her. Who do you trust after witnessing how Petulah was able to spin her web under Romulus's roof? How could a heart turn so black?

The mellow tunes from her playlist create the perfect bit of solitude before the big day. She passes back through the iron gates of the estate and slows her pace, then abruptly stops in her tracks. There it is again! Tera listens intently. Between lyrics are those whispers, more distinct than before. Even though she knows the sounds are in the music, she can't fight the urge to check around her. If she could only drown out everything but the whispers!

Tera stands-statue like trying to understand. Cutting through the morning air the sound of a roaring motor and the screeching of tires comes from behind her. She bolts off the lane while looking over her shoulder for the out-of-control vehicle, but instead, a deafening rotating wind barrels down the road coming right towards her. Its powerful momentum sucks up leaves and underbrush in its spinning fury. The tail of the rotation dances and darts from side to side, moving at breakneck speed. Tera's dark locks whip and sting her face. A random newspaper slaps her leg, wrapping itself around. With the force pushing hard at her, she shields her face for impact. Miraculously, as if a glass wall lay between her and the zephyr-like wind, she is untouched. The revolving funnel dissipates and is gone. With trembling hands Tera sweeps her windblown hair away from her face and surveys her surroundings. Expecting scattered leaves and paper, and branches torn and lying about, she finds no evidence of the occurrence. Out of breath, she leans over, hands on knees, bracing her stance. The threat feels real, but would sound like paranoia to others. When a gentle pull to take out the earbuds fails, her heart skips a beat. A stronger tug loosens one, but the other is stuck fast. Panic rises as she struggles to remove it. With some pain, she is able to work the rubbery piece out of her ear, gasping at the sight of some blood on her fingers. Wiping them on her jacket, she hurries to the safety of her home. Again, she records in her notebook.

The Madowent stands empty but ready for the important meeting. Fiery torches perch high above the rows of simple benches, soon to be filled. A supernatural light explodes through colored stained glass, depicting a strong and graceful white dove surrounded by royal sky blue. Beneath the window stands a now vacant platform. To the left are the seats for the distinguished members of the Senate. The family gathers in the back of the Madowent.

Pony breathes a sigh of relief watching his girlfriend. Sapphire smiles, her arms encircling her father's waist.

"I hope our recent battle with the darkness earned us a chance to make a significant difference again somewhere," Cashton says, "I'm not a big fan of all this waiting around,"

Growing up as a Royce, Cashton knew he was different than most, with a connection to nature, and his incredible ability to heal. After finding out the family secret and the hierarchy of the Circle of Sun, everything makes more sense to him. The young Royce found his place, and he knows who he is. He crosses his arms across his slim build. His green eyes look to Jexis, who has even less tolerance for delay.

"I dislike waiting too, but don't forget, brother, I forged the break in the circle of fire and freed you from the Caesar. And I had to be supremely patient," says Jexis.

She is the opposite of Cashton, with fair skin and light hair. She is blessed with beauty, but has little patience for primping. Looking beautiful comes with little effort on her part. What others think of her is of no concern. Once Jexis understands what must be done, she takes action. Her valiant and courageous actions during the battle with the

Cesar are rumored to have earned her consideration for Knighthood. She possesses keen intuition. She goes into execution mode, while most still ponder solutions.

Jexis says, “Later in the week, I will be introducing the vocalist Sheena McNeil from Romania, who is performing with the symphony. Father you remember her don’t you?”

“Oh I do . . . indeed,” he says, Sapphire’s arms still around him.

Surrounded by those he loves Romulus drinks in the day. Shrouded in secrecy before, these types of discussions with his family were not possible. The ability to openly discuss with his children the business of saving souls from the darkness opens a new chapter in Romulus’s life. A Polaris candidate must be part of the original Royce bloodline, but selection of the Polaris is a divine appointment. Believing his tiny daughter was swept away by flood waters, everyone, including Romulus, believed Jexis would be the next Polaris and was shocked to discover his replacement would be Quinn. A relieved Jexis seemed to flourish after the announcement, making her feelings known, that she did not want the responsibility.

Romulus says, “Yes, I remember Sheena McNeil and her angelic voice, a true gift. A beautiful lady if my memory serves me. I was quite smitten with her at one time.”

“But Father, Pony and I met with the other day at the UMKC campus, and she couldn’t be more than thirty years old,” Sapphire says.

“An ageless beauty, perhaps,” Romulus says.

A broken and devastated man, still healing after the loss of his family, had met a beautiful and talented woman. Romulus became mesmerized and regretful to move on when she chose her rising stardom over their relationship.

“I look forward to her performance,” he says.

Tera changes the subject.

“I can’t help but be a little nervous for Quinn about the ceremony and Senate meeting.”

Keefe says, “Are you certain your anxiety isn’t more for yourself? This might be the time you are placed in a more permanent role in the Circle.”

"I will do whatever is asked of me, or go wherever I am needed," Tera says with resolve.

"I agree," Chamous adds, "With the Pathfinders occupied and focused on Sleepers, numerous supporting duties remain."

Keefe nods and responds, "Damage control was critical after our battle with the River People. Both you and Tera were instrumental in making sure the community didn't raise questions that couldn't be answered and Professor Enderlee used his connections abroad to improve communication with the other regions."

Keefe is relieved for this day to arrive. Keefe is a serious man and solves problems without attracting attention. Humbleness is one of the qualities Quinn loves about him. His experience as a Guardian and his background in law enforcement proved valuable during the crisis in Nadellawick. If he is given the honor of Knight he would be pleased.

"Professor Enderlee, communication between the regions is important and has been missing," Keefe says.

The professor says, "I do know scores of folks from all around the globe. Father Mopsi and are comparing notes and share a few acquaintances. Knowing some of them are Guardians, I have a reason to rekindle the connections. The value should be evident when all the regions come together for the annual Empyrean Senate meeting. From what I understand, the Circle of Sun is a unified body, but improvements between the regions will improve our effectiveness." With one hand in his trouser pocket and the other holding his pipe, the professor continues. "With different views come new ideas and boundless possibilities. Fascinating! And more of us to keep watch on the balance of light and darkness."

Romulus alone understands more than anyone else how true his statement is. For many years the darkness slowly chipped away at the delicate balance of security by such small fractions that warning bells remained silent. More Guardians will keep history from repeating.

"I will assist Quinn. Keefe, would you join me?" Romulus asks.

Romulus and Keefe leave the group as dozens of Guardians enter the Madowent and take their seats. Romulus sends Keefe ahead to the Oratory where Quinn prepares.

Keefe pauses and watches her.

Quinn's long dark hair falls over her narrow shoulders. She is graceful and regal, surrounded by candle light.

"Are you here to make sure I'm not bolting out the back door?" she asks.

Her comment brings a grin to his face.

"Nope, I just wanted to say hello and good luck. I hope you don't mind," he says.

"I'd be upset if you hadn't," she replies. She finds confidence in his comforting embrace. "It's been a big day with the Pathfinders, and now the Senate meeting."

She raises her face to his.

Keefe says, "I want to make sure you're ok."

"I'm fine. I'm ready… but I long for some time for us," she says.

"We will have some time for us soon," says Keefe.

"I'm counting on it." She looks into his eyes.

Romulus's soft knock interrupts their passionate kiss.

"Please excuse me," he says.

"Father, come in. Keefe was reminding me, the day will come when we can share more time together," says Quinn.

Holding hands, held they lock gazes once more before Keefe kisses her forehead and leaves father and daughter alone.

"How are you, darling?" Romulus asks.

"I'll be better once my first meeting as Polaris is behind me. I want to make everyone proud."

"Oh Quinn, my dear. We are already proud," he says.

Her shimmery, sheer garment attaches on the top of each shoulder and cascades down her back, creating folds at her feet. The white and simple strapless gown underneath only needs one additional piece of finery. Romulus places the Benedict medal around her neck, with her always. Upon her finger, the Apalacid.

"Thank you, Father."

With Quinn ready for the meeting, Romulus leads her to the center of the room. Within the soft glow of the candles, he takes his daughters hand and, with heads bowed to the heavens, Romulus offers a prayer.

"Lord, there is nothing in any realm to compare to your power or to match your perpetual mercy. With every consideration of your will, I ask for fortification of wisdom, courage for our Polaris, my daughter Quinn, today. With her ordained commission to lead us, may the souls present become ignited in spirit and within her see a glimpse of your encompassing love and compassion." Romulus smiles at her and leads her from the Oratory.

The Madowent, is now filled with Guardians who stand in a show of respect as the Senate members take their places of distinction. Among them are Dr. Eudora Brazil, Etta Mollender, George Tally, Edward Carver, Mason Kidwell, Tristan Pope and Cashton. Romulus moves to a podium.

"Please welcome our Polaris, Quinn Clarke Royce."

All who are gathered stand and applaud. From beneath the round stained glass window of the dove in flight Quinn moves to the raised platform. The young, confident woman from Fireside Books, now regal in stature, addresses the gathering.

"Guardians, welcome to our Senate meeting. Only a short time ago we all gathered for the Ring Ceremony making me the new Polaris to the Circle of Sun. Each new day I humbly ask Him to make me the leader you deserve. Imperfect is our world. Darkness knocks daily at the door of innocent souls, presenting a choice to answer. The darkness loses when the knock is ignored. But our cause demands we open that door wide to look in the eye of our enemy before we drive them to damnation. Boldness, courage and power are qualities we must possess. Blessed are we who grasp the Living Stones like manna from heaven. When we truly embrace the meaning of the Living Stones, we can experience joy within our imperfect world. May our contributions swell the treasury within the Tower of Living Stones."

The crowd stands to applaud Quinn's words. Behind her, pearl-like stones levitate from the rock floor of the Madowent. The ceiling transforms, revealing a sunset. The master's brushstrokes create a sky of glistening pinks, corals, oranges and blues. The Living Stones shine like diamonds as they catch the last rays of the golden sun before their mystical journey all the way to the Tower of Living Stones. Each victory they represent saturates the air with hope for a brighter world. As they levitate upward, Quinn repeats the seven categories of the

Living Stones aloud.

"Spirit Infused Heart, Merciful Humanitarian, Concede and Live, Acceptance and Mourning, Harmony in His Will, Humble Heart and Gentle Spirit, and finally Peacemaker."

Romulus joins Quinn and she continues.

"Jexis Royce, Cashton Royce, Keefe Remington, Gunderson Enderlee, Chamous McCoy, Tera Santiago, would you come before the platform, please?"

The Guardians present themselves.

"Our purpose while we walk this earth is to lift one another up. Some are stronger than others. In times of darkness those stronger ones are a beacon. A storm raged right here in Nadellawick and revealed the value of these men and women who stand before us. We must call on those gifted with strength for leadership and defense. With great honor I bestow upon you the title of Knight."

Some in the group are unable to hide their shock at the announcement. Romulus joins her for the ceremony. He speaks with passion as he lowers his head and places his hands together.

"Guardians we are called to serve God by commission from St. Michael. The importance of this calling is immeasurable. This stands alone as God's greatest gift to humanity. Knights will provide defense in many different forms. Each of you was selected by virtue of your unique contribution during our recent battle with the darkness. This highest honor will also enhance your God-given gifts, making them stronger for service to God's army, the Circle of Sun. Please kneel."

A crystal sword appears in Romulus's clasped hands, which he uses to touch the shoulders of the candidates.

Romulus continues, "Our realm gained strong and capable warriors today. With great pride I bestow the honor of Knighthood to you."

When the new Knights rise to their feet, cheers and applause erupt from those assembled.

Romulus has a special announcement. He looks to Quinn, who nods for him to begin.

"Although they do not meet the age requirement to be considered for Knighthood at this time, they are set apart by their brave service during our battle with the Cesar. Both of them showed dedication, ability and courage. Pony Coldstone and Sapphire Royce, please take your spot among the honorees."

Pony and Sapphire join them.

"The duty of Knighthood requires much. Youth is fleeting. Perhaps this elevation will serve as retribution for having to forfeit a portion of innocence when you answered the call to service in our recent battle. With appreciation and gratitude for your servant's heart, we anticipate your full indoctrination to Knighthood."

Quinn asks the Knights to take their seats and addresses the entire group.

"Where and how can we render the most impact? Our victory over the Cesar and the River People is now a victory recorded in our history. But it is only but one battle waged in a war never ending on this earth. When the light and the security tips the scales in our favor we are winning. I hold in my hand the Quest handed down from Malachi. The great lion that guards the Tower of Living Stones sent a message for us, which I will read to you.

"Guardians of the Circle of Sun. Earnest prayers

from multitudes have reached all the way to heaven.

With loss of life and the consequences of those losses too costly to bear,

a victorious Quest will save souls and alter the annals of history."

Quinn looks up from the message to address the group.

"Some of our brave Knights will leave tomorrow for the Quest issued by Archangel Michael and Malachi. Those selected are Jexis Royce, Cashton Royce, Keefe Remington and Gunderson Enderlee. Thank you in advance for your service. Our most sincere prayers of safety go out to you. The details of the Quest will be discussed at the close of our Senate meeting. While the exact nature of the assignment is known to only a few, we ask for thoughtful prayer on their behalf. Pray for courage, strength and wisdom for these who will advance our cause.

In new business, the creation of a Sanctified Transit for our Pathfinders will be assigned to Chamous McCoy and Tera Santiago, with the aid of Father Mopsi. This kind of project can be quite delicate.

Questions will be directed to Father Mopsi."

Quinn moves closer to the group.

"Concern grows as one of the missing Fidesorbs could be lost forever. At each of the feet of the seven archangels lies the glowing Fidesorbs representing all the good of humanity. Only three more must be recovered. Our prayers are to find another during this Quest. While the appointed Guardians are away, we must be vigilant in the protection of our dear Nadellawick. Be watchful and strong and protect her with every ounce of your being. Thank you and godspeed until we meet again."

Quinn is escorted from the platform by Romulus.

The Senate rises and files out after them.

The four selected Guardians are asked to remain and join Quinn in her chambers. The atmosphere is solemn as they follow her. The four chosen for the Quest take a seat around a table along with Quinn. Romulus, Pony, Sapphire, Tera and Chamous stand around the table. Quinn speaks first.

"The worst villain known to man is man. If an intervention could occur allowing a fledgling seed of change to take root instead of being trampled, perhaps history will be rewritten. And you must know, because of Guardians, it has been. This quest is similar. Please be gathered at the Madowent at sunrise in forty eight hours and be prepared to leave for Hudovistan."

"Are we to know nothing more?" Jexis asks.

"Yes, one more thing. You may request more help in Hudovistan if the need arises," she says.

"Where is Hudovistan?" Cashton asks, looking to the other puzzled faces.

"Even I do not know, but you will in due time." Quinn says.

This statement creates even more questions.

Quinn interrupts them.

"Accepting a Quest requires an unshakable foundation of faith and to only a chosen few. And you are those."

The four look to each other for reaction. Quinn is not surprised by what happens next. With a fist thump on the table, courageous Jexis commits herself. Cashton follows with his hand on top of hers. At the same time, Keefe and the Professor show their decisions by joining them.

Chapter Eleven

Annabeth quickens her pace to arrive before Simon, a clock keeper. Navigating through the corridors and passageways of St. Paul's is getting easier. With her shoulders flat against the wall near the cleric's office door she pauses, waiting for the exact moment to proceed. With her shoes in one hand, she moves cat-like across the sanctuary floor, to the small isolated tool room of the clock keeper. He is always on time, and this time she cuts it close. Swiftly she takes her place in front of the small table, opens her catechism book and catches her breath. Seconds later, Simon enters his small work room.

"I see you are busy with your studies again Miss Chatfield," Simon says with a nod.

"Good day Simon. I am grateful for use of this space. I'm spread too thin, and finishing my lesson before I return to my duties at the Bake House is the only way. Please don't tell me you are kicking me out," she says. She uses her most charming smile.

Simon replies, "No Miss Chatfield, I must bid you good day. Until next time."

"Good day to you Simon." Annabeth waits until Simon is gone, before proceeding with her usual routine and then later another delivery.

The Diocese meeting at Fulham Palace lasts for over an hour and at midday when the Bishops break, Annabeth is graciously welcomed. Bishop Stevenson and Deacon Blaredon ask her to join their luncheon table. She is determined to make her mark on London's society.

Bishop Stevenson says, "Madame Chatfield, you bring sunshine into Fulham Palace with your presence. How are you this fine day?"

"Your Grace, I am quite well. I thank you for the invitation," Annabeth says, "I didn't know your group would be this sizeable. Have I misunderstood?"

"Not at all my dear. We are serving your confections at a small gathering tonight at my residence. May I introduce you to our tablemates? Of course, you know Deacon Blaredon," the bishop says.

"Yes," she says. She gives a slight bow of reverence in his

direction.

Deacon Blaredon says, "Is your catechism complete, Miss Chatfield?"

"Nearly finished now. The tutors at St. Paul are a blessing to many. I've met so many kind Londoners during my instruction."

"We enjoy having you at the cathedral a few times a week," Deacon Blaredon says, "and may I introduce Thomas Tobler, Bishop of Westminster?"

Bishop Tobler takes her hand as she again bows to his authority.

"Hello Madame Chatfield," he says, "I am pleased to make your acquaintance."

"Shall we sit?" Bishop Stevenson says. All wait for Annabeth to be seated.

A server pours wine from a large, heavy silver pitcher.

Bishop Stevenson says, "Madam Chatfield is an industrious young lady. She owns a Chatfield Bake House on Pudding Lane in London."

"Oh, how interesting. Proprietorship with your husband, I presume?" Bishop Tobler asks.

"I am unmarried. I carry on my father's Bake House. I was schooled in baking, but not the operations of business. I had much to learn," Annabeth says.

"Oh, indeed. Of that I am certain," Bishop Tobler says.

All nod in agreement.

Annabeth says, "My father left me little profit but a rich philosophy. He alone tended to our garden after losing my mother many years ago. My most vivid memory is working beside my father in the warm morning sun, giving our best effort. Our paltry crop would barely sustain us. He believed in reaching outside to those with more expertise and success than he. We travelled past the city walls to the small village of Croydon. Armed with only fresh bread for payment and his determination, he met the parson of the church, who enjoyed a reputation for excellent gardening. The ideas he shared with my father were uncommon. We came home and he immediately applied the knowledge. This philosophy has served me well."

Bishop Stevenson says, "We could use a wise man like your

father today, with the unsettling issues in the religious community. The Anglicans and the Catholics will never find common ground, no matter who is ruling. But I, for one, am weary of the bantering between the two factions. At our meeting earlier, my views were criticized for being… too Catholic." The bishop shakes his head in frustration and sips his wine.

"I think her father's philosophy is interesting," Bishop Tobler says.

"She is the toast of London with her magical confections. Tell us all," Deacon Blaredon suggests.

Annabeth smiles softly and humbly lowers her eyes.

"Just applying the same philosophy from my father. With a Bake House on the verge of closing its doors, I traveled to Paris seeking knowledge. A shop was making solid chocolate and I went to learn the art. I reached outside of my world for answers. My confections are so popular, my Bake House is profitable once more," Annabeth says.

"What an outstanding story and accomplishment. I look forward to sampling this new solid chocolate," Bishop Tobler says with enthusiasm.

"You will tonight, your Grace," Bishop Stevenson says.

Bishop Tobler says, "Oh that will be fine!"

"Madame Chatfield and I shared a few tea times. I, for one, appreciate a fresh voice at our table," Deacon Blaredon says.

"What a grand idea it was!" Bishop Tobler says.

After the meal, Annabeth thanks them for including her. All of the men stand as she excuses herself.

"A simple luncheon topic like chocolate leads me to a possible solution," Thomas Tobler says thinking out loud.

Chapter Twelve

After the ceremony and Senate meeting, the inner Circle of Sun gather for dinner in the Royce dining room.

Romulus Royce stands.

"I raise my glass to our Knights and to those chosen for the Quest," he says.

Quinn and Keefe lift their glasses, along with Father Mopsi, Chamous and Tera, Professor Enderlee and Pony and Sapphire.

"I am shocked over the appointments," Tera says, after sipping her wine.

"Not as much as I am," Professor Enderlee replies.

Tera's eyes remain lowered and the group sits in silence.

"This is difficult, I do understand," Quinn says, "I have had my own experience understanding and adjusting to my appointed position." A smile comes to her face." Each day I must dismiss the doubt and remind myself God doesn't call the qualified, he qualifies the called."

Quinn's testimony is like a calming elixir to everyone.

"The appointment surprised me," Sapphire says, looking at Pony. "We didn't realize we would be even considered for Knighthood."

"I wouldn't mind being a Knight," Pony says under his breath.

"Take your time, change will arrive soon enough," Romulus says.

Pony and Sapphire leave for Sheena McNeil's performance at the Missouri Repertory Theater.

Dinner is thirty minutes delayed, and Jexis goes to the kitchen to investigate.

"No explanation given for our delay, but dinner is being served," Jexis says. She seats herself, and two servants come into the dining room, followed by a harried looking Beef.

"My apologies to all," Beef says. He offers a nod of respect.

"No harm done, we quite enjoyed our conversation," says Romulus.

The diners are served prime Kansas City strip steaks, fingerling potatoes, sautéed fennel and roast vegetables with wilted red chard.

The food and the company are savored. The formality of the day fades and the group is relaxed and jovial. After the table is cleared, the servants leave them alone for conversation.

"One more toast, this one to Quinn. You honored me by your performance today. Nicely done, my dear," Romulus says.

"Thank you Father. Now I can focus on support of the Quest," she says.

"To Quinn," the group says in unison.

"This transit is long overdue. When will it be complete, Chamous?" Romulus asks.

"Your guess is as good as mine. I first must maneuver through the sanctified portion. This is new to me," he says.

"The creation of a sanctified transit is quite involved, but I am happy to assist you," says Father Mopsi.

"And what about those of you chosen for the Quest?" asks Tera.

"To be included with this group, I am honored and excited. I toast to new experiences, if you can bear yet another toast," Professor Enderlee says.

The group's laughter can be heard all the way down the hall as Beef approaches with more wine.

Romulus excuses himself from the table to take a phone call.

As if on cue, blustery winds whip branches against the massive window glass, drawing attention to its fury.

Beef offers to refill Tera's drink and she thanks him. The corners of his mouth bend up as he pours, but when his eyes meet hers, Beef drops the decanter of wine. The crystal shatters and spills out the burgundy fluid.

"What is wrong, Beef?" Jexis asks in a raised voice, moving towards him.

Two servants scurry to the mess with a broom and mop as Jexis takes Beef's arm.

He takes a deep breath while closing his eyes and then exhales with an explanation.

"Oh, how clumsy of me!" He struggles to sound calm. He turns his flushed face to Jexis. "The decanter slipped. I beg your pardon."

"Are you sure you are ok?" Jexis asks.

"My sincere apologies," says Beef. He leaves the room.

"What on earth?" Tera asks.

"I told you not to wear your hair that way," Jexis says, trying to break the tension in the room. Her comment draws laughter from some.

"Beef is usually flawless, but recently he appears . . . preoccupied," Quinn says in a more serious tone.

"Your stunning beauty knocked him off his feet, Tera!" Chamous chides.

With a forced smile, she winks at Chamous.

"Where is Father?" Cashton asks, changing the subject.

"He went out for the rest of the evening, got a text about fifteen minutes ago. He didn't say where," Quinn replies with a slight raise of her brow.

After Father Mopsi turns in for the night, a restless Jexis takes a deep breath.

"Today is a day I won't soon forget! Sorry folks, but I need a jolt of reality. Who is up for some Quoits?"

Without waiting for a reply, she heads to the billiard room. Although Quinn would prefer solitude with Keefe, she musters up as much enthusiasm as she can.

"I am, and I am going to win!"

Chamous puts his jacket around Tera's shoulders after she mentions being chilled. His jacket dwarfs her and her silly expression brings some laughs. Jexis snaps some pictures of the fun. Playing Quoits gave the group some much needed recreation.

Later before Tera turns off her bedside light, she reflects on the day and the honor bestowed upon her. Reviewing her messages, she finds the pictures Jexis snapped an hour ago. Tera laughs at Pony and Sapphire holding the Quoit rings to frame their faces, but she freezes on the last picture. Her eyes, they appear distorted. The pupil is oversized, as if someone colored them in with a black marker. With her heart beating faster, she whips through the pictures again. The other's pictures appear normal, but the last one leaves her staring. For a moment she wonders if this is what Beef was seeing. That notion sends waves of terror through her, but she calms herself with rationalization. Tera sends a text and the image to both Quinn and Jexis. After a few moments she receives a response from Quinn.

"Love it! Nice one of you two."

"Don't you think I look strange?" Tera texts back.

"Well the jacket does nearly swallow you, but you look happy!" is her reply.

Jexis's text confirms the same.

"Nice shot." Her text reads.

Beef's reaction haunts her but she's determined to stop paranoia from taking over. Tera rationalizes by recalling digital images she's seen with shadows, strange circles of light, and even red eyes. Perhaps something is wrong with her device, explaining why she is the only one who sees a problem. She dismisses the issue by erasing the picture. Out of sight, out of mind. Right or wrong, the image is gone, and she is ready for sleep.

Chapter Thirteen

Pony and Sapphire find their seats in a packed house at the Missouri Repertory Theater. Sheena McNeal's voice fills the venue with the most hauntingly beautiful music they have ever heard. The standing ovation reflects her impact. The audience begs for an encore and she obliges. Sheena's dark smooth hair glistens and her slightest move shimmers as the spotlight reflects the brilliance of her rhinestone gown. Angelic and smiling, she waves goodnight to her fans. The young couple prepares to leave but is approached by an usher, who hands them a note. Pony accepts the envelope and once in the lobby, they read it.

"Well, what do you think about her offer?" Pony asks.

"Why not? The Mosaic Lounge sounds interesting and fun. How thoughtful of Sheena to invite us," she says.

"Downtown it is!" he says. Pony holds the door open for her. The crisp and dark night greets them eagerly.

An elevator door opens and Pony and Sapphire enter the Mosaic Lounge. The rooftop night club provides most of its seating under the stars. Patrons with cocktails crowd around spacious crimson leather booths protected from the elements by supersized umbrellas. Others laugh and talk around flaming fire pits. Beyond the lounge area lay the busy dance floor surrounded by a bar, its backdrop two stories tall. Bartenders in black tee shirts mix drinks under neon lights. The list is checked over by a hostess, who leads them to a private party around one of the fires. Sheena spots them and breaks through the surround of friends and fans to greet them.

"So glad you came, Sapphire and Pony," Sheena says with sincerity.

Sapphire says, "Thanks for inviting us. The concert was wonderful!"

"Thank you, the audience was great," says Sheena.

Her attention turns elsewhere and in the same instant Finnegan appears. With his tie loosened under his evening jacket, and his dark smooth hair pulled back, he has the interest of the ladies.

"Your hands are empty," Finnegan says. He summons the server. "These two would like a couple of cosmopolitans, eh?" asks Finnegan.

Pony says, "Thanks Finnegan, but we're not of drinking age, sodas for us."

"No! Drinks for both…it's a big night," Finnegan insists.

"No, it is our law Finnegan. We're not even supposed to be in here," Sapphire tells him.

Finnegan says, "Ok, we dance."

He grabs Sapphire's hand, leading her.

With raised brows and a half smile, she glances back over her shoulder at Pony, who is as surprised as she is, but waves her out with guarded consent.

Finnegan is a good dancer. He leads her steps with confidence and flair, drawing attention to them.

A small group of women gathers and hope to be asked next, but he is undistracted; his focus is on Sapphire.

She remembers his unfamiliarity with her culture, and tolerates his closeness.

Finnegan swings her to the beat. Her hair flies behind her and the club's lights and crowd become blurred. Without warning the foreigner drops his grasp as he bends from the waist holding his arm.

Sapphire says, "Finnegan, what's wrong?" She follows as he heads to a terrace beyond the bar.

"There is… much pain."

"I will get help," says Sapphire.

"No! Pain is good sometimes," he says.

"What are you talking about?"

"When the burden is unrelenting, pain is a . . . release, you know? The . . . shoulder's out," Finnegan says, while bending again and wincing. He straightens himself and approaches a supporting pillar.

"Let me find your friends," Sapphire says, but Finnegan lowers his shoulder and rams it hard into the pillar. The painful impact is heard in his guttural moan.

"Damn!" he says his within a gasp. "Ahh, relief has come. I took action, eh?"

"Good Lord, did you pop it back into place?" Sapphire asks.

Finnegan answers, "Well, tried to... and, I think it's… a thumbs up. Time for a drink, I am not feeling too chipper, ya know?"

"Finnegan, sit down here," she says.

Finnegan's breathing is rapid, his face flushed.

Sapphire tries to conceal her gasp when she spots a small trickle of blood seeping from his ear down the side of his face. Finnegan fixes his gaze, unmoved.

"Get... out," he says. He turns his face back towards her and grabs her by both arms. His desperation frightens her and she attempts to stand, surprised by the strength used to prevent it.

"You need medical attention," she says.

"I want you… to be my girl," he says with difficulty.

Once again, Finnegan's disposition changes. Releasing her arms, he removes a handkerchief from his pocket and cleans the blood away.

Sapphire stands.

"Only a small bit of blood," he says with a half-smile. "Please forgive." He lowers to one knee in front of her. "A beautiful American girl and too much drink make me foolish."

"I am sure my boyfriend is wondering where I am," Sapphire says, her eyes searching for Pony.

Finnegan says, "Yes, you are right. Allow me to take you." He rises, bringing his face up to hers. He kisses her lips so quickly she has no time to react before he pulls her across the dance floor to a waiting Pony.

"Let's get out of here," she says, taking his hand and leading him out.

"Are you ok?" he asks.

"I'll say no if Finnegan ever asks me to dance again," she says.

Pony stops her.

"What did he do?"

"Settle down boyfriend, my honor doesn't need defending," Sapphire says. She decides not to tell Pony about the quick kiss he stole from her. "I don't like the vibe I get from him, that's all."

Sheena is absent from the party table they pass on their way to the security of Pony's car.

Pony turns the key…click, click, click.

"Damn! The battery's dead," he says, trying again.

"Oh no, and it's cold." Sapphire takes out her phone and begins to relay their predicament to Chamous.

Two loud honks in front of them capture their attention. A limousine waits at the curb with its door wide open. Sheena McNeal waves them over.

Pony slides out and Sapphire follows.

"Join me?" says Sheena.

"My battery is dead. I need to get a jump," Pony says.

"Crawl in, I will take you where you need to go, and arrange for your car to be serviced and delivered. Don't let me finish my party alone in your fine city," Sheena says.

Concern for Sapphire drives his decision and they join her.

"What is your home address Pony?" Sheena asks, after they climb in the limo. She repeats aloud to the driver who makes arrangements on his phone.

"A wonderful night. I am meeting someone later, so this will be a brief excursion. Did you enjoy dancing at the Mosaic?" she asks.

"Great place," he says, with trumped up enthusiasm.

The black car meanders through the city and comes to a stop. Sapphire is startled by a white glove rapping hard on her window. The door swings open and a chauffer offers his hand.

"Where are we, why are we stopping?" Pony asks, while climbing out after her.

"This must be our first scheduled stop," Sheena says, accepting another white gloved-hand.

Surrounded on all sides by headstones, Sapphire recognizes their surroundings. She sends Chamous their location, hoping it will be the quickest way to end this evening.

"Wait. This is Mt. Washington Cemetery," Pony says.

"Yes, you are right, Pony. I promised Finnegan and Albert we could practice some of our Romanian customs. Shouldn't take long."

Sapphire and Pony are confused.

The two limo drivers wear odd masks. One is a goat and the other an old man. The goat hands a mask for Sheena to wear, a mask of an old woman. With a full moon lighting their way, the three giggle and walk towards one of the numerous above-ground crypts. The goat and the old man force open the doors of an old crypt and enter, with Sheena following.

"You two can't hold your liquor," she says laughing.

With exaggerated gestures and melodramatic speech, the goat speaks.

"We must leave the windows and doors open for the spirit to escape."

Sapphire recognizes Finnegan's voice! The limo drivers wearing masks are Finnegan and Albert.

Finnegan continues, "Albert, did you cut the sleeves of the deceased to enable him to fly?"

"Yes, Finnegan," Albert says. He slips a silver flask from his jacket and enjoys a long drink.

"Sheena, did you place the candle in his hand to light his way past evil's bridge?" asks Finnegan.

"Yes, he's ready Sir," she responds, saluting Finnegan in the outlandish play making.

"Excellent! The coin has been placed in his hand, the toll to pay for the boat transporting him to another world," Finnegan says, using a spooky voice.

Sheena's laughter transforms to cries of despair for the departed, in keeping with character.

Finnegan says, "Don't let any of your tears fall on him or his soul could drown! Alright friends, gather for vigil over the unfortunate one. We must insure his spirit rises by sunset or it may wander for eternity."

This last remark brings laughter from all three as they leave the crypt, removing their masks.

"Shhhhh, don't wake the dead," Finnegan says, laughing.

Sapphire recognizes a healthier version of Albert this time. The scratches on his face at their first meeting are gone.

"I must get these two monkeys home," Sheena announces, while mussing Albert's hair. "They don't behave once midnight strikes."

"I like it here," Albert says.

Chamous pulls up in his truck. Sapphire breathes a sigh of relief, and she and Pony walk away.

"I don't blame you," Sheena calls out, showing some effects of her drinks at the Mosaic. "These bizarre antics won't make us many friends. I am sorry you two."

Remembering their tolerance for diversity, and knowing they may never see the three again, Sapphire downplays the events.

"Oh, don't be silly. You're just having a little fun. No harm done. Do you need a ride?" Sapphire asks, hoping the answer will be no.

"No, Finnegan's fine. Thank you for the offer," Sheena says as Pony and Sapphire get into the vehicle.

"That was weird," Pony says once inside.

"What on earth are you doing at Mt. Washington Cemetery?" Chamous asks.

"Sheena McNeil offered to help after my car wouldn't start. They stopped here to show us some of their Romanian burial customs or something. Sapphire you downplayed the whole thing with your response as we were leaving. Just having a little fun?" Pony asks.

"I didn't want to draw too much attention to the fact I was horrified and confused at the same time," she says.

"Albert looked much better than when we first met him at UMKC," says Pony.

"Yes, but Finnegan was… sick at the Mosaic," Sapphire says.

"Sick, how?" Pony asks.

Sapphire says, "While we were dancing, his shoulder got displaced and I think he nearly passed out from the pain. He rammed a pillar and put it back in place himself. He had a small amount of blood coming from his ear, his face was flushed, and eyes bloodshot. But before I rejoined you his symptoms disappeared."

"Maybe one of your visions?" asks Pony.

"I thought of that. But he fixed his own displaced shoulder and commented on the blood. I am certain it was happening. His demeanor was normal, then odd. Blood coming from the ear, what's that?" Sapphire asks.

Chamous says, "I would suggest staying away from those three."

"We are going to her performance at the Kauffman Center this week. But I don't plan to accept invites from them," Sapphire says.

Chapter Fourteen

On the north side of the estate, between the stables and Dutch barn lies the two story limestone covered in English ivy. Tera calls this place her home now. Windows with leaded glass are flanked by boxes overflowing with coral and pink flowers. An urn crowded with lavender stands next to the arched oak door.

Quinn's knock on Tera's door is more for help than permission to enter. Formalities between them long ago fell by the wayside in the name of friendship.

"Can you give me a hand?" Quinn asks. She holds a bottle of wine in one hand and a large covered basket in another.

"Whoa! What's in here?" Tera asks.

"Lunch, to give us sustenance to accomplish our goal. The wine is for sharing with Chamous next time he comes over. I asked Beef to prepare lunch for us," Quinn says.

"Perfect, I'm hungry. I am beginning to think the creation of a transit in Fireside Books may be more daunting than I realize," says Tera.

"That's why I come bearing gifts," Quinn says, laughing.

"The sun is shining, why not dine alfresco?" Tera suggests.

The spring day is mild and a gentle breeze rustles the foliage surrounding the patio.

Tera sets the basket down and Quinn spreads out the cloth covering its contents.

"I brewed up some of Mocha Joe's Italian roast. Be right back," Tera says.

Keeping secrets from Quinn weighs heavy on her, but she isn't ready to tell anyone about her strange experiences. There is no evidence anything happened.

"Professor Enderlee mentioned Elliott Kennadie's nephew Ace Kennedy, showed up at Mocha Joe's the other day with Tracie Glenn," Tera says, her voice coming from the kitchen.

"Well, we all know she's trouble. What brought them to town?"

"He was in town on business with his late uncle's estate. She rode along. He is a journalist too, but spells Kennedy the traditional way. How odd," Tera says.

Tera brings two steaming mugs of Italian roast to the patio.

Quinn sips the rich deep coffee.

"I miss a good cup of Mocha Joes'. With his uncle a journalist in the same region, the spelling change makes sense. The fact he is part of the media, explains why she tagged along," Quinn says.

"Professor Enderlee said she looked bored."

"Tracie Glenn needs a public image boost. That's the only reason she is hanging with a journalist."

"What are we eating?" Tera asks, looking over their lunch.

"Curried chicken salad, some cheese and croissants, pears, strawberries and…"

Tera says, "Looks like tiny cakes."

"I recognize those, the orange cupcakes with vanilla bean icing we raved about a few weeks ago," says Quinn.

"A delicious lunch, Quinn."

Quinn pauses to read a text and a big smile ensues.

"What's up?"

Quinn says, "Keefe and I are meeting up later."

"I'm glad. Separation is hard."

"The Quest must be the priority for now. They leave in the morning."

"Where are you two going tonight?" Tera asks.

"I am slightly intrigued. The address is… the estate." Quinn smiles as she selects from the picnic spread.

"Sounds a little mysterious. I like his style," Tera says. She samples some of her prepared lunch. "This is delicious."

"Tera, how are things at Fireside Books?"

"Different without you there, but we are getting along. We filled a rolling cart with summer reading suggestions and parked it under the awning out front. That's drawn the window shoppers inside. We also put a few small cast iron tables with umbrellas and chairs out front for the coffee drinkers from Mocha Joe's."

"Smart ideas," Quinn says.

"We've brought in some new customers by staying open later

than others on Main Street. I love the bookstore, Quinn," says Tera.

"Thank you for taking over for me. With the chaos following the defeat of the River People, we needed someone at the heart of White Oak, so we would be aware of any problems, or suspicions surrounding those community leaders who are no longer... with us. Sapphire told me about their ordeal with the Romanians over breakfast this morning. Our conversation was cut short... eavesdropping," Quinn says shaking her head.

"Eavesdropping, who?"

"Beef. He is lingering when he shouldn't. I think he cares about us like family and feels entitled to know what is happening, especially since he learned about the Circle of Sun," Quinn says.

"Normal curiosity, I bet. Put yourself in his shoes. He is on the same learning curve, but with even less information. I might be doing it too," Tera remarks.

"I want to talk to Romulus, but he has been busy away from the estate lately. Let's head over to the library and get started."

Two spiral staircases connect the two stories of the vast collection at the Royce Estate. Sunlight filters through narrow but lofty windows spanning both levels. Quinn approaches one of the high-reaching bookcases on the second level. With one finger she selects a book, tipping the bind down on its back. She does the same to six more selections on random shelves. This combination of selections causes the bookcase to creak and move and finally open slowly. Quinn leads wide-eyed Tera inside, the bookcase closing behind them.

Seven stone podiums surround a generous table. Quinn lights the candles, filling the room with warm light.

"What is this place?" Tera asks in amazement.

"This is our past and our future. This is where we find answers," she says.

Quinn lifts a substantial volume from one of the pedestals and opens the ancient book on the table.

"You begin with this and I will begin with that one."

"What are we looking for?" Tera asks.

"Anything to do with transit and portal creation."

Tea says, "Slight problem here, this book is in Latin."

"How do you know until you try?" Quinn asks.

Tera glances to her friend and back at the book. Her eyes travel across the lines, comprehending their meaning.

"I can read Latin…wow!" Tera announces.

Without raising her head, Quinn responds.

"You can do a great many things....now."

"Because I am a… Knight," Tera says.

"Yes, because you are a Knight."

Tera says, "I may be honored as one, and I am of service to the Circle of Sun, but I am not so sure."

"Remember my words? He does not call the qualified, he qualifies the called," Quinn says, looking up from the book. "You are the called. We've not only been given an honor. We are given commissions. We are given tools to perform the service we are called to. There will be much to learn. You will have what is needed when the time comes," Quinn says.

Tera leans on Quinn's strength. She takes a deep breath.

"Yes, this is the new reality. I am learning, so is Sapphire. Her commission and the whole process is frightening to her," says Tera.

"This time will pass. Sapphire will not only learn to cope with her commission, she will master it. So will you, Tera."

"I don't know what my commission is yet," Tera says.

"Neither do I, but soon we both will."

The candles flicker and burn lower as both women page through the massive volumes.

"Here is what we are looking for," Quinn says, reading from the book. "Creation of transit…the space must contain openings to the west and east, north and south."

Tera says, "Chamous and I confirmed windows are on all four sides of the attic at Fireside Books."

"The request for the transit must be submitted and granted by the Empyrean Assembly," says Quinn.

"Check. Father Mopsi petitioned them," Tera says.

"A Chi-Rho must be created with sanctified water and oil from each of the seven regions."

"Whatever that means," Tera says.

"Chi-Rho is the Christian monogram made from the first two letters of the Greek word for Christ. Father Mopsi will explain how the holy water and the sacred oil is used. This portion explains here the creation of the Chi-Rho requires qualifications as well, location of the sun in the sky and witnesses," says Quinn.

"Chamous and I will be witnessing the process and Sapphire is planning to be there too."

Some of Quinn's hair drops in front of her lowered face, and she gracefully puts the locks behind her ear. Quinn continues reading, unaware of Tera's observation.

"You should be going with them on the Quest…with Keefe," says Tera.

"He will return soon enough. More of us may be called, but perhaps not."

"Explain," Tera says.

"Depending on the difficulty of the Quest, all could be called to join. We must be ready."

"And I am sure that would be alright with you," Tera says.

Quinn ignores the statement.

"Once the requirements are met, the transit still must be considered by the Holy Dominions for final sanctification," says Quinn.

"Only Guardians may use the transit. And what does a privileged pass-key mean, I wonder?"

Quinn says,"Only those who know the code or key will be given passage. At times, the transport will be non-accessible by certain Guardians."

"And it says here, 'Knights entitlement provides sanctioned passage'. Wow, this is involved," says Tera.

"The purpose of the transit is concealment. The utmost consideration must always be taken in these delicate matters," Quinn says. She sits back and crosses her arms. "Will there ever be enough hours in the day to absorb all we must know?"

"Is that what is contained in all the other books?" Tera asks.

"Yes."

"I can't understand what I am reading anymore. Hey, what happened?" Tera asks, looking at Quinn.

"It means you've received what was needed. We are finished here," says Quinn. She closes the massive volume and returns it to the pedestal.

"I know you are looking forward to your night with Keefe. Enjoy it my friend," Tera says.

The friends leave the way they came and Tera returns to the North Lodge. Quinn prepares for her evening.

A text Quinn receives from Keefe asks text her to meet him near the lake. The afternoon sun is almost gone.

Playful breezes send Quinn's hair and the long flowing wrap she wears around her shoulders sailing behind her. This scene of the sky at dusk, the gardens, and her graceful beauty captivates a watching and waiting Keefe.

"Good evening, Keefe," Quinn says.

Guiding two horses, he leans in to kiss her on the cheek.

"I've missed you," he says.

With her foot in the stirrup he gives her a slight boost up to the saddle and they ride out.

Thick emerald grasses cover the rolling countryside of the Estate. The wind creates waves of green as the two riders gallop towards the river bluff. The sun slips low on the horizon to the west and they dismount on the south bluff. Far below, the Missouri River flows along, the limestone catching the last remaining rays of the setting sun. They stand together watching it, her back to him, his arms around her waist, his face next to hers. No words are needed as he holds her. She closes her eyes, wishing the moment would go on forever.

"Give me your hand," Keefe says.

He removes two simple rings from his pocket.

"I will miss you Quinn. I know you are feeling vulnerable with me away. But you must be strong for me. These rings were fashioned from my shield used against the River People. I gave everything to protect the light, and you. I will always shield you. I don't want you to forget that. Your name is inscribed within my ring." He shows her the ring before sliding it on his finger. "This is your ring."

In the palm of Keefe's hand lies a solitary silver band with words.

"Find Shelter," Quinn says, reading it aloud.

"Within My Love," Keefe says, reading the remainder of the sentiment inscribed inside the ring and slipping it on her finger. "I will be back in your arms very soon," Keefe says.

Quinn turns to face him.

His kiss is passionate.

"I love you. I will treasure the ring," she says.

"I rode over earlier and gathered some wood. Would you like to sit for awhile?" Keefe asks.

He lights the fire; the kindling ignites. When the flames are strong enough he feeds the fire some larger pieces.

"Would you open the wine?" he asks handing her the bottle and an opener.

"Nice. You thought of everything," she says smiling at him.

"Well, I didn't bring anything to eat, but I did remember glasses," says Keefe.

"Who needs food?" she replies, laughing. She draws her wrap closer for warmth.

The fire gains momentum and Keefe invites Quinn to sit in front of him. He surrounds her with his arms. They are warmed by the flames.

"I cherish our rings. Thank you for giving me a piece of you, Keefe."

"I am ready to go on this Quest, but I don't like leaving you."

"Your contributions will be a triumph. If and when you need more help, we will be ready," she says.

The two talked until the fire burned down into smoldering embers. They mount their horses and ride toward the estate, secure in their love and ready for the new day.

When Quinn comes back into the estate, she finds Romulus waiting.

Romulus sits holding a fluted champagne glass in front of a gentle fire in the study.

"Father, you wanted to see me?"

"Quinn. Yes I did. Please join me, I don't want to celebrate alone," he says, handing her a glass of champagne.

Quinn takes the glass and pauses, looking around the room.

"What is the celebration?" she asks.

"Well, my celebration may be a bit premature, and I am not ready for your siblings to know yet. But I want to share this news with someone," Romulus says, his happiness apparent.

"What is it Father?"

"I've rekindled a… romance with an old friend," he says.

Romulus struggles to choose words for his feelings.

"Father, how wonderful! I am happy for you. Who is the lucky woman?"

"Sheena McNeil," Romulus answers.

"Oh, the vocalist who is performing tomorrow evening with the symphony?"

"Yes," Romulus says, with an eager smile.

"I remember you mentioned knowing her before you met Petulah."

Romulus nods.

"Father, your happiness shows."

"I have only seen her a few times, but I can't deny my feelings," Romulus reveals.

"This is a good thing. Why the secrecy?" Quinn says searching his eyes.

"The depth of their mother's deception is still fresh. But, Quinn my heart is soaring. And . . . I wanted to tell someone."

He raises his glass and clinks the rim of Quinn's glass. His joy is hers and they both smile and drink to his healed heart.

"Father, Beef's behavior is an issue I would like to discuss," says Quinn.

"In what way?" he questions.

"I think he is eavesdropping," Quinn says with slight hesitation.

Romulus nods.

"Yes, I am aware. He has let some of his duties slip. He leaves the estate more than he ever has," says Romulus.

"Well, he has been a trusted servant for many years. Maybe it is time he did have more in his life."

Romulus says, "Well, I was thinking the same things. I visited his room."

"What did he say?"

"Quinn, he didn't answer. I used a key to enter and his room is empty except for this note."

Quinn reads. "I am called home to England. My family needs me. I should have left months ago. Beef."

"I can't believe Beef is gone. Will you try to reach him?" Quinn asks.

"I will try if I can." Romulus says.

Quinn retires to her room. The night still reigns before dawn and his departure, but her heart already aches for Keefe. The moon casts its brilliance across her bed. She slides the smooth ring from her finger and reads its inscription, "Find shelter within my love." And she sleeps peacefully.

Chapter Fifteen

In the early morning hours, the chosen Guardians stand in a ceremonial circle on the stone platform of the Madowent. Jexis, Cashton, Professor Enderlee and Keefe grasp hands and chant in unison as Cashton repeats the divine verses transporting them to their Quest.

"Let us soar on the wings of truth, across the seas, the valleys and the mountains, to touch the summit of our faith," the Knights say.

Brave faces mask any hesitation. A wind sweeps through the Madowent and swirls above their heads and within seconds swallows their union. Their human ring rotates with such momentum legs are swept from beneath as they're lifted by the torrential thrust. All grip is broken and they are flung apart into the unknown.

The transported ones lie upon the floor of an open faced cave. Awaking in an unfamiliar place, each are disoriented. Cashton is the first to rise and sees the Professor lying motionless.

"Professor, are you alright?" Cashton asks, rushing to his side.

Professor Enderlee rises slowly.

"Fine…a little shaken," he says.

Cashton helps him to his feet.

Keefe offers Jexis his arm and she, too, is on her feet. They face a rising sun overlooking a lush valley.

A figure bounds down from a boulder, startling all. Jexis steps back.

"Welcome, my name is Elle," she says. She moves some of her short, dark hair from her eyes. "I am your guide in this foreign place. Is everyone accounted for and in one piece? A bit of a rumbly ride, 'tis true!"

Elle's breeches and boots, along with her dialect, render the travelers speechless. The stranger stands with one hand on her hip and the other pointing to them.

"I know I look… different, but you might want to examine yourselves," says Elle.

Confused, they search themselves and one another for the familiar, but there is none to be found. They too, arrived at this place looking as odd as she.

"You won't find any of your contraptions from whence you came. Your best advantage will be your... enlightenment. You'll return to your home, the way you came. When here you must operate within the realm of Hudovistan," she says.

"Hudovistan," Keefe repeats, "where exactly is Hudovistan…in relation to Nadellawick?"

Elle says, "Ah, the emphasis is not on where but on when, my fine fellow. Hudovistan refers to a specific span of time. I am sorry I do not claim to understand. You do know of London town, am I right as rain? Try to fit in as best you can. In London there are plenty of odd ducks, so I wouldn't put a powder keg of worry on that one."

"Who are you?" Keefe asks.

"Like I told you, I'm Elle, Pathfinder in the Circle of Sun. Romulus and my Uncle Thomas are friends. Your presence is answered prayers. Please follow me to fresh horses for our short journey. Once there you will find the answers you seek."

With their minds reeling, they ride in silence, not yet accepting what seems obvious and impossible. They emerge into a clearing where Professor Enderlee pulls back on his reins, stopping his horse at the same time the others do, seeing a castle tucked in a valley. The fortress, with towers and moat, stands gallantly at attention awaiting their arrival. The weary group share astonished glances as they approach. Elle leads them through an outer gatehouse, across a court to a drawbridge.

Elle says, "Welcome to Tobler Tower."

Children run in their direction and, a dog scampers at their feet.

"Elle, you are back! We wanted to come along," one of them says.

"I missed all three of you," she says. She hugs each and they scurry out of view.

Elle says, "Tia will show you to your quarters."

The four wide-eyed travelers follow Tia through corridors of stone, passing curious house servants on their way to a staircase.

"This is the most secure place in the castle," she says.

Her comment brings more questions in their minds.

Tia says, “The first door is for the gentleman, and the next door is for the lady. Dinner is served a quarter past the hour. I will be back then.”

Jexis follows the three men through their door. A window from the castle captures a view only imagined in storybooks.

“May I speak frankly?” she asks.

“Do we have an option?” Cashton answers.

“I’m glad you can inject humor, brother. But I am…concerned,” Jexis says.

Professor Enderlee says, “I share that concern. My head spins with questions. But let’s remain calm until dinner, when our questions will be answered.”

“He is right, sister. We are chosen for a specific purpose. We must not allow our vulnerability and fear of the unknown to chart our course. Stay cool, Jexis,” Cashton says. He puts his hand on her shoulder.

“We can’t even communicate with Father or Quinn. We no longer have our phones, or….contraptions as Elle pointed out!” she says, exasperated.

“I am as baffled as you all, but the professor is right. We should wait until we have more answers. It’s too early for panic,” Keefe says.

“Ok, I am reserving judgment....for now,” she says, leaving for her room.

Jexis wonders how she can do anything. She is without her clothing, personal supplies, her phone, her weapon, and most importantly, her confidence. She plops down in a chair by the window, trying to make sense of things she exhales, allowing her weary shoulders to fall with an audible sigh. Closing her eyes, she whispers, “St. Michael, you know my commissions better than I even do at this point. I’ve been like a foreigner in my own land, why should this be any different? Calm me and empower me. Although I am unaware, you know how I will aid these people. Please dispel my fear, confusion and apprehension, and I pray for those to be replaced with wisdom and courage… I am ready to offer all I can,” Jexis prays.

She rises, takes a deep breath and looks for a libation.

Before long, Tia knocks and the four join her for a long walk to the Great Hall where Elle waits. At the far end, between two windows spanning the distance between the floor and the canopy of this massive hall, lies a seat of authority. Elle makes her way to the dignitary as they follow. The room is silenced as she bows.

"This is Thomas Tobler, Archbishop of Westminster and my uncle," Elle says.

The Guardians make quick glances to one another, then bow as Elle did.

"May I present Knights from Nadellawick? This is Professor Gunderson Enderlee, Keefe Remington, and Cashton and Jexis Royce," she says.

Thomas, a large robust middle-aged man with flushed cheeks and wavy copper hair, stands. His kind smile sets the group at ease.

"Come here niece. Is that any way to greet me?" Thomas Tobler says.

Elle climbs small steps in front the Archbishop and he sweeps her into a hug as a slightly stiff Elle accepts. The three children who greeted her in the courtyard swarm her and lead her off to a table setting. The big man bounds down and greets each, beginning with Keefe.

Thomas Tobler says, "You must be Keefe Remington. I have heard much about you from Romulus. Allow me to shake your hand?"

Keefe obliges.

"Gunderson Enderlee. Your enlightenment will be our advantage," Thomas says. He shakes the hand of the professor.

"Cashton Royce, son of Romulus, warrior and healer and Jexis Royce, daughter of Romulus, warrior, courageous and independent thinker," he says, and shakes their hands as well. "Welcome to you all. You arrive from a distant time, but you are Circle of Sun. Together we will defend the light. Thank you, thank you for coming."

Tia seats them at the long table next to Thomas Tobler. Servers pour wine and serve food. The four can do nothing but observe this scene in awe, but they are hungry and thirsty and accept the sincere welcome and the sustenance with gratitude.

Thomas says, "Two hundred years ago sickness swept across our land. Entire villages were affected, leaving many with few inhabitants.

The loss of life was so profound, and the effects of the sickness so far reaching, that history was changed. The good people of London fear history is repeating. We have lost two important spiritual leaders from a mysterious affliction. They believe if God cannot save the men of the cloth, they are doomed themselves. Rumors and doubt are spreading faster than this suspected plague. We need a miracle before it is too late. Recently, I took some advice to heart. Reach beyond what you know, seek answers outside of your own understanding, which is precisely why you are here. My days are spent in worry and my sleep in nightmares. I am perplexed by the meaning of a recurring dream, and dismayed by its influence upon me."

"Explain your dream," The professor suggests.

"In a valley lies a tree filled with the fruit of life. Any who eat from the tree are instantly cured of afflictions. Desperate people make the long and difficult journey through barren wilderness. A raven waits upon a rock, collecting their toll to enter the valley. Beyond the rock lies a path into the lush green valley. A traveler reaches in his pouch for coins, gladly willing to pay any amount required. The raven has a warning. He tells him to stay away from the swift flowing river, which will carry him over the waterfall to certain death. The man thanks him for his warning, and counts his coins for the toll. The raven laughs at the man and explains he does not accept payment in coins. The price of the toll is loss of his eyesight." Bishop Tobler continues.

"The man lowers his head and contemplates his options, death or life with no sight. Both carry a steep price. But the man agrees to the toll, like the rest of those before him. He steps one foot upon the soft green grass of the cool valley and immediately his eyesight is gone. He searches far and wide across the valley, heeding the Raven's warning, when his fingers touch the water, never knowing the tree lies a short distance on the other side of an insignificant brook that poses no danger. Eventually the man dies, never finding the tree. The raven deceived every traveler in the same way. The dream visits me nightly and its meaning haunts my days. Perhaps the panic surrounding us has affected me like everyone else. Can you help us?"

Cashton speaks for the group.

"You are asking for help in determining if there is a spreading sickness, a plague, and if there so, you are trying to prevent history from repeating itself in loss of lives. Is that right?"

Thomas says, "If anything can be done, we must do it. As Guardians you would be shielded if an illness exists, as part of your entitlement. Your character will not be discounted if you refuse this Quest. Discuss this among yourselves. Prepare any questions you would like to ask Tia will escort you to the courtyard." Tia does so, leaving them to dicuss their Quest.

"What are we going to do?" Jexis asks.

"Help, I am not sure how. This is what our Guardianship is all about. We have the endorsement of St. Michael, after all," Cashton says.

"He's right," Keefe says, "our faith is our guide. We need nothing else."

Professor Enderlee puts his hand on Keefe's shoulder.

"Yes, I agree. Or else I would not have consented to making the journey. Jexis?" the professor turns to her.

"My doubts were squelched earlier. My heart is peaceful. I am ready," she says.

The four rise and Tia leads them back to the Great Hall and Thomas Tobler.

Keefe says, "The master plan is only known by Him, but we are here today, in this place and time, armed with knowledge and faith and our willingness to serve."

Thomas stands, his relief evident in his beaming smile.

"We must understand the gravity of the situation before we can proceed, and make sure we are dealing with facts," Keefe says.

"What are the physicians saying about the spreading illness?" Cashton asks.

Thomas says, "This afternoon you will meet with a group assembled to answer your questions at Gresham College in London. This will give you a place to begin. You will be meeting with the Professor of Divinity and the Professor of Physics. You will also be joined by Deacon Simpson and Archbishop of York. Your horses are ready. Elle will show you the way."

Chapter Sixteen

With a wrapped sandwich under his arm, Chamous dodges heavy drops of rain while opening his umbrella. He walks the two blocks back to Fireside Books, through streets saturated from the steady precipitation. Water gurgles out from the shop's downspouts. The droplets bounce from his raised umbrella, sounding like popping corn. The moisture and cooler temperatures, mixed with the heat of the ground from an earlier warm afternoon, creates a misty and foggy evening in White Oak. Chamous pulls the shop keys out of his pocket and eyes two figures on the other side of the street. A red glow from the end of a lighted cigarette brings the two men into focus. A dog barks in the distance and the men watch Chamous in silence.

With Father Mopsi arriving soon to begin work on the transit, Chamous follows preparation instructions from Father Mopsi and builds a good, hearty fire. It crackles while catching momentum and Thomasina rubs herself against his legs, purring for attention. Father Mopsi gave specific details about the hours they would be working on the transit and who could be present. The priest also told Chamous to make sure Tera would be there at first light. She would be serving as some kind of witness. The existence of Guardians shatters his reality and supplies a large dose of the unexplained. For a man who relies on logic like a compass to guide him, he must now operate on faith. A screech, followed by a car horn from behind the bookstore, signals the arrival of Father Mopsi. Chamous first glances out the front shop window, confirming the empty street. He pulls shutters from either side of the large window and secures them before rushing back to let Father Mopsi in.

Chamous takes an oversized satchel from Father Mopsi's hands to lighten his loaded arms. He grossly misjudges its weight and uses both hands to keep the package from hitting the floor.

"What's in there?" he asks. His question goes unanswered.

"Where have you been? There is no time to waste!" Father Mopsi says, sounding agitated.

Chamous takes the satchel inside while Father Mopsi returns for more.

He joins Chamous with a smaller tote. A soggy Father Mopsi removes his damp coat and hat and hangs both on a rack near the back room entrance while Chamous secures the back door for the night.

Father Mopsi warms himself by the fire.

"This small table is not sufficient, Chamous. Anything taller?" Father Mopsi asks.

Chamous says, "Yes, one in the back room."

"Those two small sofas will need to be slid back some," Father Mopsi says. He surveys Fireside Books in preparation for their work. After switching the tables and clearing the sofas back Father Mopsi seems pleased. "Ok, this is good. What time is it, Chamous?"

Before Chamous can respond, Father Mopsi makes a request.

"Please brew up some tea? I am chilled to the bone," he asks Chamous.

"Sure I can Father, I will be right back."

A small light illuminates the dark Mocha Joe's kitchen enough to prepare tea.

Father Mopsi is eating his sandwich when he returns.

"I am famished," he says, while chewing.

Chamous sets down the pot and two cups.

"Just save the other half for me, Father," he says.

"Oh, Chamous I am sorry I took your sandwich. I am a little nervous," Father Mopsi says.

The two men sit in silence eating.

Father Mopsi's leg bounces all the while.

"Shall we begin, Chamous?" he asks.

Still chewing, Chamous can't respond right away.

Father Mopsi doesn't wait for an answer. He removes the sandwich wrapping and tea and transforms their dinner table. He covers it with a purple cloth from the satchel. A Circle of Sun emblem is stitched into a starched white runner, which is laid over the top of the purple. Mopsi checks the front of the table facing the fire to ensure it is centered. Using both of his hands, he heaves a dark metal cauldron from the satchel to place upon the fireplace hearth. From the smaller satchel he retrieves a bundle and unwraps a glass decanter with great care.

"Sacred chrism oil," he whispers.

Another glass decanter with silver handle is positioned alongside.

"Holy water from each of the seven regions within the Circle of Sun. We will combine them and fuse their properties with the perpetual fire," Mopsi says. He next places a miniature chest on the center of the table. "Chamous, stand next to me."

With the rain still falling and the wind beginning to howl, Father Mopsi mumbles the words of a prayer. He opens the small chest and removes a gold box adorned with jewels of amber, gold, jade and turquoise. Father Mopsi gingerly lifts its golden lid, revealing a burning flame. Chamous' gasp is drowned out by a stifling crack of thunder rattling the windows of the bookstore. The blowing wind howls and whips the structure with rain.

"Please fetch me a small piece of kindling, one with a forked end." Mopsi instructs.

Chamous stares at the holy candle with amazement and wonder.

"Did you hear me Chamous?" he asks. "That is the Perpetual Flame, the fewer questions, the better."

"Oh,... um, ok," Chamous says.

He sifts through the bucket of twigs and small branches and finds one about the length of his forearm.

Father Mopsi nods in approval. The experienced Guardian pours small amounts of the chrisom oil and the holy water into the iron cauldron. From the fireplace he lights the left fork of the branch. Returning to the table, he lights the right fork of the branch from the Perpetual Flame.

Father Mopsi explains, "Solitary flames, until they travel to the center and become one."

Seconds away from fusing together, thunder rumbles and lightening crashes. Father Mopsi lets neither deter him from his task. When the two flames burn as one, Father Mopsi drops the flaming branch into the cauldron igniting the brew. Both of them stand back as flames rise toward the ceiling. The father stirs the mixture once it subsides, then motions for Chamous to take over the stirring. The thick, oatmeal-like mixture boils and bubbles, filling the shop with a spicy sweet aroma.

"Will you assist me? We must pour the sacred mix into this mold," says Mopsi. "This is one of the oldest symbols of Christ, called a Chi-Rho, the first two letters in the Latin word for Christ."

Together, they spill the boiling liquid into the mold.

"Careful now. Slow down the flow…that will do just fine, good man," he says. "Now we wait."

Chamous adds wood to the fire, and plops down on the sofa next to Father Mopsi. The fresh logs crack and smolder before burning bright and hot. They sit in silence watching the flames leap and flicker while a storm rages outside. Father Mopsi pulls a flask from his breast pocket and takes a swig, then offers it to Chamous who accepts. Together they wait for the mold to harden and both fall asleep.

Thomasena pounces on Chamous's lap, waking him up as Tera arrives. The large table he and Father Mopsi worked on is now gone. In its place sits the coffee table.

"Good morning," Tera says. She pecks Chamous on the cheek and hands him coffee. "Long night?"

"Where is Father Mopsi?" he asks.

From a small room upstairs they hear him respond.

"I am up here. Please come up so we can prepare before our sunrise deadline," he says, yelling down to them.

Tera attempts to tame his mussed hair.

"How did it go last night?" she asks.

"Fine and weird....holy," says Chamous.

Tera says,"That sounds about right. From the research Quinn and I did, I would say those words describe it."

Chamous climbs the narrow and squeaky flight of stairs to the attic. The Chi-Rho sits on a table in the center of the small room.

"The cast is perfect," Father Mopsi says with pride.

Chamous examines the smooth, wheat colored symbol as Father Mopsi crosses his arms and nods his head.

"Yes, all is going as planned. We will discover if our request is granted from the Holy Dominions when we try out the transit for the first time," the Father says.

Tera enters the attic room.

"The doors are locked, but Sapphire is late. She planned to drop off some books and be a witness to the first transport of the Sanctified Transit. I've received no text," Tera reports.

"I'm afraid we can't wait for her." Father Mopsi says.

"We should proceed," Tera says, agreeing.

Mopsi says, "All right then, first and foremost, Guardians are the only beings privileged to use the Sanctified Transport." Father Mopsi paces the floor of the small attic space peering out of the four windows while explaining the process.

"The procedure is as follows. A Guardian who wants to access the transport must request a specific periodical, Dr. Wiley Oliver's Bird Watching Bible. You lead them to the landing of the stairwell, and from there they will know what to do."

Allowing his excitement to show, Father Mopsi stops his pacing and puts his hands together with enthusiasm.

"Let's send someone to the Madowent. Chamous will you approach the table?" he asks.

A reluctant Chamous moves to the center of the room beside Father Mopsi.

"Now, take your hand and trace over the Chi-Rho, like so," says Mopsi.

Chamous imitates his action.

"Yes, that is how it's done. Cross your wrists and place them over your heart and focus on your destination," Mopsi tells him.

Anticipation grows as all three wait. A sound is heard, a faint, distant shrill becomes louder and closer. Like a sheet floating in a slow motion breeze, the room rises and falls as transparent waves of movement roll over all. Chamous keeps his wrists crossed but Tera covers her ears as the high pitched sound becomes unbearable. Clothing and hair are whipped by a wind storm in the tiny room. The shrill sound stops, the winds cease and left on the floor next to Father Mopsi lies a ghostly shape.

Chamous looks around the room, eyes wide with wonder.

Tera stands against the wall, astounded.

Before anyone can say or do anything, the apparition rises, dusts herself off and says in a breathless British dialect, "Pardon me, but what am I doing here?" She adjusts her glasses and attempts to tame her disheveled hair.

With astonishment, Father Mopsi gasps as he recognizes the former tutor at Royce Estate.

"Calista...Calista Twinning?" Mopsi asks.

"My question remains unanswered, where am I?" the apparition says, looking all around her, then focusing on Father Mopsi's face. "Clarence Mopsi, is that you? Great Gatsby, it is! We're not at the estate?" she asks.

"Calista it's been years. If I may ask, Calista, where did you come from?" asks a sheepish Father Mopsi.

"Royce Estate, of course. I am a permanent fixture, don't you know? Taken from this world in a cruel accident. But I've got me a surplus of duty to the Royce family still," Calista Twinning says.

Chamous and Tera stand speechless as Father Mopsi checks each window.

Mopsi says, "Here is our problem. This east facing window is only partially open." He thrusts the stuck window all the way up. "That should do it. Chamous come back to the table. Let's try again. I speak with the utmost confidence when I give the next instruction. When you reach the Madowent please remain on the receiving line of the transit for a few hours. Calista, would you like transport back or will you use your own means of transportation?" the Father asks.

"Conserve energy is my motto," Calista Twinning says.

She moves to the table alongside a blank-faced Chamous. They both trace the Chi-Rho with their hands and cross wrists over their hearts. Once again the room is transformed as it rolls in waves. A gust blows around the table in the center. And then, as before, the wind ceases.

Chamous is gone, and Calista Twinning is gone.

Father Mopsi takes stock of the room and a very frightened Tera.

"My dear, everything will be fine. Please sit for a moment," Father Mopsi says. He stands a toppled chair upright in a far corner of the small attic and leads her to it.

Tera's phone signals a text, which she ignores. Her face is void of expression as she searches for logic.

"The woman, she knew....she was...I saw..." Unable to complete her thoughts, Father Mopsi comes to her aid and pats her hand.

"Yes that was an apparition and it was Calista Twinning. Yes, she traveled via the Sanctified Transport from the Royce Estate. Yes, Chamous traveled...somewhere." Father Mopsi tries to reassure her but ends up sounding as perplexed as Tera looks.

Tera's phone continues to buzz.

Father Mopsi breathes a tremendous sigh of relief when he reads the text from Chamous.

"Safely at the Madowent! The....lady is not with me," the text reads.

"There Tera, you see? Chamous is just fine. It looks like our Sanctified Transport is operational, and it's a dandy!" Mopsi says, sounding very happy.

Tera takes the phone and reads the text. With shaking hands she responds to the text. "Ok." is all she manages to respond.

Her phone buzzes again.

"Are you alright?" Chamous texts.

"Yes, trying to calm myself," she responds.

"Another new experience! I will meet you back at the estate later and we can talk. We should leave for the Symphony by five thirty," Chamous writes.

"Until then," Tera replies.

She takes a deep breath and stands.

"Dear, are you alright?" Father Mopsi asks her. He rests his hand on her shoulder.

"Yes, I think I am fine now," Tera says.

She receives a text from Sapphire.

"Change of plans today. Sorry! Later," the text reads.

"Will you be riding with us to the Symphony?" Tera asks in her text. When Sapphire's response is not immediate, she turns to Father Mopsi.

"I better get back downstairs and prepare to open the bookstore," Tera says.

"I will see myself out the back way, Tera," Father Mopsi calls out. He gathers his things to leave and Tera makes her way down the small crooked staircase.

Chapter Seventeen

Tera unlocks the door and goes through her opening routine. She puts a sign on Mocha Joe's door to enter through Fireside Books, as she will be handling both businesses solo this day. She discovers a light left on when she decides to brew some calming chamomile tea for herself in the kitchen at Mocha Joe's.

Back behind the counter at Fireside, Tera breathes deeply and allows herself time to sit still. She recalls her strange experience while running. She takes her small notebook out and reads the phrase whispered over and over. She prays for the courage to face her fear. Today her concerns seem even more absurd and she dismisses her thoughts and distracts herself with paperwork. After a quarter hour of progress, the dangling bells announce a delivery. She signs for the boxes and thanks the delivery man. The shop is still empty. Immersing herself in the mundane tasks helps Tera to feel grounded after her unusual morning. But again and again her hidden fears resurface and she knows she can't continue to bury them. The whispering voices and the chasing wind rotation are connected. It's time she tells Chamous and Quinn about what she has been experiencing. She searches for possible translations to the words she does not recognize as English. With her pen she makes notes. She copies the first two words and says them out loud.

"You lock," she says. At least that is what they sound like, she thinks. She copies the next two words and again repeats them aloud. "We ask." She writes down the last two sounds. "In tina."

She reads aloud the phrase buried in her music. At first it was barely audible, then grew louder during her run. "You lock, we ask, in Tina."

She enters the phrase into the translation search bar, with no results. Almost as quickly, her resolve fades. Could her mind be playing tricks on her? She shakes her head, thinking Quinn can help. Her decision clears her head again, and she once more deals with the tasks at hand. She focuses on putting the package of supplies away. With her hair piled high on her head and a pencil tucked on top of her ear she adjusts her glasses and scoops up the packages. Tera notices an odd scent in the air and is startled when she sees a man sprawled out on a chair in the reading nook.

She jolts, dropping everything to the floor.

"Oh ma'am, forgive me for giving you fright," he says.

Tera's guard goes up immediately as he bends down to help her. His hair is ratty and he looks at her through bloodshot eyes, dark with circles.

"Thank you," she manages to say in a soft voice.

"Yes, let myself in. I'm up for a good read. What's good, eh?" he asks.

"You don't sound like you're from around here," she says. She remains calm as she walks the supplies back to the sales counter and the safety of her phone.

The man runs his fingers along the bookshelves, shopping for a title.

"Righto, ma'am, I'm from across the pond as they say. Just here for a few days." He looks over the book in his hand. "This one's not quite grabbing me. I prefer something a little edgier… perhaps a dark romance." he says. He forces a natural laugh.

Before Tera can speak, a car horn blares.

"My mate's here to collect me. Hope ya' don't mind a brewed a lil' Mocha Joe's too. I must come back and shop when I'm not so rushed. Cheerio!"

With a badly bruised hand he waves goodbye and leaves.

Tera's eyes follow him as he slams the door of the bookstore. She races to the window, watching as he enters the passenger side of a car driven by another man. As they speed off he looks back at her and salutes. She immediately calls Chamous.

"Hi sweetie, what is it?" he asks.

"Someone was inside before we opened," Tera tells him as calmly as she can.

"What do you mean, Tera?" Chamous says.

"After Father Mopsi left, I prepared to open and made myself tea. After working for almost forty-five minutes I see this creepy guy sitting in one of the reading chairs and it startled me so badly I dropped an armload of supplies. He looked sort of beat up, and he had an accent," she says.

"Is he still there? I'm coming right over," Chamous says.

"No he's gone now. He made himself at home and even made coffee in Mocha Joe's for himself. He tried to intimidate me, and was flagrantly rude. When we were in the attic, I suspect he was inside," she says.

"I'll be right there. Secure the door for now so you can choose who you'll allow in," says Chamous.

She closes her eyes in relief that he is on his way. Her phone signals a text and she assumes it from him but she is wrong. The text reads, "You lock we ask in tina." The words take her breath away!

"Oh my Lord!" she says.

She drops her phone from her hand. With her mind reeling, she confirms with herself that, she had shared the phrase with no one. Before realizing what any of this can mean she begins to wonder if she is alone right now.

Suddenly her phone vibrates from the floor. She takes a deep breath and scoops the phone up, heart racing as she reluctantly peeks.

"Eu Locuiesc InTine," the text reads.

Tera holds the phone in her shaking hands as she reads. She attempts to sound out the words. In one horrible second she understands. Eu is what she thought was 'you'. Loc is the word she was pronouncing as 'lock'. 'We ask' must be all one word, 'loc we ask' or Locuiesc. And then 'in Tina' was In Tine. Eu Locuiesc In Tine.

This is what she heard! What could the strange phrase mean? Allowing panic to rise, she races to her computer. Her hands tremble as she struggles to enter the phrase into the translator. The hasty and clumsy attempt yields no matches. She tries desperately to calm herself and takes her time to enter the letters correctly. Tera waits for information after hitting the enter key. She literally feels her heart thumping in her chest, her cheeks becoming flushed, as she waits wide-eyed for the translation. Her hand flies to cover her gasp. It is a Romanian translation.

"I live in you."

Chapter Eighteen

The Kauffman Center is crowded with concert goers when Tera, Quinn and Chamous arrive.

"Tera, are you alright?" Quinn asks. "You are quiet."

"Nothing a good night's sleep won't cure," Tera says casually.

Tonight's show is a sold out performance. Thousands want to hear the voice of an angel, Sheena McNeil. After she performs two songs she interacts with the audience. Her speech is eloquent as she talks about her European heritage. When she mentions Kansas City's heartland charm, the crowd gives her a standing ovation. Ace's article in the Star had offered a poignant picture of an artist's humble beginnings and rise to superstardom. Sheena McNeil performs brilliantly. She bows after her encore, the fans not wanting the evening to end.

Quinn, Tera and Chamous planned to meet Romulus at the after-event cocktail reception in Brandmeyer Hall. They all three enjoy a glass of wine while waiting for him.

"Any word from our travelers, Quinn?" Chamous asks.

"Not yet."

Tera says, "You two probably know me better than anyone. I have something I want to…"

"Good evening, my name is Ace Kennedy, with the Kansas City Star. My uncle, Elliott Kennadie, was a journalist for the White Oak Advocate."

Chamous says, "Yes, he covered all the news in town. I am sorry for your loss. My name is Chamous McCoy. These are my friends, Quinn Clarke Royce and Tera Santiago."

"I am pleased to make your acquaintance. May I introduce you to a friend of mine, Tracie Glenn? Tracie is the county prosecutor," says Ace.

Tracie Glenn seems all too eager and wedges herself around the table until she is front and center.

"Is your entire family represented this evening?" she asks.

"Not everyone," Quinn replies.

"Ace showed me around this incredible venue, where I saw

Romulus earlier. He appeared star-struck as he gave a private tour to Ms. McNeil," Tracie Glenn says with slight sarcasm. "I'm seated with the VIPs on the other side of the large column. Please ask Romulus to stop over and say hello when he shows up. The mayor and his wife are waiting for a glass of champagne. I hope you enjoy your evening."

Ace nods to them and follows her as she continues her mission to rub shoulders with the right people.

"She is very easy to dislike," Tera says, sipping her wine.

A buzzing phone distracts the group as each check for its source.

Tera says, "I wonder where Pony and Sapphire were seated."

"And when Father and Sheena will join us," Quinn says.

Tera says, "And Sheena?"

Quinn smiles but doesn't divulge what she knows about the romance.

"Don't tell me, let me guess. Romulus has fallen for Sheena McNeil? I'm not surprised, when I saw him talk about her at dinner. They knew each other before, right?" Tera asks.

"Yes, they did. I will let you judge for yourself what the state of their relationship is when they join us," Quinn says.

Tera says, "If Sheena takes his arm for the evening the whole city will know."

"I think that's the idea," Quinn says.

* * * * *

Romulus had arranged for ten minutes of privacy after her performance. He waits for Sheena with roses and champagne. He plans to escort her down the grand staircase to Brandmeyer Hall for the reception in her honor.

"This is lovely, Romulus. Thank you for this and for the tour earlier," Sheena says, accepting the chilled Dom Perignon poured for her.

"You made me very happy when you told me about the song," he says.

"It was written many years ago…the first time," Sheena says, lowering her eyes.

"All those years ago we parted ways. I didn't realize," says Romulus.

“The song has been with me, always. I’ll be held up for a short time, once the reception is over. Here is my hotel key, why don’t you go ahead of me and chill some wine? I would love to show you our song.” she says, smiling at him.

“I would enjoy that,” Romulus says, putting the key is his pocket. “A magnificent performance tonight! Please accept these roses, along with my congratulations.” He places the flowers in her arms and kisses her on the cheek.

“There was no reason for you to do this, Romulus. Just spending time with you is celebration enough. Roses and champagne; you are spoiling me,” she says.

“I think I will like spoiling you,” he responds.

Sheena sips her champagne while Romulus looks over the Kansas City skyline from the large window. Far below, traffic snakes between tall, narrow buildings. He identifies the golden dome of the Cathedral of Immaculate Conception.

“Sheena, come to the window. I want to show you the cathedral,” Romulus says.

After a pause with no immediate response, he turns. Sheena’s head lies on her right shoulder, her eyes appear glassy. The abnormal sight jolts Romulus to her side.

“Sheena!” He touches her arm.

Sheena’s head snaps upright, her face is flushed, blue veins in her throat stand out against her light skin.

“My Lord, what is happening?” Romulus says as she slumps forward, falling into him.

She labors for breath as the neckline of her dress grows tighter.

He rips the collar of her garment away to free her breathing. There are bruises and scratches on her back. As he leans her back to rest in his arms, there are similar abrasions on her chest. Romulus reaches for his phone to call for help.

Sheena slaps it away from his ear, scratching his face.

“You are unwell, you need immediate care, Sheena,” he says, trying to remain calm. He bends down to retrieve his phone, when Sheena leaps on him. She strikes him over and over. Romulus manages to stand and free himself from her grasp. She bolts to the large window and pounds it with her fists.

"Let me out of here!" Sheena runs out of the room and down the corridor.

He follows as she reaches the balcony overlooking the guests attending the reception, afraid she may hurl herself over the edge. Reasoning leads to restraining her. She is a danger to herself.

"Don't touch me!" Sheena screams.

Their struggle now comes to the attention of everyone below as Sheena twists right and left to break Romulus's grasp. Despite his efforts to stop her, she jerks away with force, and plunges over the balcony.

Romulus stands paralyzed and, as if in slow motion, his beautiful Sheena falls.

Unified gasps of horror and screams ensue from the onlookers below as she crashes to the floor.

Two security guards run to the victim.

Romulus breaks his immobility and bounds down the staircase to Sheena, who lies in a growing pool of blood.

"Sheena! Sheena! Dear Lord have mercy!" Romulus cries in desperation.

Pandemonium erupts as the majority of the witnesses begin to close in around a kneeling, distraught Romulus. Other concert goers, too horrified and shocked, sit with their hands over their mouths.

Quinn, Tera and Chamous rush to Romulus while paramedics ask everyone, including Romulus, to move back.

He tries to catch his breath while struggling for glimpses of her through the kneeling group of first responders.

"Father, are you alright?" Quinn asks. She uses a napkin to stop a trickle of blood oozing from a fresh deep scratch. "Tera would you get him a glass of water?" Quinn asks.

"Her scratches are…gone… she flung herself… her scratches," Romulus rambles while his eyes dart, taking in the flurry of activity surrounding Sheena. "Did you see? I don't understand."

Quinn says, "Father, please drink this water. Come and sit down here."

An officer approaches Romulus.

"Sir, my name is Douglas Sollmer. I am with the Kansas City Police Department. We would like to ask you a few questions. Could you come with me?"

"Yes," he says blankly and follows him.

Another officer addresses the crowd.

"My name is Officer Matthews I will be taking your statements on the accident at the table in the far corner. We'll go one at a time."

Sheena McNeil is now a statistic as the bag containing her body is zipped shut. This is the scene as fresh-faced Pony approaches Quinn and the others. His concern and confusion are evident. Panic grips him, his voice frantic.

"What's going on?" he asks.

"Sheena McNeal fell from the balcony... she's dead," Chamous tells Pony.

"What…she's dead?" Pony asks, stunned.

Tera says, "Wait! Where is Sapphire?"

"She texted this morning she would be riding with you tonight," Pony says with a hint of panic.

"She never showed at the book store! Her morning text informed me she wasn't coming and she would see me later, I assumed with you," Tera says. Her trembling hand rests on her forehead, the expression showing what they all were feeling. Both she and Pony check their phones for word from her, and send messages that will go unanswered.

Chapter Nineteen

With an hour's ride ahead of them, the Guardians head to Gresham College.

"How are you faring, Professor?"

"Never better, Keefe! The prospect of seeing Gresham College, one of the most important institutions of the time, is remarkable!" the professor says with vigor. "The evolution of human thought or enlightenment has roots in this place and with a group called the Royal Society. These men are the first to question tradition and challenge ideas. Even in the twenty-first century, lectures from the Royal Society are still recorded and available. We are actually witnessing this. Extraordinary!"

Cashton says, "What we know now about pandemics and isolation is substantially advanced. We have that on our side," Cashton adds.

Anticipation grows as they approach the city walls of London. Carts and carriages, horses and pedestrians form a bottleneck at the entrance of Bishopsgate. The streets are narrow and crowded, making passage challenging. The group is surrounded by two- and even three-story, wooded Tudor houses, all squeezed and stacked.

"Look, the second level projects out further than the first, and the third level even more," Jexis says, pointing up.

"I'm dizzy," Cashton says.

A tight hold of the reins is needed to maneuver around children waiting for their mothers to purchase fish or bread. Vendors take advantage of their captive audience by approaching with poultry, fabric or fruit for sale. Hackney carriages navigate around those milling in front of the blacksmith's shop. Musicians perform, hoping for good will. The travelers are silent while observing the centuries' old-culture from horseback. They meander through the city's cobblestone streets until they arrive at Gresham College.

With windows at the end of the library and book shelves lining the other walls, the Circle of Sun members are eventually seated at a large table in the center of the room. Tea service and a chocolate seashell upon a lace doily grace each setting. Introductions include the Professor of Divinity, George Gifford, and the Professor of Physics, Robert Hooke. Among those attending are the Archbishop of Canterbury and the Bishops of Salisbury and Oxford.

The meeting is brought to order by Sir John Cutler.

"Fellow members of the Royal Society, today we address the rising panic and declining health of London. Archbishop Tobler brings guests who may offer solutions to some of our issues. I would like to turn the floor over to George Gifford, Professor of Divinity."

Professor Gifford says, "My good fellows, I regret to inform you that Deacon McGivens, spiritual leader at St. Clement in Eastcheap, will not be joining us as planned. I am not sure of the seriousness of his illness at this time; however, remember him in your prayers for a quick return to health. I would like to offer reports on the most serious outbreak regions. It looks as though . . ."

"Wake up, men of London! We don't need another stack of reports to show us people are getting sick at an alarming rate! A pattern is emerging. The Catholics are taking matters into their own hands. King Charles won't repay their loyalty with tolerance. No choice remains but to balance the scales of power with the Church of England. We are losing clergy…" says Professor Hooke, being then interrupted himself.

"What are you suggesting, Hooke? Religious men are being eliminated with some intent or grand scheme by the Catholics? Come to your senses. Look around you man. Illness has no prejudice!" Professor Gifford argues.

Hooke fires back, "Apparently your awareness ends with the reports you hold in your hand! The parish of St. Nicholas Olave reported no illness, yet their spiritual leader is dead. The same can be said about All Hallows Honey Lane. The Deacon is the only one to fall ill."

"Excuse me Robert, another possible case with Deacon Dante. I heard from Dr. Culpeper this morning," one of the deacons adds.

Robert Hooke continues, "Perhaps now, but these parishes were healthy before these casualties. We must understand religious persecution comes with a high price. Those who stand to gain by the deaths of some of our most prominent leaders in our church may be the

Catholics. The wedge widens between King Charles and his Catholic wife, a queen who is criticized by English society."

Professor Gifford says, "I struggle to understand the nature of your insinuation, Professor Hooke! Are you suggesting our own Queen Catherine is part of a scheme to eliminate spiritual leaders, because of her opposition to the Church of England? There are not enough hours in the day to entertain such outlandish speculation. The Anglicans are using ignorance to fan the flames of hysteria." George Gifford stands at the podium in frustration. He pauses and the group is silent for a moment. "The religious intolerance in our society today is an issue worthy of discussion; however, the panic surrounding the illness is the most pressing concern of the day. If we cannot identify who our enemy is, hysteria itself or the Black Death, we will be unprepared to mount a defense. The whole city of London may be wiped out if history is to repeat. I would be interested in a fresh view of our situation."

Professor Gifford turns attention to the wide eyed-visitors.

Professor Enderlee ends the awkward silence.

"Good afternoon, I am Professor Gunderson Enderlee. I would find it most challenging to offer an opinion unaffected by panic if I were in your shoes. I believe we should begin with an investigation into the untimely deaths of the clergymen. We will start with St. Clements in Eastcheap to observe Deacon McGivens. My colleague, Detective Keefe Remington, is experienced in these matters," he says. The Professor looks to Keefe, who nods to the gathering. "Dr. Cashton Royce, a gifted physician, may be able to shed some light on the matter. Permission granted to begin our investigation and report back to you?" The Professor glances around the room and back to Professor Gifford, who seems pleased.

"Thank you, Professor Enderlee, for your offering of reason. Until more facts are collected, devising a strategy would be foolish. The results of your investigation will be eagerly anticipated," he says.

Professor Enderlee signals for Keefe and Jexis, Cashton and Elle to follow him out of the meeting and the college. They mount their horses and set out for the parish of St. Clements Eastcheap. Jexis rides up next to the Professor.

"Professor Enderlee, thanks for taking the floor, but....Cashton, a doctor?" she says with a playful laugh.

Cool Cashton is unmoved by her comment and winks in her direction.

"Everything from surgeon-barbers to apothecaries and midwives and even housewives were called upon in this time of history to administer to the ill. And with Cashton's unique talents, he more than qualifies," the professor explains.

"Professor Hooke is more interested in who is getting sick than why they are getting sick," Jexis says.

"I find that interesting too," Keefe says. "A conspiracy theory is unlikely, but we will check both angles by visiting the sick clergy."

The wind stirs up dust from the streets as they head in the direction of London's Bridge. The church on Clément's Lane sits on a corner with the parsonage next door. Elle waits with the horses while they knock on the door. They are met at the door by a thin woman with a handkerchief to her nose.

Jexis says, "Good day, Madame. We are the deacon's colleagues from Gresham College. May I introduce Dr. Cashton Royce?"

Without any hesitation, and without removing the handkerchief from her nose, she opens the door and welcomes admittance.

"Deacon McGivens is two doors down," she says. She points out their destination and scurries in the opposite direction.

Cashton enters the room and the others follow.

"Who visits me this afternoon?" the deacon asks weakly, but with a slight smile.

"I am Dr. Cashton Royce. I hope you don't mind, I was sent by your colleagues from Gresham College. May I introduce my associates, Miss Jexis Royce, Professor Enderlee and Keefe Remington?

"I am pleased to meet you and quite grateful for a physician's visit. I fell ill last night."

"I am very pleased to see you are sitting up. How are you feeling?" Cashton asks as he examines the deacon. He checks for swelling of the lymph nodes in the neck and under the arms.

"Stomach cramping and pounding headache. I'll be leaving for the Pest House right quick, I suspect," the Deacon says, lowering his eyes.

Professor Enderlee translates his meaning in hushed tones to Jexis and Keefe.

"The Pest House is an isolation hospital."

Cashton says, "I wouldn't be so sure. Your symptoms do not indicate the spreading sickness. I suggest you stay isolated from your parishioners, until you are better.

"May I ask you a couple of questions?" Keefe asks. "We are conducting an investigation surrounding the serious health threats and your answers can help us a great deal."

"Surely, I will do all I can. I am so grateful for the visit, doctor. My good friend Deacon Clarence Dante in our neighboring parish, fell ill last week and I am concerned for his welfare. Would the kind doctor call on him? Dr. Culpeper is very busy," says the deacon.

"Which parish is he located in?" Cashton asks.

"He is at St. Martin Orgar on Martin Lane. Blessings to you, sir! Blessings to all of you!"

"I would like an account of your schedule from the last few days. I will also need a record of anything you consumed including liquids. Please list individuals you came into contact with, and locations. Indicate which of those you knew were sick and those who are not. I will need this within the hour. Perhaps the woman who answered the door would make the necessary notes from your dictation. We will return in a few hours to collect the report," Keefe tells the deacon.

"Sir, I will do as you ask, but we have had no reports from anyone in our parish who has been sick. I am the first," he says.

"Why do you assume a spreading sickness, if no others have taken ill?" Cashton asks.

"The whole city has been talking for weeks about the… sign. Six months ago a comet seared through the winter night, beginning the whispers of impending doom! Londoners spread the word that God is angry. More souls are abandoning their faith and giving in to panic I'm afraid," he says.

A cold rain joins the wind, making their ride to St. Martin Orgar Parish a challenge. Similar to their last stop, they are greeted at the door by fearful servants who wear bonnets strong with the scent of vinegar and nosegays of lavender tied to their necks. Once again,

Cashton examines the ill man and Keefe asks a report of his last few days. Like the first patient, Cashton does not find the typical symptoms associated with the plague. The deacon proves to be quite helpful by providing them with a list of other clergy who are ill, and parishes reporting illness.

"Most of the deacons attended a dinner a few evenings ago, ate something sour I suspect," the clergyman says, "or perhaps it was too many sweets, those decadent chocolate shells!"

Once outside, the group makes their plan.

"I wonder if those chocolate shells were the same confections we had at Gresham College." Jexis asks.

"I ate mine, it was delicious," the professor says.

"Death by chocolate? What a way to go!" Jexis says, making light of a serious situation.

Keefe says, "Let's split up. Professor you come with me, and Jexis, you go with Cashton. We will see the last deacon and then visit the apothecary. You two check in on the final parish on our list and then check out the docks. See what the fishermen from the parish who lost their deacon have to say. We can compare notes at the pub we passed the block before, at sundown. Stay safe."

Jexis and Cashton ride to the busy port of London to talk with the fishermen on the piers. Multitudes of trading companies, fishing boats, and the home of the Royal Navy crowd the river. A lady in her Sunday-best looks out of place on the grimy docks that sit in the murky water of the Thames. She is handed a parcel she tucks by her side and the hackney coach drives her away. Cashton approaches a docked boat, where a group of men is working.

"Excuse me, are any of you from the parish of St. Nicholas Olave?" Cashton asks.

Every man stops his activity and stares at Cashton.

"Yup, that'd be every fisherman you're looking at, Sir. Has the new Deacon paid a visit to bless our vessel?"

Cashton smiles, but he is the only one. The men are stoic and serious.

"I am not your new Deacon, I am Cashton Royce. Today I am collecting information for Gresham College about the illness in your parish. This is my sister, Jexis Royce."

"We need a new Deacon, ours is dead," one fisherman says.

"I am sorry to hear that unfortunate news. Are there records being kept on the numbers of sick parishioners?" Jexis asks.

"Yes, the number is zero," a fisherman in a red cap says.

"No one else has been sick?" asks Cashton.

"Not yet, but we all will be soon, I suspect," the same fisherman says, "Everyone knows that our time for punishment has come. Our sins have caused the loss of Deacon Thornbush. We will soon all succumb."

Jexis says, "The numbers do not reflect that a spreading sickness is the cause at this time."

"That might be what you say Ma'am, but we don't need no proof. We've been hearing the word from the streets for months that it was coming. And now we have lost our deacon. Our prayers have gone unanswered. We press forward knowing our time is short," the fisherman says.

"Do Londoners come dockside to buy your fish directly or to collect shipped items?" Jexis asks.

"No, boats are unloaded and items stored or picked up in the warehouses by retailers," an older fisherman responds. "Most avoid the docks. Can't blame 'em."

"That's why I like to be a fisherman, left alone mostly," the one in the red cap says.

"I noticed a proper lady who left in a hackney coach."

"That would be Miss Chatfield from the Bake House. She comes to the docks often. She delivers bread to us. It is delicious. She says she has to give away bread before it goes dry and we are the most worthy. She is an angel, that one. She slips a sweet confection in every now and then to boot!" the elder fisherman says. "Now that our days are mostly dark, we can use a kind gesture."

Jexis and Cashton thank the men and return to their horses.

"The woman who makes these chocolates and delivers day old bread to hopeless fisherman might shed some light on our investigation," Jexis says.

"I say we pay her a visit. But if you are offered one of her infamous chocolates, I would pass," Cashton says jokingly.

The Bake House on Pudding Lane enjoys a steady stream of business this day. The door is propped open with a shoe-sized stone, allowing smoke to exit. Jexis and Cashton enter a crowded room of patrons, who don't seem detoured by the remaining haze. An elegant woman stands next to a distraught lady.

"Miss Chatfield, I burned the bread again, I will never be a baker. I am sorry you put your trust in me," a crying lady says.

"Miss Bellmore, collect yourself," says Miss Chatfield.

Miss Bellmore's shoulders are rounded and her head down. A slight woman waiting in the wings offers Miss Bellmore a handkerchief.

"Thank you, Miss Jones," Annabeth Chatfield says on Miss Bellmore's behalf.

"It is only bread," Annabeth tells her, "no reason to ruffle your feathers. Come now, the yeast is ready for your next batch."

A crisp white apron is taken from a hook and Annabeth helps her into it.

"You are still in your learning stages. I've burned my share of loaves! We are much too busy for tears. Miss Jones and I have some business." Annabeth sends her back to bake and turns her attention to Olivia Jones.

"Oliva, I'm afraid I have yet another interruption. Mr. Helms is arriving to collect his order. Would you mind wrapping the bread and tarts for those three customers while I help him?" Annabeth Chatfield says, pointing to three waiting customers.

"Certainly," she says.

Olivia quickly packages loaves of bread, a pie, some confections and tarts for the customers.

Mr. Helms leaves his wagon in the street out front.

Annabeth gives him two large covered baskets. She is interrupted by Olivia's question.

"I don't see any more Sweet Basil Bread," Olivia says.

"That's right, sold the last two loaves before noon," says Annabeth.

Olivia nods to the gentleman who wanted the bread.

"You heard the baker, come earlier tomorrow, I guess," she says.

Mr. Helms takes the baskets from Annabeth laden with bread.

"I won't be able to pay for the bread until tomorrow's eve." Mr. Helms says.

"Nonsense, I will accept no payment," Annabeth says in a business like tone.

Mr. Helms protests, "But Miss Chatfield, this would be the third time and you are in business to make a profit."

"The sustenance is needed and I want to help the cause," she pats Mr. Helm's shoulder and his eyes twinkle with gratitude. "Those loaves are fresh and still warm. Make haste back to school."

The Bake House has been refreshed by the outside door and Annabeth removes the rock and closes the door behind him. Left in the shop is Jexis, Cashton, and Olivia.

"May I help you?" she says to the brother and sister.

"We are interested in your confections, the chocolate shells?" Jexis says.

Olivia interjects, "You and the whole of London!"

Annabeth smiles humbly and uses long tongs to select a few of them.

Jexis says, "We sampled them yesterday and found them to be delicious. Four shells please. They are like nothing we've seen."

"You are quite right. They are the first solid chocolate confections in London," Annabeth says.

Cashton points to the glass case.

"Not to trouble you ma'am, but I would prefer the ones with the delicate etching," Cashton says.

Annabeth's eyes lock on Cashton, but for only a second.

"I was planning to… dispose of that row of chocolates. But I am more than happy to sell them," she says, her pleasant smile returning.

"Is there something wrong with them?" Jexis asks.

"Yes, there is," she says pausing, "Those with etching, as you call it, were dented by the tongs before they were set. They are imperfect but still delicious."

"They will be just fine." Cashton says.

"I don't believe we've had the pleasure of serving you before," Annabeth says as she wraps the confections.

"I am Jexis Royce and this is my brother Cashton. We are from

Liverpool visiting friends."

"You've some lofty friends at Gresham College," she says.

Her comment surprises both of them.

"I don't believe I mentioned Gresham College, did I Sister?" Cashton asks, looking at Jexis. Both turn their attention to her response.

"An astute woman of commerce knows where her chocolates are being served," she says lowering her head and peering from under her brow at Cashton. The awkward silence ends with Olivia's comment.

"I see there is one imperfect one remaining, would you mind? I haven't eaten all day."

"Not at all Olivia, please enjoy," Annabeth says. "May I introduce you to Olivia Jones? She prepared the meal served at the Deacon's dinner two nights ago. There is some concern about the illness affecting three of the deacons. I offered to go over the menu with her."

"I wouldn't want to be responsible for others suffering," Olivia Jones says. She wrings her hands in her lap.

"Rabbit pie should not be allowed cooling time, for it quickly becomes sour. One of the six pies she made was not served from the oven," Annabeth says.

"A sour pie is sweetened again with pickling spice, a trick I learned from my mum," Olivia says.

"A practice to abstain from," Annabeth adds.

"Oh dear, I may have done something wrong," she says, and then stuffs the entire chocolate into her mouth, chewing quickly. Her eyes remain fixed in front of her. Her hand trembles as she uses a linen cloth to wipe a smidgen of almond cream from the corner of her mouth. "I will be sacked for sure, and homeless. I wonder if my cousin from the country would take me in. I won't be ever allowed to cook again. How will I earn my keep? Oh, whatever shall I do?"

"You will not be sacked, I am sure of it," Annabeth says, patting her on the arm before lifting a tray laden with loaves of bread.

A youth enters the Bake House carrying a box so large he barely sees over it.

"Apothecary delivery. Back room alright, Miss Chatfield?" he asks.

"No, I am able to do it myself." She drops the tray hastily and loaves slide down, nearly toppling onto the counter. Annabeth takes the box from him and scurries past Miss Bellmore and the ovens to a drawn curtain. She deposits the delivery on the floor, in front of the curtain. The delivery boy is gone, and Annabeth arranges the toppled loaves.

Miss Bellmore stops her baking to open the newly arrived package.

"Lots of fresh basil," she says loud enough for all to hear.

"Looks like Sweet Basil bread will be available for tomorrow's patrons," Olivia Jones says.

"Is there anything else I can help you with?" Annabeth Chatfield says to Jexis and Cashton, handing them the satchel of chocolate.

"No, good day, Miss Chatfield," Jexis says as they leave the Bake House.

* * * * *

Keefe and Professor Enderlee make their last stop of the day at Apothecaries Hall.

"We may find some answers here," Keefe says.

Phillip Culpeper's office is at the end of a long hallway. Keefe knocks but there is no answer. He waits a bit longer and knocks louder.

"Be still, I am coming to answer your call," a voice from inside the room says.

After a rustling of keys, their knock is answered by a middle aged man of average height with wavy hair and short bangs. His moustache is turned up at each end and his nose has a slight hook, his eyes brown and gentle. Dressed in a black doublet buttoned to the top of his collar, and he sports a knotted neckerchief.

"How may I help you?" he asks the two men in a breathless rush.

"We are looking for Dr. Phillip Culpeper," Keefe said.

"You have found him. Does someone need care? I am just leaving," the doctor says.

"No, we are gathering information for an investigation into the spreading illness," Keefe explains.

"The spreading illness? Yes, my concern deepens. Some days I am convinced the frenzy is justified. But I am treating many who do not have the symptoms. Perhaps it's too early to tell. Are you physicians?" Dr. Culpeper asks as his eyes dart around his office.

Keefe says, "No, we are gathering research for Gresham College."

"Ah, I understand," he responds.

"I am hoping to warm up with a spot of tea. Could I bother you for some?" Professor Enderlee asks.

The doctor pauses.

"I don't keep sundries, I am sorry," says Culpeper.

Professor Enderlee says, "Panic has superseded the facts concerning the spreading sickness in some cases. Our findings will be reported back to the Royal Society, which in turn will share the information with the Lord Mayor."

"You also dispense medications. You are an apothecary as well?" asks Keefe.

"Yes, indeed I am," Dr. Culpeper says as he prepares to close his office. He extinguishes lanterns and puts his cape around his shoulders.

Mesmerized by the living history, Professor Enderlee walks around the room while Keefe talks with the doctor.

"Well, of course, any effort that can cast light on the problem..." Culpeper says, fidgeting with the papers on his desk.

"May I also request your assistant's presence so I can gather as many facts as possible?" Keefe asks.

"Oh, an assistant would be a luxury. It's only me," he says.

The professor is distracted by the oils, powders, flowers, scales and containers. Nearly forgetting the reason for their visit, he blurts out a question of his own, leaving Keefe to hold his fact finding off for another few moments.

"Must you store some of these ingredients in the cellar?" he asks, glancing at the only other door in the room.

Dr. Culpeper keeps his gaze steady.

"Ah, no cellar here… but I do keep some in my root cellar at home," Culpeper says.

"Have you treated symptoms that could indicate the spreading sickness?" Keefe asks.

The doctor's fingertip runs over his notes.

"My first patient, Mrs. Shaver, had a broken finger but still offered to serve me a hearty breakfast. I was most grateful. Let's see, hmmm . . .William Shoals followed after Mrs. Shaver. He had a rough night after ingesting tobacco, but by lunchtime he recovered nicely. No concerns of spreading sickness on those two. I delivered a tonic to Timothy Weiss in the pub on Bushtail Lane where I took my midday meal, and then....let's see." He turns the page of his notes. "Next I looked in on Sir Alfred Jameson and his bad knee. There was nothing to suggest the spreading sickness either," he tells them. "However, yesterday at St. Giles in The Fields, a woman did display all the classic symptoms of the illness. She is isolated and I am trying to make her comfortable. She is a cook for the parsonage. In the last several weeks I've treated no other cases symptomatic of the spreading sickness. My last call of the day was to a young family. I examined their new baby, a tiny beauty. Reminded me of my little Cora, God rest her soul. Losing our child changed my direction to further my education in medicine, from apothecary to physician."

"I am so sorry about your daughter," Professor Enderlee says with sincerity.

"Thank you, my wife and I are parents of two girls now. They are the darlings of my life. In fact I was leaving to return home for our evening meal when you came calling," he says.

"Thank you Dr. Culpeper. I think we have gathered enough facts from your recent patient list. Good day," Keefe says.

Night falls and the rain stops as the two men are detoured by a mob in front of a modest home. Three men pound on a door marked with red paint.

"Stand back, stand away from the door," one of them shouted to the inhabitants inside.

The angry crowd tightens around the men.

"And the lot of you back up! We need some room!" someone else shouts out.

"Help them!" a woman cries.

"Leave them isolated or they will sicken us all!" another voice yells.

A struggle between the opposing parties ensues and the altercation draws more. A few of the men try to free the isolated patients within the house, as others begin fighting.

"The Justice of the Peace gives reason to quarantine. So be it!" a deep voice shouts out.

Wood cracks and the door is broken down, while frightened inhabitants flee down the streets. A tangle of men throws punches at one another. London is in turmoil and Keefe and the Professor are glad to reach the pub.

The two pass by a gathering of men drinking ale and debating the scene in the street. Professor Enderlee spots Jexis and Cashton at a table near the back.

"Welcome gentlemen. What kept you so long? Elle arranged lodging at Gresham College, before she left for Tobler Tower," Jexis says.

Keefe takes a long drink of his ale they had waiting for him.

"Of all the patients Dr. Culpeper has seen in the last few days, only one shows symptoms of the spreading sickness. His suspicious nature is what I found interesting," Keefe says.

"What do you mean?" Cashton asks.

"He is a nice enough gentleman and a caring doctor. But our presence made him quite nervous," says Keefe.

"Yes, I noticed the same thing," Professor Enderlee says.

Keefe adds, "We heard the sound of fumbling keys when he was answering, so I questioned why his door would be locked. I also found some inconsistencies. A tray sat on the side table near the only other door in the room. A hook beside the door held a lighted lantern. If my eyesight is correct the tray held a steaming cup of tea or soup. Looked like he wasn't alone. I asked about an assistant, but he told us he works alone. When the Professor asked for tea, he responded by saying he didn't keep any sundries."

"Perhaps his meals are delivered," the professor offers.

"Yes, but his first patient, the lady with the broken finger, made him breakfast, and he mentioned eating his midday meal at the pub. When we arrived he was leaving to have evening dinner with his family. So I don't think food was being brought in for him," Keefe says.

"Maybe he has a lady friend…who is not his wife," Cashton suggests with raised brows.

"Perhaps. When the Professor inquired about a cellar he seemed nervous. I'm suspicious of his demeanor," Keefe says.

"What are you thinking?" Jexis asks.

Keefe replies, "My hunch is he's treating someone in his offices... taking care of someone who's requested discretion."

"But why?" the professor asks.

"The Justice of the Peace is isolating all those suspected of having the plague. We witnessed how the folks of London feel about that," Keefe says.

"We need to keep tabs on him," Cashton says.

"The word on the dock and in the streets of London is doom and gloom. The fishermen believe it is only a matter of time until they become sick," Jexis says. "Here are the reports from those who are ill. I discovered a link between them. The clergy who are sick attended the same dinner two evenings ago."

"Food poisoning?" Keefe asks.

"If it were food poisoning, wouldn't more of the attendees be ill?" Cashton asks.

"Perhaps they are and we're unaware," Keefe says. "Did the stricken men all eat the same thing?"

Jexis says, "The menu is in the report, Keefe. Looks like rabbit pie, potatoes, bread and chocolates."

The bar maid interrupts them.

"I'm sorry, but I overheard ya referrin' to the shells of chocolate. A pure sinful delight! They've taken flight, and I kna' their maker!" she says with her shoulders back and chin elevated. "She's the lady from Chatfield's Bake House on Pudding Lane. We call her a witch!" And with a hearty laugh she sets down more ale at the next table before continuing. "I mean who else could make the cocoa solid? None in all of England, 'cept for the lady. If ya haven't yet tried 'em you best git to it. It's a delicacy made for a King. I can't afford the likes of 'em, but I tasted them at the Bake House."

A voice from behind the bar calls her away.

"Chocolate in solid form would be something new for this

society. Wait, those sound like the same chocolates at the meeting of the Royal Society at Gresham College. I ate the confection, and it was delicious," the professor says.

"We visited Annabeth Chatfield's Bake House on Pudding Lane, the maker of the candy. We happened to see her at the docks. The fisherman said she brings them bread. Perhaps the confections have something to do with all of this," Jexis says.

"How could food not become a source of illness under the conditions in which it is stored and prepared during this time in history?" the professor notes, looking around the pub.

"With the numbers of customers who purchase and consume her bakery food daily, it's unlikely there is a problem there," Jexis says.

"Who would know the Deacons who attended the dinner became ill? Are other inquiries being conducted?" Cashton asks.

"None that we know of. The dinner was only a couple of nights ago. Why do you ask?" the professor says.

"Miss Chatfield was discussing the menu with the caterer of the dinner. They seemed to be going over it to determine if something Olivia Jones prepared was part of the problem," Cashton tells them.

"How did they know about any of it?" asks Keefe.

The four look to each other for answers.

"One of six rabbit pies was not served hot, and Olivia Jones added a pickling spice to a suspected sour pie. Concerned about the responsibilities of her error, she was calmed by Miss Chatfield and warned about using the pickling spice," Jexis says.

"They would not be privy to the information about the illnesses. Perhaps the chocolates are the issue and Miss Chatfield is moving the blame to Miss Jones," Cashton says.

"It seems silly to spend so much time focusing on this angle. Food poisoning is common in this time period. It seems insignificant to me," Jexis says.

"Unless it's intentional," Cashton points out. "We talked to the fishermen about the extent of the illness in their parish. They reported no cases of illness prior to the death of their deacon," Cashton recalls.

"Some of the professors at Gresham College believe the clergy are in danger, being singled out," Professor Enderlee says.

"Based on the facts we have all collected so far it looks that way, but our investigation is young," Cashton says.

"We have seen the quarantines and the hysteria. People are afraid," Keefe says.

Jexis notes, "The fishermen believe the rumors they hear about impending doom. They believe it is just a matter of time before they all will die. God is mad at them, punishing them and spreading an illness to kill everyone. In their mind, losing their deacon just confirms that."

"Perhaps we do have some kind of conspiracy here. It would only take a few hand-selected victims to whip the rumors to an all-time high," Keefe says.

"Our investigation may be finding evidence of a conspiracy, but would our suspects be all the Catholics? That's absurd," Cashton says, as he motions for the waitress to bring another round.

A few minutes later she delivers more ale to their table.

"Do you know Olivia Jones?" Jexis asks the bar maid.

"I do sir, she's a caterer, lives on Byward Street at the Tilly Boarding house. Figured she'd dive in and be Miss Chatfield's assistant, Lordy kna' she could use another set a hands, and she kna's 'er way 'round a kitchen too, that one. Mattie's not suited for bakin' anyway," says the barmaid.

"Mattie?" Keefe asks.

"Baker's helper.... left the bake house one day and never came home. Thinkin' she found 'erself a fellow, I wager," she says with an obvious wink.

Jexis thanks the busy barmaid.

"Let's pay a visit to Olivia Jones." Keefe says.

The Guardians were told Olivia Jones resided at Tilly's, a boarding house on Byward Street near All Hallows Church. A full moon lit their journey down the cobblestone streets. Cashton is nearly thrown from his horse when a cat weaves between its hooves. His quick instincts bring the horse back to submission and he is able to stay in the saddle.

The Tilly house is tall. They enter a door with no markings and begin the trek up the long narrow staircase, while a set of golden eyes watches. A particularly loud creak of one stair sends the feline scurrying away, while they climb yet another staircase, even more constricted than the first. The landing ahead is dimly lit from the single flame of a burning candle sitting on a chair. A haunting violin tune becomes louder as they ascend. Jexis notes the familiarity of the melody and her mind filters through composers, trying to place it. The long journey from the street leaves them all winded and they fill their lungs with stuffy spiced air.

Keefe's knock is followed by complete silence and hurried footsteps inside.

Olivia Jones only partially opens the door.

Cashton steps forward and extends his hand.

"Miss Jones, remember me from the bake house, I am..."

"Cashton Royce, who could forget?" she says, drawing her words out. She slides her hand through the small space to accept his hand.

"My friends and I would like a couple minutes of your time. May we come in?" he asks.

Olivia's eyes become wide. Before opening the door all the way, she glances behind her and opens it.

"It's the rabbit pie! Am I right? Damn that rabbit pie!" she says.

A fireplace warms the small room. A woman lies on the couch sleeping. At least four cats lay across the available sitting spaces. French doors lie open wide, and night air rushes in from the terrace. Sheer panels billow in and then out of the room freely from the gentle breeze. Wine and glasses sit on a low table, along with a dozen lit candles, their flames flickering from the draft. A violin rests near the fireplace. Incense smolders in various locations, creating a lingering haze before melting into the night.

"We are only here to gather some information. You remember my sister Jexis, and these are our colleagues Mr. Remington and Professor Enderlee. I apologize for coming unannounced," Cashton says.

Olivia glances at the woman on the couch and replies.

"Oh, you are just in the nick of time, actually." she says. She takes a long drink from her wine glass.

"Sit down if you please," she says, looking to her cats, "Banish!" Every feline in the room scatters.

"Who told you the deacons were ill after the dinner a few nights ago?" Cashton asks her.

Before she can respond the woman on the couch begins to wake up. She moans and sits up slowly.

"Oh, don't mind her, she's blind as a bat for a while yet," Olivia says.

"Where am I?" the woman asks.

"You are where you were before you slept," Olivia says, sounding annoyed. "Allow me to introduce Doris." She takes another drink of wine, and empties her glass. She pours more for herself before she offers wine to her guests. They decline, but the lady on the couch begins to feel the table in front of her and finds a glass.

"I will," Doris says.

"The wine will only make you sleepy again... oh, hell, why not," Olivia says and pours her a glass.

Doris smiles but struggles to focus on anything.

"Are you alright?" Cashton asks.

"Will be soon enough. I best be making myself beautiful. My party starts at midnight" she says standing, only to slump back down on the sofa, some of her wine spilling out.

"Sit yourself down! You will be right again within the hour," Olivia says.

"What is wrong with her eyes?" Cashton asks.

"She's drunk a potion to mesmerize a man," Olivia says, rolling her eyes and drinking more wine.

Doris says, "The lady dropped it in my eyes. Beware, men of London! Simply try to deny my seductive power now!"

The lady's comments throw Olivia into a tailspin of giggles. She covers her mouth but her giggles grow to hearty laughter. With her head thrown back she falls against the back of her chair, holding her stomach. Soon the other lady joins her, leaving the four visitors out of the joke. It appears they will not be getting too much information from Olivia on this night, when the French doors slam shut with such force the entire sitting room vibrates. Simultaneously the lazy fireplace flames grow beyond the firebox, licking the mantle, and the violin explodes, sending wood fragments throughout the room. Two glass vases shatter, cut flowers and water spraying over all. Instantly, the room falls still once more.

"What was that?" Keefe asks.

Olivia, with eyes as wide as saucers, holds her hand over her mouth, surveying her surroundings.

"The lady does not appreciate my antics," she says. She raises her goblet to the heavens. "I apologize to the goddess of goodness," she says.

"My vision returns!" Doris exclaims and drinks all the wine in her glass.

"What exactly is going on here?" Keefe asks.

"Are you sure you want that information? This scene is for the ladies mostly," Olivia says.

Keefe says, "Yes, who is the goddess of goodness and what potion are you referring to?"

Olivia moves to sit next to Doris, who is pouring again.

"The lady is a midwife, a doctor and a friend. When we hurt, we go to her for solutions and she always gives something to reduce suffering or solve a problem. Doris comes looking to seduce with her beauty and the goddess gives her the potion. The pain of bearing children is lessened as well as women's monthly terms handled and better controlled. Not a woman in London wants to be without the help of the goddess," says Olivia.

"Why don't you just call her a witch like most of the others?" Doris says, before a hiccup and giggle.

"Call her whatever you will, she is an angel! Look what she brought for me today," Olivia says. She leaves the room and comes back with circular box covered with a pretty white linen. She sets the covered box on the table and pulls the center of the linen up revealing a round cage.

Olivia says, "This is Charles and Catherine, my royal pets."

Two black rats scurry around in a soiled cage.

Olivia tears a small piece of bread and delivers it through the cage.

"Aren't they adorable? Charles holds the bread with his little claws, so sweet," Olivia says.

Jexis moves herself back, away from the rodents.

"You are saying the witch is merely a woman with potions, like an apothecary." Cashton says.

"Yes, now you understand. She was here a moment ago. We were relaxing and drinking wine after she made two potions. One was the Bella Donna potion for Doris, and the other was the flying ointment. That stuff smells nasty!" Olivia says. She belches and covers her mouth. "Pardon me!"

"We didn't pass her on our way up," Jexis said.

"No you wouldn't have seen her leave. She went that way," Olivia says, and points to the French doors.

The professor walks through French doors to the terrace, and then asks, "How would one get down from here?"

Olivia checks around the room and leans in, motioning to the others to do the same.

In a whisper she says, "She flies!" With wide eyes, she nods her head up and down.

"What do you mean she flies?" Keefe asks.

"What do you think the flying ointment was for?" Olivia asks with complete seriousness. "She knows about everything, too. Who do you think told me about the deacons? It was the goddess! I was afraid I'd done something wrong, and she offered to help me. Isn't that right Mr. Royce?"

Before he can respond, Jexis does.

"Annabeth Chatfield is the goddess, the witch?"

"Indeed," Olivia says, finishing off her wine.

After leaving Olivia's, each of the Guardians shares their opinion on what the next step should be and no one can agree. Weary and hungry, Keefe suggests they head back to Gresham College for a late dinner, then to discuss the next course of action.

* * * * *

Jexis allows her body to sink down as steam from hot bath water rises, creating a veil of mist all around her. The strange experiences at Olivia's had given them more than their share to think about. The day had been long and tiring. In some ways the information gathered at Olivia's made things more opaque instead of clear. The steamy water relaxes her muscles. She rests her head all the way back to enjoy the sweet tranquility. Her racing mind slows enough for a peaceful melody to surface. Humming softly she savors the remaining moments of her temporary retreat. This melody is fresh in her mind, and then she remembers why. It's the haunting violin music they heard at Olivia's. Renewed and refreshed, she finds Keefe and Cashton seated at a table and Professor Enderlee near the fire, sweet tobacco smoke wafting above him.

The meal consists of roasted chicken, root vegetables and bread, served with ale and wine. The warm fire and nourishment provided a break from the intensity of the day.

The professor lights his pipe after dinner.

"What do we know about Annabeth Chatfield?" Keefe asks.

"We have a list of positives and then we have the other... list." Jexis says. "Flying? Was Olivia serious?"

"I think she was drunk," Professor Enderlee says.

"We know she helps people with herbs and such," Jexis says.

"You mean her potions and brews?" the Professor says, taking his pipe away from his lips.

"That would explain the large order she received from the apothecary when we were in the bake house," Cashton says. "The herb used to make the eye drops is Bella Donna or Deadly Nightshade. The drops actually dilate the pupil of the eye. Expanded pupils were considered attractive, seductive. It is not uncommon in the seventeenth century."

"But Doris could barely see," Jexis said.

"It was a dangerous practice, causing loss of eyesight and even blindness," Cashton tells them.

"Deadly nightshade has been used for centuries. The Romans put it on the tips of their arrows for instant death, and it was the poison of choice if you wanted to murder someone," Professor Enderlee says.

"Could deadly nightshade be used in the Chocolates?" Keefe asks.

"Indeed," says the professor.

"What kind of motive would she have? Her confections are the toast of London, she has a thriving bake shop, and her potions help a lot of people," Jexis says.

"Yes, she is all of those things you mention, Jexis. But we have many red flags to consider. When we were in the bake shop and requested different chocolates than the ones she had selected, she looked at me in a knowing way. The feeling is hard to explain, but I sensed something," Cashton says.

"I agree with you on that. I also found it suspicious she knew we were at Gresham College," Jexis says.

"The illness of the deacons, there would only be one way for her to know," Keefe says.

"If she was doing the poisoning," the professor finished.

"I also found our visit to the bake shop strange in another way. It was staged, like she knew we were coming, Olivia there at the exact time we came in," Cashton says.

"I think she was throwing the attention off herself," Keefe suggests.

"And she was putting her best face forward, helping Olivia while supporting the less fortunate in the community. It was a large dose of presentation," Cashton says. "Since she was presenting the things she wanted us to see, we weren't able to see anything else."

"The woman we met in the bake shop, Annabeth Chatfield, is not the same lady described as a goddess or witch by Olivia," Cashton says.

"That's right, Cashton. We were presented a lady with an aptitude for business and a generous spirit. We didn't see the other version. Not sure I want to," Jexis says.

"I think we need to revisit the bake shop… tonight," Keefe says.

Chapter Twenty

Romulus rejoins Quinn and the others after providing details to officers about Sheena McNeil's accident. As soon as Quinn sees Romulus she rushes to him.

"Father, are you alright?" asks Quinn.

Romulus closes his eyes during their embrace.

"Having you here…thank God," Romulus says.

Then Tera embraces him while Chamous rests his hand on the broad shoulders of Romulus.

"Can you tell us what happened, Father?" Quinn asks, as she leads Romulus to a table.

Chamous and Tera sit along with them.

Pony paces in front of one of the windows with his phone to his ear.

Romulus says, "I am still unsure myself. Sheena and I were drinking champagne and talking before she went into… a seizure. Her throat swelled, the neckline of her gown grew tight. She was laboring to breathe so I ripped the collar away. When I called for help she became enraged and slapped the phone away and attacked me. Her behavior was out of control as she pounded on the windows and ran out of the room. She was a danger to herself. I followed and yelled out to her."

Romulus shakes his head and thrusts a tight fist into his open palm, then rests his forehead against his palms.

Quinn touches his arm as he continues.

"We struggled on the balcony. She wouldn't allow me to draw her away from the overlook. She didn't sense danger, as she backed against the railing. I tried to hold on to her while she scratched and flung herself. I couldn't save her," he says. The distinguished, strong man shakes his head, steel blue eyes wet with emotion.

"Romulus, I am so sorry," Chamous says with sincerity.

After a couple seconds of silence, Chamous leans to Quinn.

"Pony needs some help, so Tera and I are going with him," he says in hushed tones.

Tracie Glenn approaches Quinn and Romulus, her elegant white silk blouse tucked into a scarlet pencil skirt. She pulls a chair out, taking a seat next to Romulus. She crosses her long legs and places her manicured hand on top of Romulus's folded hands. With as much respect and empathy as she can muster, she speaks to him.

"Mr. Royce, are you ok?" She studies his eyes before looking to Quinn and back to Romulus. "A tragedy of this magnitude surely has put you in a state of shock. Do you need anything, anything at all?"

"No, Miss Glenn, not at this time," Romulus says stoically.

Tracie Glenn says, "I am afraid I am going to insist you be seen by a medic." Despite Romulus's objections, she waves a young man over, giving him orders, and turns back to Romulus. "Don't be a hero. The first concern is always for the physical self."

"Miss Glenn, I have been seen by the medics," he says.

"Mr. Royce, my apologies. I tend to be bossy during a crisis. My car can deliver you home, you shouldn't be driving," says Tracie.

"A kind offer, but my family is here," he tells her.

Tracie says, "What about your car? I would like to make things easier a the family that trouble calls on again."

"Miss Glenn your courtesy is graciously declined. We are from opposite camps but your goodwill is appreciated," Romulus says. He slides his chair out and stands; showing her the conversation is over.

Tracie Glenn stands and crosses her arms.

"I've made some errors in judgment in the past but this provides a perfect opportunity," Romulus cuts her off.

"I again thank you for your concern, but may I be frank?" Romulus says. His voice commands the attention of anyone in earshot. "I don't agree with your politics and question your character. This evening is a personal tragedy. Those who identify the situation as an opportunity are the kind of people I try to avoid. Good night."

"You are accusing me of opportunism? Perhaps those in glass houses should not throw stones," Tracie says, as Romulus ignores her and takes Quinn's arm.

"An exasperating end to this nightmare," Romulus says.

Father and daughter ride in silence until they are out of the parking lot and on their way to the estate.

"Sheena was possessed… by something. I believe she is a victim by association. Quinn we are under attack! Where is Sapphire?" he asks, before Quinn had her chance to tell him.

"She didn't show tonight. We just discovered an hour ago. Pony and Tera believed she was with the other," Quinn says. She takes a deep breath and continues. "Everyone has lost contact with her since this morning. Tera, Chamous and Pony went to Fireside Books to compare notes."

"Take me there!" Romulus says with urgency.

In less than a half hour they pull up to the book shop, seeing smoke coming from the chimney. Romulus is greeted with compassion by his Circle of Sun family.

Tera goes to Romulus immediately.

"I am so sorry for your loss Romulus. A terrible tragedy!" Her voice quivers and her eyes fill with tears, dreading to tell him. "We can't account for Sapphire." The brimming tears spill over to her cheeks.

Pony begins pacing.

"What's going on? Where could she be?" Pony asks, panicked.

Quinn, who is the only member of the group who does not sit, goes to Pony.

"Pony, remain calm. We will find our sweet Sapphire, please sit down." She leads him back to his seat and she seats herself on the fireplace hearth, facing them all. "Romulus thinks Sheena is a victim of... possession"

All eyes go to Romulus.

"Unnatural is the word I would use to describe her behavior, the seizure. I believe we are under attack."

"The fact Sapphire is now missing makes his theory possible. We must be prepared. And we must keep level heads, stay vigilant in our faith," Quinn tells them.

In a soft and tentative tone, Tera speaks up.

"Possessed?" she asks. She closes her eyes, not wanting an answer.

Knowing her best friend even better than Chamous, Tera's comment raises Quinn's concern.

"Why, what is wrong?" Quinn demands.

"Strange experiences," Tera says with dread, her palm holding her forehead.

Chamous pulls her arm away.

"What is it? What's happened?" asks Chamous.

"I heard whispers, the same phrase over and over, in a strange language. At first the whispers were in music and I assumed it was static. While running the other morning, a forceful whirlwind came after me. I sound insane. But when Beef dropped the decanter in the dining room... I know why, I know what he was seeing," Tera says with tears in her eyes.

"Seeing?" Romulus asks.

"Distortion of my eyes! The picture Jexis took. I'm scared," she confesses.

"The picture appeared fine to me. Jexis didn't mention anything," Quinn says.

"Beef saw something in you? You sense another spirit trying to overtake you, is that it?" Romulus asks.

Tera can't hold back her bottled emotions over this fear.

"Will I suffer the same fate as Sheena?" Tera asks, her voice cracking.

"What phrase were you hearing?" Romulus asks.

Tera moves to the window of the bookstore. She puts her arms around herself as if to bolster her confidence.

"I live... in you!" Tera says, her voice breaking.

Chamous rushes to her side and puts his arms around her.

Romulus addresses them all.

"Possession…spiritual warfare . . . the battle to dominate and eliminate the spirit…and claim its body. Sheena was possessed, and possibly Tera is being attacked in the same way. A deviant spirit seeps into your psyche and battles for the dominant thoughts. Any doubts the evil spirit can create in the victim's mind provides leverage. The attack is subtle and leaves little evidence. The victim's spirit is stolen, little by little. Tera, your strong spirit, your will is protecting you. Not everyone has a strong spirit. Tonight, we must give you what you need to protect yourself. I can't help Sheena I pray I'm not too late for

Sapphire."

"Who knew Sapphire's plans for the day?" Quinn asks.

"She left early to help with the Sanctified Transit. She didn't show and once Father Mopsi left, I received a text around eight. Her plans had changed. I assumed I would see her at the Kauffman Centerwith Pony," Tera explains.

"What about you, Pony?" Quinn asks.

"I planned to pick her up at six for the concert. But this morning around eight o'clock her text said she'd be riding with Tera tonight… helpful since I was already in the city," he says.

Romulus reads the text on Tera's phone.

"Sapphire would've offered an explanation of why she changed plans," Romulus says, and reads the messages on both phones. "Sapphire wants you each to think she is with the other." Romulus calls her number.

In the complete silence they wait, praying this time she will pick up her phone and they will find her.

"Sapphire, pick up your phone!" Pony pleads, his voice breaking.

"Wait…listen!" Quinn says.

The faint sound of a muffled ringtone sends both Chamous and Romulus hunting.

The search leads Chamous to the reading nooks. Everyone freezes, straining to hear as Chamous pulls a ringing cell phone from deep in a chair cushion.

"She was here!" Pony says.

"Wait, the creepy guy sat there," Tera says.

"Who?" Romulus asks.

"A stranger with a foreign accent . . . looked like he'd been in a fight. He broke into the shop and sat watching me until I noticed him," says Tera.

"Sounds like those damn Romanians! Finnegan liked Sapphire. Finnegan must have her!" Pony says.

"Did you watch this guy leave, Tera?" Chamous asks her.

Tera responds, "He got into a yellow jeep with another guy,"

Chamous paces.

"He was following her. They took her before she showed at the bookstore. He used her phone to send out texts, hoping to buy time," Chamous says, thinking out loud.

With her hand trembling, Tera holds her phone out for all to read the phrase that haunts her.

"I discovered the phrase is in Romanian," says Tera.

Quinn studies the message.

"I think that is too many digits for a phone number, 00902166600," Quinn says.

Chamous examines the number and pushes redial.

They all are silenced in anticipation of who will answer, but Tera's phone does not connect to anything. The display remains lit on the number, but nothing happens. Chamous turns the phone off and back on, then removes the battery. Despite numerous attempts, her phone lodges on the number.

Chamous jots the number down.

"I will investigate the number further," he says.

Romulus says, "These two men, we must find them. Sheena was a guest at Hotel Phillips. I am assuming they are part of her entourage."

Pony puts his jacket on, and takes one last glance at his phone. He slides it in his pocket. Whatever the plan, he will be part of it.

"Quinn, take Tera and go back to the estate in case Sapphire comes home on her own. Take a look around her room and let me know if you find anything to help us discover what has happened. Pony and Chamous will come with me. Before I return home I will file a missing person's report. Although I am certain they can't help in this situation, the more eyes looking, the better," he says.

"Please stay safe. Come together for a moment before you leave. While attacks come to the Circle of Sun in many ways, spiritual warfare is waged in the shadows, a battle for our very souls. With Sheena now a casualty, Sapphire missing and Tera being attacked, we must assume we are all in danger from our spiritual enemies. But a battle like this is not fought alone. Our Lord and protector leads the battle and we stand protected behind him. Satan has been defeated, our victory is secure. But the victory is through Him, not through us. As strong spirits we surrender to his power and give him the authority to defend our soul. The most effective tool the enemy uses against us is doubt. Doubt weakens our resolve, causing cracks. A crack can turn into a river of doubt. We must never give the enemy his chance and fortify ourselves with our faith in Him alone. Let this verse be your tool…'Do not be afraid of them; the Lord your God himself will fight for you!'" Quinn says.

Romulus, Chamous and Pony leave the bookstore.

Waves of relief flood over Tera as she embraces Quinn.

"Those words I will repeat over and over," she says to her friend.

Quinn and Tera begin the drive back to the estate. Moonlight spills across the Missouri countryside and trees flash past the window of the moving car.

"Wishing Keefe were here?" Tera asks Quinn.

"You are reading my mind, I wish they were all home. No word of any kind since they left. Keefe prepared me, no contact for the first several days," says Quinn.

"Shouldn't they be called?"

"We can't communicate yet," Quinn says.

"I wonder why Beef was the only one who could see what I saw in the photograph." Tera says.

They ride the remainder of the way back to the estate, Tera whispering over and over the words to protect her soul.

Chapter Twenty-One

The Guardians tie their horses in front of a lively pub a short distance from Chatfield's Bake House. Pudding Lane is quiet and filled with shadows. Cashton wedges the lock open and they enter. With heavy drapes pulled shut, one lamp is lit, revealing a neat and tidy bakery.

"Let us not repeat history by persecuting an innocent because of their differences. The Puritans of Salem, Massachusetts used the label of witch for anything they feared," Jexis says.

"She's right, differences were misunderstood and many suffered because of ignorance," the professor says. "Because this woman understands uses of herbs and oils, we don't want to jump to any conclusions."

"We are looking for evidence to support poisoning and conspiracy, whatever that may be," Keefe says.

Jexis adds, "So far, we're grabbing at straws. I don't feel much progress is being made."

"I agree, our fact-finding is drawing us further in the wrong direction," Cashton says.

"Investigation often takes you down many dead ends," Keefe says, "that's part of it."

"Thomas Tobler recognized impending disaster in the form of the plague or Black Death. Enough is known about the devastation the pandemic caused when it ravished Europe in the fourteenth century. Threat of pandemic is what brought us here, but our investigation has been so heavily saturated in religious conflict we've barely focused on the possible pandemic," the professor notes.

"There is so much confusion, we are only beginning to unravel the causes," Cashton adds.

"I think the reason we are here has little to do with the plague and more about the state of mind of these Londoners. I can't put my finger on it, but it was something with Bishop Tobler's dream. I sense a connection, but I am unable yet to understand it," the professor says.

"These are study books of some kind," Jexis says, examining

Annabeth Chatfield's items. "Catechism of the Anglican Church, The Book of Common Prayer."

Cashton lights the lamp on the desk and helps Jexis.

"Here is a roster of clergymen. There are indicators by some of the names listed," says Cashton.

"Those are the ones who are sick or have died," Jexis says.

"I found something, a stain," Keefe says from the area behind the curtain. He holds the lantern low to the ground.

"It looks like blood, not sure what kind," Cashton says.

The room behind the curtain is cluttered and dirty. Unlike the front of the bake shop, this room would be off limits to customers.

"This is the curtain Miss Chatfield was tentative about opening when we were here. She set a delivery down in front of the curtain, not wanting to draw the curtain back," Jexis says.

"You wouldn't want your patrons to see this mess. What went on back here, and what's that odor?" Keefe asks.

"Look up," the professor says, pointing to the herbs hanging in bunches from the ceiling.

Cashton says, "Don't touch the one with the large purple leaves! Bella Donna, extremely toxic. The root is the most potent, complete loss of voice first, and then parts of the body would become debilitated. Pupils would be dilated. You could be made sick, or with full doses you would not survive."

"This door is locked," the professor says, trying to force the door in the rear of the curtained-off room.

Keefe uses a mallet to break the lock. He opens the door to multitudes of scratching rodent claws scampering for cover.

"My Lord, what is that?" Jexis asks in horror.

There is not a square inch of space that isn't moving. The room is filled with rodents. Cages stacked upon cages. Pretty fabric lined baskets are inhabited by rats who scurry over the basket handles in their haste to clear out. Rodent tails hang thick from the rafters. One tries to crawl up the leg of the professor. He shakes it loose moving back out of the room. Keefe does a quick survey of the room before pulling the door shut.

"My skin is crawling! Why keep rats?" Jexis says, holding herself.

"That is peculiar, and crazy!" Keefe says.

"Remember, Annabeth Chatfield gave rats to Olivia," Cashton says. "Why would she do that?"

"We've seen our share of rodents in London since we arrived, but she collects them? They are pets to her?" Jexis muses. "Completely bizarre and creepy! I am ready to get out of here."

The four congregate around Annabeth's desk.

"If this woman is putting poison in her chocolates, could she also be spreading disease with rats?" Keefe asks.

"I thought she was helping people," Jexis says.

"Perhaps that is what she wants you to believe," Cashton replies.

Professor Enderlee says, "She is making people sick with the Yersinia Pestis bacterim, the plague! It is not the rats she wants as much as the fleas that are crawling on them. The fleas on the rats carried the disease aboard ships that brought them right to the port of London."

"But how would she know fleas are the carriers? That wasn't known at this time in history was it?" Keefe asks.

"No, not identified until the late eighteen hundreds!" the professor says.

After Keefe's question it only takes a few moments for each to arrive at the same chilling conclusion; Annabeth Chatfield is not from this time.

Keefe wastes no time. He opens the door of the stone oven with red hot embers still glowing within. With a shovel he throws burning coals into the rat infested room. Instantly the commotion sends the rats scampering for cover and the coals sizzle and smoke and combust into flames.

"What are you doing?" the professor asks.

"We must stop the spread of the disease. This is a good start. No good can come of this place. We will find this Miss Chatfield next," Keefe says.

With great force the room ignites and the four Guardians run out through the front door.

"The proper authorities will need to be notified immediately to prevent the fire from spreading!" Keefe shouts.

Flames are already leaping out the windows of the Bake House.

The Guardians knock on doors and windows and Cashton warns everyone in the pub.

Chapter Twenty Two

The midnight hour has long passed when Pony, Chamous and Romulus drive through the quiet and dark streets of downtown Kansas City on their way to the hotel.

Romulus uses Sheena's key to gain entrance.

"See if you can find anything with a list of those she's traveling with. Sheena was going to give me something she had written for me, I hope it's there," Romulus says as they take the elevator up.

Everything in the room is neat and tidy. Romulus sifts through the notebook next to her bedside, and some papers on a desk, but does not find what he is looking for. Pony searches for anything that might reveal the last names of the men traveling with her.

"You never met Finnegan or Albert?" he asks Romulus.

"I didn't ever see anyone else, and she didn't mention them," he says.

"I'm going to check out the parking garage and ask a few questions at the front desk. Trust me those two would stand out. I'll meet you downstairs," Pony says.

The hallway is empty; thus no chance of running into others in her entourage. He takes the stairs to the parking garage and after scouting out both levels he finds no yellow jeep. In his frustration he shoves open the door and it slams into the wall of the stairwell on his way back into the hotel. The sound echoes throughout the quiet lot of parked cars behind him. With the accident, Sheena's entire entourage would be thrust into the spotlight, but where would they be? Pony's ringing of a bell, brings a young woman to the front desk.

"I am looking for friends of Sheena McNeil. She was traveling with a whole group of people from Romania," Pony says.

The desk clerk continues chatting on her cell phone.

The young woman says, "Yup, something big is going down right now. I thought nothing ever happened on this shift!" she says into her phone, laughing.

With all patience gone, and overcome with a sense of urgency, he grabs the cell phone right out of her hand.

"I am sorry, but this is a matter of life and death. She was traveling with two Romanian men. It's critical we find them," Pony tells her.

"I will call security if you don't leave the hotel immediately." she says, grabbing the phone back from him. "McNeil checked in alone, I was working that night. I've seen no one else; not sure I would tell you if I did," she says with attitude.

A man in a suit bustles to unlock the front door. He leads three police officers to the elevator.

"They are in her room right now," the hotel staffer says as the elevator doors close.

As soon as the doors close he hurries from the hotel. Pony walks about halfway down the block and hides in the shadows. His pocket vibrates, signaling a text from Quinn.

"Romulus is not answering his
cell, police came here looking
for Romulus. No word from
Sapphire, what about you?"

The doors of the hotel open and Romulus emerges with the officers. Chamous follows. Romulus gets into a squad car. Chamous lingers, hoping Pony might be watching before he gets into the car. Once gone, Pony goes over to where the police car had been. In the gutter of the street lie car keys. Once safely back in Romulus's car, he replies to Quinn's text.

"R. is on his way to the station...looks
like Chamous went along."

Quinn texts back,

"I am on my way then. Come back
here and stay with Tera. We can get
this all straightened out by morning."

"K." Pony texts back.

The street is empty and Pony feels hope slipping away. Where is Sapphire? He turns the ignition and heads for Washington Cemetery.

With the massive iron gates locked, Pony parks the car. He will be on foot now. With only a partial moon, he must maneuver past the acres of headstones on his way to the oldest part of the cemetery. He chooses his steps carefully, out of respect for where the dead lie. To find the place the bizarre scene took place a few days ago with the Romanians he can't be so worried about where he is stepping. But desperation outweighs respect for the dead. He begins running. Pony's feet pound hard on the ground beneath him, the final resting places to legions of souls. The eerie hoot of a watching owl carries across the shadowy grounds. With his determination wavering, he finally recognizes his surroundings and where the limo was parked. As if the wind knows, everything becomes still. In front of Pony lie rows of mausoleums, their entrances emerging from a grassy slope, ready for mourners to call. Years of vandalism left one crypt door hanging on its hinges and Pony remembers it as the one where the bizarre scene took place. He doesn't entertain the fleeting thought Sapphire might lie inside hurt or dying, however, the thought shakes him to his core. But what did he expect to find, coming here to the cemetery? His hope would be perhaps two Romanians grieving for their friend Sheena. And if he did find them, lying on the floor having indulged in too much liquor as they had done before, he would need restraint. Pony enters but does not find Sapphire, or anyone. A gentle breeze finds its way in too, and catches the dry leaves from the lonely floor swirling them around him. With most all of his hope spent, he falls, resting on the cold tomb, all fear drowned by the ache in his heart. Pony regrets ignoring the warning signs they both felt about the Romanians. He speaks out, his words echoing through the dead of night.

"Where can she be? Lord, I beg of you. Please help me. Please help me," he cries.

He rests his head on his arms. He closes his eyes to hold the tears in. In his mind's eye he sees her. Together they smile in the sunshine, her beautiful jade eyes full of happiness. The scene allows peace to his heart for a few moments. He opens his eyes and instantly his attention is diverted to radiance from the corner of the crypt. He straightens and wipes at his eyes. He plucks an oddly glowing stone from the floor and with a flicker of hope, he reaches in his pocket, retrieving the glowing stone from the tunnel under Bordeaux's. Two similar stones! He thrusts both back into his pocket and bolts from the crypt, running all the way to his car.

When he arrives at the winery he turns his headlights off. He passes Bordeaux's, parking his car near the vineyards. He finds the underground tunnel they discovered before. Into the darkness he descends, using his flashlight to light the way. With courage he runs as fast as he can, and once again, he comes to a glowing portion. The wall where he collected the stone still glows faintly. He continues past, down the opposite way for any sign of her. His search brings him back to the glowing arch-like area on the stone wall. Pony feels the glowing arch; it's edges are warm, the center almost hot. He steps on something hard, diverting his focus to the floor of the tunnel. A silver ring! He recognizes Sapphire's ring she had been here. With renewed hope he puts his hands upon the stone wall again.

"What are you doing? Get away!" a voice bellows out.

"Who's there?" he responds.

Pony stands ready to protect himself, but a familiar face greets him.

"Father Mopsi, you startled me!" Pony says, relieved.

"What on earth brings you down here, and at this hour?" Father Mopsi asks.

"With all due respect, I could ask you the same thing," Pony says, hungry for answers.

"Son, you really don't want to know!" Father Mopsi says.

"Sapphire is missing! Some lunatics have her," Pony pleads and grabs Father Mopsi's arms. "They're not normal, Father! Finnegan was the last to see her, he used her cell phone!"

"But why would you think she was here?" he asks Pony.

Pony releases the priest. He digs the two glowing stones out of his pocket and shows them to Father Mopsi.

"One I collected when Sapphire and I explored the tunnels, and the other from the cemetery where we spent time with the Romanians," Pony says. "Something is not right about these guys, Father Mopsi!" says a frantic Pony.

Father Mopsi grabs Pony's arm.

"You must get out of here, Pony, the tunnels are dangerous," he says.

Pony pulls his arm away from Father Mopsi with force.

"I don't care! They have Sapphire!" he says. "This is her ring!

She was here! What is this place, Father?" Pony asks desperately.

Father Mopsi examines the ring.

"I was afraid of this! This winery was home to Carolynn and Adam Langford, these tunnels a transport for their dark army! After their defeat in Nadellawick, Quinn asked me to guard the tunnels. In the last few days I've seen evidence of activity again! Right where we stand is a passageway. Where it leads is a place none of us wants to go!" Mopsi says.

"But that is where Sapphire is. I must go there," says Pony.

"Pony, this transport is foreign to me," says the Father.

Pony does not care what the Father has to say about the unknowns. With Sapphire's ring upon his little finger he places his palms against the wall. Father Mopsi tries to reason with him.

"Remove your hands Pony. We don't know where . . . "

And suddenly the archway glows a brilliant white, evolving into red embers before igniting into flames that leave Pony completely unharmed. A mystical wind whips through the empty tunnel. Its force blasts Father Mopsi away from the opening, pinning him helplessly to the opposite tunnel wall.

Pony's palms melt the stone away creating an opening much like the Madowent. Without hesitation, he steps inside as the burning arch becomes a spinning circle of fire, sending sparks flying several feet either side of the opening. Once inside, he begins to run.

Pinned to the wall by the forceful wind and flames, Father Mopsi watches helplessly as Pony goes deeper and becomes smaller and smaller. When it is too late to follow, the flames subside and the opening is gone. Only a glowing arch remains, and a distraught Father Mopsi. He runs as fast as his legs can carry him out of the tunnel.

Chapter Twenty-Three

Vic Buffington arrives at the police station before Quinn, just as Romulus is questioned about the accident again.

"I gave you a statement already. It's very late," Romulus says to investigators.

One of the investigators says, "We need a few more minutes of your time."

"My client won't be answering any questions at this hour. The sun is nearly up," Mr. Buffington says.

Romulus says, "No, Vic. I am innocent and I did nothing wrong. I will answer their questions."

"What were you doing at the Hotel Phillips, Mr. Royce?" the investigator asks.

"Miss McNeil wrote a song for me many years ago. She wanted me to have it," he says.

"Mr. Royce what is the nature of your relationship with Miss McNeil?"

"I knew Sheena in England before I married my first wife. I loved her, wanted to marry her, but her focus was her career so we both moved on. I never saw her again until this week. We picked up where we left off," he answers.

"Mr. Royce, would you mind telling me exactly what happened before Miss McNeil's death?"

"I gave her a tour of the Kaufmann Center earlier in the day, after her sound check. The afternoon went without incident."

"Go on."

"After her performance, I planned a private champagne reception in one of the suites. She was in good spirits and health. Suddenly, everything changed. Sheena became agitated and went into some kind of seizure. She had trouble breathing. The high necked gown was suffocating her, so I tore the seams. I was shocked to find scratches and marks. She bolted from the chair and pounded on the large glass windows. I called for help. She slapped the phone from my ear and jumped on me, hitting me over and over. I struggled to hold her arms from striking me. She ran out of the room and headed for the balcony. I raced after her, convinced she would fling herself from it. I caught up to her and she became combative and would not allow me to stop her. She jerked violently as I tried to help her. One of those violent motions sent her plunging over the rail," Romulus concludes.

The loud knock on the door, followed by the exit of the investigator, leaves Romulus and his attorney alone. Outside the room and down the hallway, a waiting Chamous is joined by Quinn. He arrives just in time to see Romulus being taken away in handcuffs.

Vic Buffington goes directly to Quinn.

"What on earth is going on, Vic?" Quinn demands.

"Romulus threatened Sheena. A witness has come forth," Vic says, shaking his head.

"What? That's absurd!" Quinn says, exasperated.

"The witness's information proved credible when your father returned to Hotel Phillips in the middle of the night," Vic says. "In a story about Miss McNeil she was quoted as mentioning how helpful her journal would be in writing her life story someday. If she wrote anything about her relationship with your father, it would be in that journal. Whether a journal exists or not, your Father made an error in judgment by putting himself at the hotel," Vic says.

"There is more to the story, Vic. My father had a reason to be there," Quinn says.

"Quinn, I am on your side. I don't doubt his innocence for a moment. We will mount our defense after a few hours of sleep. I am meeting your father first thing in the morning. You need to get home and sleep yourself. We can and will get to the bottom of this. Until then, good evening. Oh, I nearly forgot, your father asked me to give you this note." Vic Buffington gives Quinn the note and leaves the station.

Quinn opens the note which reads, 'Do not file a report'

Quinn had hoped she would be driving her father to the estate with them.

Chamous says, "Why doesn't Romulus want us to file the report about Sapphire?"

"Where Sapphire was taken would not be in their….jurisdiction, if you know what I mean. That being the best reason, but now that Romulus stands accused of murder, it would not be wise to report his daughter goes missing on the very same day. It will only complicate everything and slow us all down. I am assuming these are his thoughts," Quinn says tersely.

Tera meets them both immediately when they arrive. She leads them into the sitting room. A distressed Father Mopsi sits on the couch with a handkerchief to his face. Dr. Brazil tries to console him.

"What is wrong, is it Sapphire?" Quinn asks with urgency.

"No, it's not Sapphire. Quinn, oh Quinn, the dark transit! It is active and Pony is gone!"

"The transit is active? How did Pony even know if its existence?" she asks.

Father Mopsi says, "As I reported to you there were signs of activity again. I found Pony investigating on his own tonight. From a glowing stone, he connected Finnegan to the dark transit, and then he discovered Sapphire's ring at the base of the glowing arch. He is convinced she's been taken through it. I am afraid he might be right. Despite all my attempts, he entered the dark transit, and I was helpless to stop him." Father Mopsi buries his face in his hands.

Seeing Father Mopsi so distraught affects Quinn deeply.

"Father, we will find them both. You did everything you could," she says.

"I don't do well, when our kids are involved. Look at me, I am a puddle," he says, whimpering. Tera offers him another tissue.

Quinn goes out into the hallway with Dr. Brazil.

"Please take Father Mopsi to his quarters. He will be needing a sleeping tea," Quinn says.

Dr. Brazil escorts Father Mopsi back to his room.

Chamous and Tera sit together on the sofa. Quinn doesn't give it a second thought.

"We will leave immediately for the winery. I have to enter the transit. I have to find Pony," Quinn says.

"Quinn, you can't do that alone," Tera says.

"I will go with you," Chamous offers.

"Are you sure, Chamous?" Quinn asks.

"No doubt at all," he replies.

"Tera meet Vic Buffington and my father at the station first thing tomorrow morning. I must find these innocents first. I will return to help my father fight for his freedom," she says.

Chamous and Quinn rush to Bordeaux's and enter the underground tunnel in the vineyard per Father Mopsi's recommendation. Once they are standing in front of the Dark Transit, she asks Chamous to take her hand and together they stand beneath the glowing arch.

"Chamous, I want to make sure you understand, I can offer no guarantees. You know the evil of those who used it before us. I do believe the attacks are coming from dark angels. This transit, guarded by Father Mopsi lay dormant after our battle. Since the Romanian foreigners arrived, this transit has become active. I am only to conclude this will lead us to answers. I will give you one last chance to decline," she says.

"No, I have no doubts about it. Tera's with me on this. I am privileged to help," he says.

Quinn holds her palms flat on the wall. Once more the glowing arch dazzles as bright as the sun. It ignites into flames and an unnatural wind whips through the tunnel. The arch becomes a circle and spins, spraying sparks everywhere. Instead of an opening, the whole face of the wall bursts, sending Chamous and Quinn back from the firewall. They use their arms to shield themselves from the heat and flames. Quinn aggressively moves back to the center of the tunnel, her hair whipped by the wind, the fire licking her. Bravely and defiantly, she lowers her head as if she is bowing to the power. She remains steadfast for a moment before lifting her chin to the heavens and raising her arms overhead. She puts her fingers together leaving an oval of space between her palms and shouts firmly above the thundering wind and flames.

"I command control of this transit for the good of mankind!" she shouts over the wind.

The oval opening between her palms harnesses the light of goodness and explodes through it. The flames fall under her command and leave the Circle of Sun branded around the entrance. She turns to Chamous who grasps her hand and together they step within the transit. But, unlike before, the opening does not close again. Neither one looks back as they travel deep into the unknown.

From the shadows a figure steps inside the transit and follows.

Chapter Twenty-Four

"You are not eating anything, Miss," Culpeper says to the beautiful young woman.

"My name is Sapphire! I keep telling you," Sapphire says.

"Your Aunt Annabeth explained everything to me. To save you from the Pest House, I am to keep you hidden," Phillip Culpeper says with kindness in his eyes.

"Who is Annabeth? I assure you I am not ill," she says.

"Disorientation and confusion, even physical outbursts can surface in some cases like yours. I assured her I would care for you, but you must eat if you are to regain your health, please Miss," he says.

Sapphire cannot recall anything after her abduction. She does not know where home is, only she is far from it. She wonders if this doctor might be right about her mental state, because she can't find any signs of the twenty first century. The cellar has no electricity, no running water, a sack of straw for a mattress and her clothing and that of the doctors are garments from another time in history. No one would ever find her here. Her hopelessness grows, along with her hunger. She begins with the clear soup.

"What kind of soup is this?" Sapphire asks.

"My wife's recipe, onion and barley broth," says Culpeper.

"It is good. Thank you. Where am I and what year is this? I am confused perhaps."

"This is London and the year is 1666. Does that refresh your memory?" he asks.

His response sends her mind reeling. How is this possible? What has happened, and how will she ever find her way home? It is almost too much for her to take in. Sapphire does not want the doctor to suspect illness, so she does her best to carry the conversation forward.

"Yes, I think the fog is… clearing." Sapphire says slowly.

The doctor has been kind, he has helped her, not harmed her. He presents her only hope of escape.

"Please tell me about your family," she says.

Culpeper lights up at the question.

"My wife Gwendolyn and I lost our first little girl to illness. But we have been blessed twice since then. Martha is 6 and Millicent is 3. Losing the first child led me to practice medicine. Before, I was only an apothecary," Phillip says.

"Your family sounds wonderful. Do you live nearby?" Sapphire asks him.

"You did not eat your bread and I must insist you drink this tea. Please sleep now, you need the rest and I must tend to my family. Millicent has taken ill. There is much demand for a physician. The spreading illness is feared to be the dreaded plague it nearly wiped our land clean of life 200 years ago. I am busy," he says avoiding her question.

Culpeper climbs the small flight of stairs and closes and locks the door at the top. She will not find answers in the cellar. What if Finnegan and Albert return? Who is this Annabeth who claims to be her aunt? How did she end up in another century? Her mind races with questions with no plausible answers. The uneaten bread is moldy, an indicator of the time she has been captive. No one is coming for her. Sleep takes over and along with it comes a nightmare.

* * * * *

A summer's day, mild and colorful. A meadow stretches as far as the eye can see. The gentle breezes bend the tall grasses and they move like waves in the ocean. Through the center of the meadow a trail leads into the sunset. A line of people follows a horse drawn cart carrying a tiny coffin. The funeral procession is silent except for the cries of the grief stricken family. Doctor Culpeper holds up his wife as they walk to the cemetery to bury their child.

"Why, God? Why did you take another child? Our little Millicent... why, God?" his wife asks. She collapses in a heap of dark despair.

The family surrounds to console her, knowing nothing can.

Doctor Culpeper must run to catch up to the driver of the cart to implore him to delay. He is surprised to find his friend Annabeth driving.

"Annabeth, whatever are you doing here?" he asks her, completely

stunned.

"Don't you understand, you stupid, trusting fool? I am the orchestrator of this blackness! You helped me to make my chocolate of death with your poison belladonna. Yes, I used the root of the bush, the most deadly, to grind into a paste. It blended beautifully with my almond and honey cream. Those chocolates are my arrows I shoot into the heart of the highest ranking clergymen within earshot of my presence. Stupid ignorant Londoners are easy to scare. They think every comet flying through the night sky is a sign from their weak God," she pauses to laugh at the expense of mankind.

"No, No!" Culpeper says as he tries to grab her arms and pull her from her seat on the cart.

The pleasant summer day gives way to bone chilling winter. The ground is now barren and the trees leafless. The wind whips her once golden hair to black silk. Her skin is deathly pale and her smile evil.

"Get away from me!" Annabeth says. She kicks Culpeper to the ground. She takes her whip and draws it back to strike the horse carrying Culpeper's baby away.

Culpeper uses all the strength he can muster and attacks again, but he is no match for her.

She throws him to the ground like a rag doll. She jumps to his side, and puts her boot on his chest.

He cannot move.

She looks to him, her face becoming gaunt and tight, and her teeth looking more fang-like, her eyes sunken.

"How did I create a good panic? By choosing religious leaders as the first victims! I like panic. They all believe their God is mad at them. Erasing their leadership provides loss of hope and makes a ready harvest to the darkness. Another spark of brilliance hit me: Why not bring back the plague? It worked so well two hundred years ago!" she says. And with this, she laughs, her mouth almost animalistic now.

Ignoring everything, Culpeper's grief-stricken wife rushes to the side of her fallen husband.

"Phillip, Phillip, are you alright? I do not blame you. You did everything you could. All we need is our love, and each other," the distraught woman cries.

"Look at the display of love!" Annabeth says sarcastically.

Phillip manages in his pain to reply, not caring if it meant his death.

"Yes, we value something you will never be able to understand: eternity with our God in heaven, and we have experienced love," he says.

"Your love, so grand! I too had the miracle of love, albeit from a fool. Yes, love can set you free!" she says. She raises her hand to the heavens and a bolt of lightning answers her summons. A jagged force cracks dangerously close to the cart sending the horse rearing up, disturbing the tiny coffin. It lands upon the ground, spilling its contents. This turn of events sends the parents into motion and Annabeth laughs while savoring the gruesome and hopeless darkness.

The parents rush to find the tiny casket is empty. The wind becomes calm again. Color and life return to the world.

The confused parents hold each other.

All eyes turn to the meadow.

Walking towards them is a magnificent lion, their beloved Millicent on his back. She scampers off his back and runs to her parents, happy and healthy.

Annabeth is unable to move in the presence of the Lion Malachi.

The parents embrace their child, kissing her, tears streaming down joyous faces. Phillip holds her up to the heavens as the sun beams warm and golden upon her.

Millicent laughs with delight. She shows them both the pendant Malachi placed around her neck.

"It is a pomander," Phillip says.

Little Millicent brings the pomander to her tiny lips and kisses it.

Phillip and his wife are joined by their other daughter. Together they all walk hand in hand through the meadow grasses, safe and happy.

Only then can Annabeth move. She advances on Malachi and lifts her sword of death to him.

Malachi rises up on his legs and crushes her.

Sapphire wakes from her dream and immediately reaches around her neck. IT IS THERE! The pomander Malachi placed upon her neck in the first dream she had of the great lion. She finds a pebble and writes upon the stone wall.

"Sapphire was here! Beware!

ANNABETH SPREADS SICKNESS

AND DEATH! Saving Culpeper's daughter."

She takes the pomander from her neck and examines the ball of gold. With little effort, it unlatches and falls open like the sections of an orange. Upon each section is an inscription: blue bread, sugar, starch, potassium, water. Sapphire is uncertain of their importance. She reads the sections again. Is this why she is here? She remembers the words of the lion in her first dream.

"You will save a life, thereby saving your own."

Culpeper mentioned his daughter is sick. In this dream, the Culpepers are preparing to bury her. But Malachi delivers her back to them with the same pomander around Millicent's neck as this one. Does this hold the key to saving Millicent's life?

With her hope soaring on wings, she throws the straw mattress from the bed and uses her foot to smash through the frame. She carries the longest portion of the wood frame up the stairway and rams the door over and over until the door busts through.

She sets about her work, but doesn't get too far before Culpeper returns.

He is stunned to find Sapphire upstairs.

"Miss, what are you doing? How did you get out from the room below? You must not be out of bed!" he says firmly.

Sapphire produces a knife.

"Now wait, doctor. I am only using this knife as protection while I explain myself. I was sent here to help you," she says.

Culpeper moves towards her, and she lunges at him, forcing him back.

"Please trust me," Sapphire says.

"But right now you are acting like you've lost your senses, as Annabeth warned," he says with sincerity.

"But if I were not telling you the truth, why would I wait around for you to come back? If I broke out from the downstairs, I could easily have escaped through this door or out the window. But I didn't! I am staying with you. I am going to help you to save your child!" says Sapphire.

Phillip Culpeper's expression changes and he takes two steps back.

"But what could you possibly know about medicine? You are only a young lady," he says.

"I have a remedy. It comes from the future, a future free from the spreading sickness known as the Black Plague. It is called penicillin. It could save your Millicent," Sapphire says to the man.

"How do you know about my Millicent?" he asks her.

"I am not sure Phillip, but I had a vision that your little girl was.... deathly ill. A terrible lady whom you count among your friends,is really your enemy. She is trying to make people sick. In my dream your Millicent becomes healthy again and is saved by a remedy. Believe me, Annabeth is not a friend," she says.

"I just tended to Millicent; she grows worse," Culpeper admits. The worry and desperation show on his face.

"This is why I am here! I will see this through! I will do all I can to save her. Please let me try. What do you have to lose?" Sapphire begs.

"Yes, you are right. I have nothing to lose. Where do we begin?" Culpeper says.

"Here is the list of ingredients. I will need your help. But first I must get something from downstairs," she says. Sapphire retrieves the moldy bread from the cellar.

"What is that for?" he asks.

"The discovery came by accident right here in London. A specimen is left uncovered by accident. A mold forms on it. A growing blue and green mold, like on this piece of bread, contains properties that will fight the kind of illness that affects Millicent. To harness its properties, it must be filtered," she says.

A stunned Dr. Culpeper looks to the bread with both fascination and confusion.

With the ingredients inscribed within the pomander, they begin their work. Sapphire carefully scrapes the mold from the bread into a glass beaker, and the doctor filters it with heat. After a couple of hours, Phillip and Sapphire have the rustic penicillin ready. They leave for Culpeper's home.

Chapter Twenty-Five

Fire spreads from the Bake House, fueled by relentless east wind gusts. The blaze is fed by the timber buildings that make up the whole of London's structures. The primitive methods of fighting fires with a relay of buckets to douse the flames prove ineffective. From horseback Keefe, Jexis, Professor Enderlee and Cashton view the escalating crisis.

A man from the group yells out to a young bystander on horseback.

"Inform the Lord Mayor and the Royal Army! Make haste!"

The adolescent gallops across the cobblestone to summon the highest officials.

Keefe takes the opportunity presented.

"Jexis, I want you to do the same. Allowing a young boy to deliver such a critical message is risky. I am confident as soon as the Lord Mayor is informed, he will mount a strong defense. We will meet up with you at Gresham by nightfall. They must understand the extent of the crisis," Keefe says.

Without hesitation, Jexis follows.

"Do you know the whereabouts of Annabeth Chatfield?" Cashton asks a group of onlookers.

"She spends most of her time at the Bake House but goes to St. Paul's at noon like clockwork," a woman tells her.

Cashton says, "Thank you madame."

"We passed St. Paul's earlier, let's go," Keefe says.

"Sounds like she is a regular at St. Paul's," the professor comments.

"I guess we know why," says Cashton.

* * * * *

Quinn and Chamous's journey ends abruptly as they tumble across the floor like dice thrown from a cup.

Disoriented but unhurt, Quinn goes directly to Chamous, who rests against a wall.

"Chamous are you ok?"

Chamous opens his eyes. He shakes his head in an effort to

refocus.

"I think so. That is quite a ride. Are you alright?" he asks her.

"Yes, just tossed and tumbled."

"Where on earth are we?" Chamous says wide-eyed.

"Well, it can't be too good. We are behind bars, and we're not wearing our own clothing. We've been captured," Quinn says.

"What are you wearing?" Chamous asks in hushed tones.

Quinn looks down at her clothing, and then to his.

"The same thing as you," she says.

"Costumes of sorts?" Chamous suggests.

"We are in some kind of… dungeon," Quinn says. Without making a sound, she approaches the bars, peers out of the cell, then dashes back to the wall. She closes her eyes and breathes in deeply, regaining composure.

Chamous takes his turn to look outside of the bars.

"Good Lord, what is that?" he asks.

"I don't think we are wearing… costumes," Quinn says.

Slender and tall, black-robed figures glide across the stone floor. One approaches, and at first Quinn is speechless in the presence of the faceless hooded figure, but manages to speak bravely to him.

"Where are we?" she asks.

The figure drops his head back laughing, his hood down now, exposing a hollow skull. In a curious childlike voice he speaks, "She a lost soul too, or she's too much ale!"

He runs the tip of his sword across the bars, sending a metal clatter echoing throughout the dungeon.

"Who are you?" she asks.

"I am no one," he says in the same innocent voice. He points his bone finger to the other guards.

"And that one over there, he's no one, too. As well as him and him," he says.

"What is your plight?" Quinn bravely asserts.

"We are the former prisoners of these cells. The Black Witch offered us freedom in exchange for our souls and we gladly accepted. We are on the other side of the bars now," the guard says.

"Why do you sound like a child?" Quinn asks hesitantly.

"We speak with the voices of our lost innocence," he answers.

"What is the name of your Black Witch?" Quinn asks.

"Madame Chatfield, she is who we serve. From the catacombs of Saint Paul's she arrives soon to give us orders," says the guard.

"Release us immediately!" Quinn demands.

Laughter again comes from the skull.

"You sound like the one who came before you. This is no place for beginnings; only endings. She will see to that," he says.

Quinn slides the back of her St. Benedict medal down, allowing a destructive beam to bust the cell door wide. Next she aims her weapon at him, slicing off the boney hand that raises a sword to them.

"Pony, where are you?" Quinn shouts as she and Chamous escape their cell.

"Quinn? Quinn, get me out of here!" Pony says, recognizing her voice.

A few cells down they find Pony.

"Stand back!" Quinn says, using the all-powerful shaft of light to free him.

Dozens of black robed guards make their way towards them, Quinn extends her hand out.

"Stop!" she orders.

An invisible wall of protection prevents their aggressions.

"You gave your soul to the wrong master, living in darkness for centuries. You are to be judged by only one master. I am offering you the judgment day you have been robbed of," she says with authority.

Hundreds of childlike voices chatter and accuse and debate.

Quinn shouts loudly over them all, "Declare the name of my Lord and Savior as yours and you will rise from these dungeons, earning your due judgment day."

At first there is no movement, but within minutes many of the guards ascend in a vapor, leaving their black robes lying in a heap.

"This is your chance to break the bond of darkness," Quinn says.

"Kill them!" a voice calls from the group.

They rush the invisible barrier, slightly bending the powerful wall. The dungeon fills with dozens more of them. Quinn stretches her arms in front of her. With palms open, cobalt rays explode towards them from every fingertip. As they fall, Chamous and Pony begin their escape, with Quinn following shortly behind them. The three create distance between themselves and the enemy, running through tunnels of the ancient dungeons. Pony is first to arrive at the dead end. Within reach hangs a rope ladder. He climbs and the others follow. There is nothing but darkness and three hopeful souls seeking freedom. Just when doubt begins to creep in, the air becomes fresher, and the night sky appears. Pony is the first to crawl through to the land of the living.

All three emerge from the old well, relieved.

"I don't know where we are, but any place is better than that!" Pony says.

Quinn asks, "Pony are you alright? Did they hurt you?" She moves Pony's hair out of his eyes.

"Mostly they ignored me, while waiting anxiously for the Black Witch," he says.

Quinn embraces him.

Pony says, "Thank you for saving me. If I wasn't just whisked through a dark transit, dumped in a dungeon, guarded by ghosts, I would be more blown away by what you just did Quinn," Pony heavy irony.

Chamous tousles Pony's hair.

"I am so relieved you are ok, Pony. What were you thinking, going alone?" Chamous asks.

"Romulus needed you. There was no time to waste. I found Sapphire's ring at the base of the dark transit under Bordeaux's and I think Finnegan brought her through to this place. The guards told me the Black Witch waited anxiously for a girl to arrive."

"What on earth?" Chamous says. He created a view by sweeping branches away.

Quinn and Pony stand shoulder to shoulder in astonishment, observing the unfamiliar and chaotic scene.

Villagers with over-packed wagons crowd the streets, struggling for passage. Panic-stricken citizens with packages and bundles under their arm frantically herd their families away.. Wooden wheels clack as they roll over cobblestone surfaces. Smoke fills the night air. A spooked horse rears up in protest at the disorder.

Quinn heads towards more unknown.

"We are dressed like them!" Pony says as they follow her.

Quinn approaches a woman walking behind a wagon.

"What is happening here?" she asks.

"Are ye blind? Away from here, if this wagon can get through. Fire burns through most of London by now. Even St. Paul's is in danger! We are fleeing to camps outside the city walls, God willing," the lady says.

"What is the year?" Quinn asks.

"Have ye lost yer bloody mind? This is the year of our Lord, sixteen sixty six," she says as she walks away shaking her head.

"I bet I can guess the rest," Chamous says knowingly. "September second, sixteen sixty-six." Chamous opens his fist and shows them the numbers written on the palm of his hand, 00902166600.

"If you leave the zero off at beginning and the two on the end, a date remains. September second, sixteen sixty-six. This is the origin number of the text Tera received," Chamous says. After pausing he says, "I don't want to even ask how this is possible."

"We will start at St. Paul's Cathedral," she says.

Uniformed soldiers wrangle their way through the crowds towards a corner building, where the blaze has spread.

"Make way…make way! We are here to fight the fire!" one of the lead soldiers shouts.

The Londoners in the streets cheer while clearing a passageway. At the end of the procession rides the commanding officer and beside him a woman on a white horse. Her long blonde tresses flow with each smoky gust of east wind, her face sprinkled with ash.

"Wait, that's Jexis!" Pony says.

A surprised Jexis sees them among the onlookers. She speaks to the officer and then navigates away from the crowd, sliding off her horse. The trio is stunned. Quinn runs to her first, embracing her.

"Quinn, is this reinforcement? Because we surely need some," she says breathlessly.

"I am shocked to see you here! Where are the others?" asks Quinn as she looks around.

"Just passed them a ways back," says Jexis.

"If the Quest led us here, and our trail to find Sapphire led us here . . . ."

"Wait, Sapphire?" says Jexis, her response comes with a firm grip of Quinn's arm.

Quinn proceeds delicately.

"Jexis, Sapphire's been abducted, and we believe taken through a dark transit under Bordeaux's. That is what brought us here."

"What do you mean abducted? My Lord!" Jexis says.

Jexis keeps her serious and composed disposition, her eyes brimming with tears.

"What are your leads? She is more important than anything we are doing here! Whoever is responsible will regret the day they were born!" Jexis says. She walks quickly to her horse and adjusts her saddle, jerking the cinching straps sternly.

Quinn grips Jexis' forearm.

"Wait, that is not all. Sheena McNeil fell from a balcony to her death at Kauffman Center after her performance."

"What?" Jexis says, stunned.

"Father believes her body was invaded, possessed. He couldn't stop her from falling. He is being held responsible."

"You have got to be kidding!" Jexis says exasperated.

"The justice system is being manipulated somehow. I left before knowing all the details. I needed to follow Pony first. We must find Sapphire. Afterward, I planned to have Keefe return to help Father. Two different challenges landing me in one destination."

"I can take Keefe's place," says Chamous.

"Good man," Jexis says.

In the middle of the chaos the four try to fit the pieces of the puzzle together.

Jexis begins to pace.

"Where does the dark transit end?" she asks impatiently.

"Behind the row of trees over there is a well. A rope ladder in the well leads down to the underground dungeon and transit guarded by black robed spirits," says Quinn.

"She did a number on quite a few of them," Pony says proudly.

"I just passed Keefe, Cashton and the professor on their way to

St. Paul's not too long ago," Jexis says. She takes two of the army's horses and puts reins in both Quinn and Chamous' hands. "Pony, hop on with Quinn. Follow me."

Smoke-filled streets and droves of people in exodus make progress slow. Jexis veers away from the congestion of the streets to a courtyard offering quicker passage across to the next street.

Quinn spots the rest of her Circle of Sun family. Keefe's confused expression gives way to pleasure when he sees Quinn. He promptly dismounts and rushes to her as she slips off her horse. With her feet barley touching the ground, he sweeps her into his embrace. Pony goes to the professor, Cashton and Chamous greet each other, all of them pleased to be reunited.

"Quinn, are you alright? Why are you here?" Keefe asks.

"We are under attack in Nadellawick. Sapphire was taken and we believe, brought here. Chamous and I traveled through a dark transit, the same way Pony did. We think the Black Witch has Sapphire. We are headed to St. Paul's."

"So are we. The Black Witch may be responsible for the chaos you see," says Keefe.

"That is not all. Romulus has been arrested, the charge is murder."

"What…murder…who?" Cashton says in disbelief. "My sister, taken?"

Jexis says, "Sapphire was taken by someone and they believe, brought here. Their search has led them here!"

Quinn adds, "Sheena McNeil is dead. Romulus believes she was possessed, and whatever lived inside her, flung her from a balcony. But he is being held responsible. I don't know all of the details of his charges. Keefe, Father needs you in White Oak. Chamous and I will stay. We will join in these efforts to stop this fire and to find Sapphire!" Quinn struggles to conceal her emotion and all that has happened.

"My Lord, Quinn," says Keefe.

Quinn quickly wipes at her eyes.

Keefe looks to the others before taking her hand, leading her to privacy near the trees. Standing chest to chest, he lifts her chin.

"Quinn, are you alright?" he asks.

Welled tears spill onto her cheeks.

"Yes, I am just relieved we are united. I need your strength to add to mine," she smiles at him. Her voice is strong, masking any weakness.

"Quinn it's me…you are allowed your emotions. You can always show me your vulnerability, and I in return can reveal all of me. That is ours alone. I am sorry all of this occurred back at home, without me by your side," Keefe says with compassion.

"I am gifted with great power, I have the endorsement of St. Michael himself, Polaris to the Circle of Sun. I am the example for others to follow," Quinn says with courage.

"Oh, Quinn, vulnerability escapes no one; it is the action we take in spite of it. Your actions to move forward in the face of fear is what reveal your character as a leader. I am confident in your wisdom, and authority. It is my greatest joy to think a part of you needs me. I have never been more proud of you, or more in love with you," Keefe says.

His words and his tender kiss blast away the emptiness and fortify her resolve.

"And I am afraid we will be separated again," she says with regret.

Keefe says, "It won't be for long, my love."

He leads her back towards the group.

Keefe offers all the information they have gathered to Quinn, Chamous and Pony concerning Annabeth Chatfield, the spreading illness, the Bake Shop and his responsibility with the fire.

"You did what you had to do, Keefe," Professor Enderlee says.

"But now the flames are out of control," Keefe says with disappointment.

"Many pleaded with the Lord Mayor to act swiftly," Jexis said. "But he laughed it off, saying even a woman could squelch the blaze with a few buckets. Creating fire breaks would mean destroying other's property and he didn't want the city to be liable. When the Lord Mayor opened his eyes to the widespread deterioration, his actions came too late. The King ordered the Royal Army after he discovered the Lord Mayor washed his hands of the situation. But I am not sure, with the fire so widespread that London can be saved."

"I thought it was the right thing to do," Keefe says.

"We had no way of knowing the threats of the fire would not

be taken seriously until it was too late. If others did what they are supposed to do, we would not be in this position. You had to destroy the housing of all those infected rats," Cashton says.

"I agree, you had no choice," Quinn says. "Jexis, take Keefe to the dark transit. Chamous, ride along and tell him what he needs to know about Romulus."

Keefe mounts his horse, his eyes locked on hers, before he turns his horse and follows.

Chapter Twenty-Six

Small flames are beginning to burn the east side of St. Paul's Cathedral when the Circle of Sun arrives. First, they must locate the catacombs to find the Black Witch.

"We are looking for openings to an underground," Quinn says loudly as they all scatter quickly, exploring in the church.

"The hole is outside," a voice says from a church pew.

The Guardians rush to a man holding a cloth to his bleeding head.

"May I help you, Sir?" Cashton says. He uses the sponge filled with holy water and dabs away the blood, then rips strips from the man's cloth to wrap his wound.

"Thank you, kind sir. I've seen the hole and the witch who lives there," he says.

"Take us to her," says Quinn.

"She ain't here. She left when the sun went down. I stay far away from her," he says.

"Will you show us?" Quinn asks.

The man rises and leads them through the length of the nave to a door on the other side of the vestibule. He lights a lantern and they follow him out into the churchyard. Amid headstones and crypts, he leads them behind a row of bushes. He stops alongside a long metal plate, similar to most that mark a resting place. The man lifts a corner of the plate and points to the hole. As debris flies through the windy smoke-filled yard, Quinn lowers herself into the crypt-like opening. The old man gives her the lantern and leaves. The others follow. At first glance, the hole is nothing more than an ancient cellar space. Quinn holds the lantern high. Nothing but a dusty old travel trunk sits against the far wall.

"Now, what?" Cashton asks.

Quinn hands the lantern to Pony and heaves the trunk open. Dozens of rock steps lead far below the earth's surface.

The Guardians look to one another. Anticipation builds. They all make their way carefully down the dark descending hole. When they finally reach the bottom the lantern guides them to a storefront, complete with window dressing and light, as if they were on a street corner in London, hundreds of feet up. Six stone steps lined with pots of herbs and living flowers lead them to a massive door that creaks open on their arrival.

No lantern is needed inside. The space is expansive and grand with a roaring fire pit in the center, its flames leaping and simmering. The wall opposite is made of looking glass and reflects the visitors.

"It's bottomless, how does it burn?" Pony asks, inspecting the fire pit.

The heady scent of burning incense smolders on an immense table piled high with books. Cashton and the professor more closely examine one of them lying open-faced.

"How about the name of this massive book, ***Raven's Grimoire***? Potions and spells for anything you could want. Here is a list of items with Culpeper's name on it. He's been linked to Annabeth more than once," the professor says. "She gets herbs and supplies from him. We questioned Culpeper, and he was nervous while we were there. Keefe and I both suspected he wasn't alone that day"

From the shadows, a figure emerges with tattered clothing, and a body covered with scratches and cuts. It is not the Black Witch.

"They said you would come," a voice says.

All eyes turn, the sight freezing them in their tracks. Before them stands the man who once served all of them with loyalty and grace.

"Beef, what are you doing here?" Cashton asks with dismay.

"Haven't you figured it out yet? This is my only home. I took the transit after Quinn and Chamous," he replies.

"You are injured," says Quinn, moving closer.

"Don't come near me. I serve only one master, the Black Witch," he says.

His comment leaves the Guardians looking to one another with confused expressions.

"Let us help you, Beef," Cashton pleads.

"I don't need help. I have been a prisoner in your world for far too long. My reason for living was service to your mother. Romulus could never love Petulah the way I did," Beef says, raising his voice.

These words confound them all.

"I knew what she needed, before she could even ask. I understood her, and earned her respect as the only one who did. She wanted each of you to be by her side in her allegiance to the darkness, but she was alone. You killed her!" Beef yells, his words sputter out with disdain. Beef's jaw becomes tight, his eyes wild. He raises a knife and rushes Quinn.

Cashton quickly and easily disarms him. He falls to the ground weak, but still defiant. He stumbles away from Cashton and back to his feet.

Beef says, "It doesn't matter. She knows I love her. She knows it was I who set her free!"

"What do you mean, Beef?" Quinn asks.

With a coy smile, he repeats out loud:

"Dancing in the midnight sun,
knowing that our work is done.
Serpents, snakes and stains on souls,
found within the darkest hole.
Trapped forever, darkness gone,
but fear the lover's tears at dawn," he says, before breaking into curious laughter after repeating the verse. "Yes, the understanding dawns on your faces now."

But his laughter turns back to despair.

Beef says, "You took her from me! The depth of my despair had no measure. One stormy night I planned to drive off a bluff and end my misery, but she stopped me. My shock at her return paled in comparison to my joy when she revealed I liberated her from eternal rest." Beef's tears stream down his face. "The morning after she died, I collected her favorite flowers to ease my pain, and placed them on the spot she perished just hours before. Don't you see? The miracle of her resurrection is love! Can the heart of one so dark be loved by another? Yes! Yes it can! My tears permeated the soil and broke the spell of death. I freed my love! She is forever in my debt and I am forever in her service."

"What do you mean…she is freed?" Cashton says with a raised voice.

The Guardians stand frozen, awaiting an answer with far-reaching ramifications.

"She lives! She lives to destroy the Circle of Sun!" This announcement sends Beef into jubilant laughter. He again refocuses on them.

"But once defeated on the soil of Nadellawick, her destiny can only be fulfilled elsewhere. So my Black Witch draws you to her like puppets on a string, my powerful Petulah!" Beef says with pride.

Without warning, a wall of water explodes through the looking glass, flooding into the Black Witch's den. The force knocks the professor down and Pony races to his side.

Quinn points to the wall opposite, sending a brilliant jet of destruction which busts it open, giving the water a place to go. The river of rushing water seeks the lower passage, creating escape back from where they entered. Standing between Quinn and the flames of the fire pit, stands a distraught Beef, hatchet in hand.

"Beef come to me. The water will soon be over our heads. Put down your weapon. We can get out of here," Quinn says, shouting above the roar of rushing water. She holds her hand out to him.

Beef recklessly swings at Quinn, narrowly missing her.

"I want to be the one to end your lives," he says, spewing the words out bitterly.

Suddenly water swirls around his legs and topples him backwards. He grasps for safety but there is none to be found. He falls into the pit of perpetual fire. Quinn rushes to get as close as she can to the flames. Beef's screams echo as he drops to the depths, consumed by its fury.

"Quinn we've little time left, the water still rises!" Cashton yells out.

With both Pony and Cashton on each side of the Professor, they lead him out as Quinn follows quickly behind. With water rising at an unnatural pace, they make their way up the rocky steps, the turbulent waters chasing them. They emerge to find the night sky brilliantly lit by the fires consuming London. The entire roof of St. Paul's Cathedral is now engulfed in flames. The mighty structure simply begins to break down, the lead roof melting and pouring into the streets. Quinn finds an area thick with trees to act as a shelter from smoldering ash falling all around them. Cashton and Pony lower the Professor to the ground and he leans against the trunk of a tree. Cashton looks the professor over for injuries. The professor holds his knee.

"I twisted my knee when the water forced me down," he says wincing.

Cashton places his hand upon the Professor's knee.

Above the chaos Quinn's name is called.

"Listen, it's Chamous!" Quinn says.

"Chamous, Chamous! We're over here!" Pony shouts while running towards him.

He puts his arm around Pony.

"I am glad you are all ok. I was concerned to see the Cathedral in flames," he says breathlessly. "I am assuming you did not find the Black Witch?"

"No, but…"

"Wait, where is Jexis?" Cashton asks.

"She talked of unfinished business and will rendezvous with us later at Gresham College," Chamous says.

"Beef was in the Black Witch's . . . den, he's dead now," Cashton tells Chamous.

"Beef, why? How is that possible?" Chamous asks.

Quinn says, "Looks like he held quite a grudge for us putting an end to Petulah. His tears shed upon her grave… reversed death's grip. She's alive, and spinning her evil threads as Annabeth Chatfield. Since she could never set foot in Nadellawick again, she devised a grand scheme to bring the Circle of Sun to her doorstep."

"She's responsible for the possessed souls, I assume." Chamous says.

"She wants to destroy Romulus. She would find a way to get us here," Quinn says.

"The Quest, and perhaps one of the missing Fidesorbs," The professor says, "how would she…"

Cashton says, "She is influencing people, manipulating clergy, even Archbishop Tobler. I didn't think I would ever encounter her again." Cashton shakes his head. "How can this evil ever be destroyed?"

"We will find Sapphire, and we will find a way to destroy her. I pity Beef," Quinn says.

"You tried to save him, Quinn," the professor says. "I think Cashton's touch soothed my injury."

"Can you take us to Culpeper?" Quinn asks the professor.

"Yes, I can," the professor says.

Chapter Twenty-Seven

Tera opens the door to Keefe's knock. For a moment she is speechless.

"What are you doing here…the Quest?" she asks.

"The search for Sapphire led Pony, Quinn and Chamous to us. Quinn explained the urgency here, so they both stayed and I came back to help."

"The transit led to...the Quest? How is....where is Sapphire, has she been found?" Tera asks with deep concern.

"Not yet, I'm afraid," Keefe says.

"I know I cannot ask you specific questions, but I'm very concerned and confused. Sapphire's trail and the location of the Quest are connected? I pray the day will soon be here and I will no longer be in the dark. I am glad you are back here. We need you," Tera says.

They share a friendly embrace.

"Come in from this bitter spring wind," Tera offers.

Keefe notices Tera's bloodshot eyes.

"How are you Tera? Are you ok?" Keefe asks with concern.

"My eyes are irritated, something in the air this spring. Sheena McNeil's accident, Romulus arrested… I'm sure Quinn explained the situation," she says.

"Yes, but she lacked details. Tell me everything before I meet with Romulus," Keefe says.

Tera asks, "Would you like something to drink?"

"How about some strong coffee?" Keefe says as he sits in front of Tera's fireplace.

"Romulus being held, it's hard to imagine. The pieces don't fit together. Our problem involves Tracie Glenn," Tera tells him.

"I've dealt with her before. She is completely self-serving," says Keefe.

"You do not want her for an enemy!" Tera admits.

"I suspect things are moving quickly, and the wheels of justice were being heavily greased by Tracie Glenn," says Keefe.

"Oddly she did everything she could to offer help. She even

admitted she made some mistakes in the past."

"I wouldn't buy her act, not for a minute."

"It would be a feather in her cap, if her compassion at Romulus's time of need earned her some respect," she says.

"How did Romulus react to her behavior?"

"Skeptically… and he accused her of being opportunistic."

"Exactly what I am thinking," Keefe says.

"If she were out for blood, wouldn't she be the one bringing the charges?" Tera asks.

"What do you mean, who did?"

Tera says, "Someone in her office, one of the assistant attorneys. Vic said her name doesn't appear anywhere."

"How strange! If Tracie Glenn wants to destroy Romulus, repair her public image and bolster her political future, why would she allow someone else to take the reins? The entire department is a team, but I would be surprised if Tracie Glenn allowed anyone else to capture her spotlight," says Keefe.

"Exactly what we are thinking."

"Only one reason I can think of," Keefe says, after he sips at the hot brew. "She can't be a witness against him if she's the one doing the prosecuting."

"She witnessed the accident, along with the rest of us. We all saw the same thing."

Keefe says, "Enhanced version, perhaps? She hates the Royces. I wouldn't put it past her. This coffee is good."

"It's the new blend from Mocha Joe's; the professor calls it Missouri Morn," Tera says. She savors some of the rich roasted brew herself. "Tracie Glenn holds disdain for both the Royces and White Oak."

Keefe says, "What do you mean?"

"The professor served her on a weekday recently when she and Ace Kennedy stopped in to Mocha Joe's."

"Ace Kennedy? Oh, yes. Quinn mentioned him. He is the young journalist, nephew to Elliott Kennadie, right?"

"Yes, he stuck to her like glue at the concert. She wants a friend in the media, and he is making connections through her, for mutual gain. Ace had business with his late uncle's estate, and she rode along. She was totally bored and wanted to leave even before she finished her coffee."

Keefe pauses and then laughs under his breath.

"A county prosecutor has little time for country drives in the middle of a workday. She's soliciting information from Kennedy, about anybody and anything! If she's befriended this Ace, maybe I should pay him a visit."

Tera nods her head in agreement.

In a flash, Keefe pictures Tera lying on the grass with her eyes closed, blood oozing from her mouth. The vision makes his heart pound and his disposition switches to defender, but Tera sits comfortably on the sofa.

"Tera, you are in danger! You will be...challenged!" Keefe says.

Tera's gaze is strange, her eyes look hollow.

"Tera, Tera!" Keefe says. The sight is frightening, but still he reaches for her. As soon as he touches her, her beautiful brown eyes appear normal.

"Stay away from me, Keefe! You can't help me; this battle is within!" Tera says.

She sinks down in a chair, wrapping her arms around herself. With a forced smile, she does her best to put Keefe at ease, but there is trembling in her voice.

Tera says, "It will pass. I am fighting the good fight." Tera holds her head, wincing in pain. "The headaches are getting stronger. My medication is on the counter next to the sink, would you mind?"

"Yes, I would be happy to," he says. Keefe is relieved to do something to help her. He foresees what is coming and considers how he can protect her. A pill bottle sits next to the kitchen sink and Keefe fills a glass of water. The wind howls for his attention and through the window, trees are slapped by a fast approaching storm.

The scene is altered when he is approached from behind. The window reflects Tera rushing him, knife over her head, ready to deliver a fatal stab.

In a split second, he moves from her advance, and the counter stops her charge. Keefe dodges her, while the dropped glass shatters.

He grasps Tera's forearm as she raises the long blade again. His strength is challenged by the supernatural enemy, and the sharp point comes dangerously close.

Then, as if her spirit commands the victory, her eyes once again soften and Tera is back. She drops the knife, horrified at her own actions. She bolts from the lodge. The grey skies are pregnant with rain ready to fall. The wind whips her hair around and she holds herself. With hollow eyes again a guttural voice speaks.

"I live in you."

Tera is thrown to the earth, convulsing. With every ounce of strength she can muster, she pulls her body from the ground and runs towards the trees.

Keefe chases after her as she reaches her destination.

One oak stands alone in a clearing, but she falls short of reaching it. Red welts surface on her arms from an invisible whip.

"No! It will never happen," Tera screams out. She heaves herself up, fighting the driving winds that nearly prevent her from going forward. She reaches the place she's prepared. She slips her wrists and feet into leather straps, pinning herself to the tree.

Keefe gets closer but is blasted yards back and immobilized by the evil force.

The rain begins to fall.

With hollow eyes Tera speaks in guttural sounds and groans from deep within her.

"No mercy! You are weak!" As if she is being slapped by an invisible force her face falls from side to side. Blood comes from the corner of her mouth. Defiantly, Tera battles the evil. "Is that...all?" She repeats herself louder and with conviction. "IS THAT ALL YOU HAVE, I SAID?" Tera starts to laugh. "You can beat my body, but I won't be moved! My body is one with this tree!"

With a force of great magnitude, the mighty oak begins to rock back and forth. Roots crack and rip deep below the ground.

"You can do anything you want to my body, but you will never own my soul! It's spoken for! The dark ransom of death has been paid by my redeemer!" she screams.

While the tree remains steadfast in the ground, Tera's body is further attacked. Her head leans to the side and is forced hard to her shoulder. She winces in pain as the loud wind nearly drowns out her voice. With fierce courage she continues.

"I stand committed and promised to Him alone! With the authority of Jesus Christ, I command you, leave this body!"

Nature explodes sending rain in fast falling sheets, stinging her skin. A glow begins at her feet and slowly moves up her body. A brilliant radiance covers Tera, protecting her as she clings to the tree. Her pain lifts she powerfully prevails.

Tera shouts, "I gladly serve Him! I am honored to fight His battles! If I die today, I will spend the rest of eternity with Him, so I win no matter what. LEAVE MY BODY!"

Her head falls limp; remaining breezes blow hair over her face. Soon all is calm; the campaign of attack is over.

Keefe rushes to her side.

"Tera, Tera!" he raises her face.

With eyes opened slightly, she speaks.

"It is gone. I think I did it," Tera says in a weak voice.

Keefe says, "Oh Tera! Let me help you out of here." He removes her restraints and her soaked body falls limply into his arms. He carries her back to the lodge and wraps her in blankets. He places her on the sofa in front of the fire. Keefe rushes to the bathroom to gather first aid for her injuries. He finds her sleeping restfully, with most of the blood and injury vanishing before his eyes. He calls Dr. Brazil and asks her to come immediately and to bring Father Mopsi along. Fresh logs crackle and warm the room. He drops in the chair with relief, watching her and waiting.

"Thank you Keefe. I am so sorry," a weakened but relieved Tera says softly.

"We've known about the threat of possession and the dangers. Quinn shared her concern with me, but…"

"I couldn't wait much longer. I had to drive out the darkness myself, but would need someone to witness. I'm so sorry it had to be you," says Tera. Filled with light and peace, she pulls the blanket over her shoulders. The flames consume the logs and warmth once again fills her world.

"You are strong, Tera. The Circle of Sun has a fierce warrior in you," Keefe says, but Tera is fast asleep.

He leaves Tera in the care of Dr. Brazil and Father Mopsi and drives through the rain to the offices of the Kansas City Star. He hopes to find Ace Kennedy. It's unrealistic to think Ace would divulge any information about Tracie Glenn, but he has to try. His hope fades when he finds only one person left in the office this late afternoon. A young woman clears some things from her desk and fills a tote.

"I am looking for Ace Kennedy, would you know if he is still around?" Keefe asks.

"Sorry, most everyone is gone. That desk is Kenney's, take one of his cards," she says as she carries her tote through the sea of desks.

"Good night, Art," she says passing a maintenance man standing on a ladder.

"See ya… off to Lipardi's for happy hour?" the man asks.

"No way, too much to do, good night," she says as she leaves.

Keefe finds the desk of Ace Kennedy and takes one of his cards.

"Happy hour at Lipardi's huh?" he asks as he passes the maintenance man.

"Yup, it's the hangout I guess. Heard it's a real dive, somewhere in the west bottoms."

Keefe heads back out into the wet Kansas City evening. He figures Lipardi's might be a good place for a drink.

Chapter Twenty-Eight

With the sun already sunk into the horizon, the air is chilly. A strong gust of wind causes Keefe to draw the collar of his coat up as he rounds the corner to Lipardi's. The neon sign in the window is only half lit. Smoke, mixed with the lingering odor of nightlife, greets him at the door. He walks through the room and chooses a booth. Lipardi's is definitely off the beaten path.

Constant news blasts from the old television over the bar, but is ignored this night by the few patrons who are there. Keefe orders a beer and takes out his phone to review a few notes. He lays Ace Kennedy's card down, but before he can make the call, the rush of cool night air enters along with two men who take seats at the bar.

"Are you covering the city council tomorrow, or is Brad?" one man says to the other.

"I won't be back in time, he can take it," the other replies.

Their conversation resumes after being served cocktails.

"Kennedy wanted it, but he is too tied up," the first one says.

Keefe perks his ears when Kennedy's name comes up. The man continues.

"His days are probably numbered at the Star,"

"Kennedys got a truckload of contacts and connections, thanks to Glenn."

"Lucky stiff!"

"Are you kidding? Trust me. You don't want her...help."

"I take any help I can get," one of the men says, as he motions to the bartender for more peanuts.

"I'm telling you, you don't want the headache. Ace is all wrapped up in the frenzy surrounding the McNeil investigation. I told him to walk away from that Glenn. Just stop taking her calls."

"What journalist would trust her information? With her epic error in judgment with that case last year, you could be left hanging on a wire, by putting all your eggs in her basket."

"Ace says he's not following blindly. He wants her in his corner. The more she confides in him, the better his position will be as she rises politically."

The other man says, "She's pretty clever. Politicians know better than saying anything which could be used against them."

Keefe can't believe his luck at overhearing this conversation. The men each order another drink and one asks the bartender to turn the channel to the game.

"Ace is walking a fine line right now. He needs to be careful," one of the men says.

"What do you mean?"

"Glenn is stacking the deck; now Ace is tight-lipped."

"Yup, sounds like he will either be ruined or be up for the Headliner Award," the other man says.

"Kennedy is on his cell constantly since the McNeil woman died. Once he rolled his eyes, confirming it was her. Before he finished the conversation he took the call out into the corridor. Now he takes most of his personal calls there. I am assuming he is talking to her. Just a hunch," he says, chewing peanuts.

Keefe writes down notes about what he has heard. He orders another drink and develops his plan based on assumption. There is nothing to lose.

The next twenty four hours keep Keefe, Romulus and Vic busy mounting a defense. Romulus is pleased Keefe can be his eyes and ears. The details are combed through time after time to discover the vulnerable places in Romulus's account of the day Sheena McNeil died. His patience wears thin knowing Sapphire is in danger and he can do nothing.

While the process of proving innocence goes on at the police station, an exciting diversion is taking place at the prosecutor's office, and Tracie Glenn wants Ace Kennedy to be the first to know about it.

Ace's cell phone vibrates in his pocket as he sits at his desk at The Star.

"Are you ready to pen the most noteworthy story of your young career?" Tracie Glenn asks.

"What's up?" he says.

"A public relations opportunity! I'm on the gratitude list for the new Governor. I will meet him in person finally, after directing my friends and their funds his way. The office nearly went in shutdown mode when the call came in," Tracie says with excitement in her voice. "Pick me up tomorrow at seven a.m."

"Ok, I'll see you bright and early tomorrow morning," Ace says.

The day Ace and Tracie are on their way. The ride to Jefferson City through the sloping green of the Missouri countryside is picturesque. A sense of patriotism overwhelms Tracie as they travel up the long drive to the Governor's mansion.

"Ace, like I have told you dozens of times, someday I will occupy the highest position in our state, and this will be my home. All the pieces are coming together. The passion for my goals has never been stronger," Tracie says.

The mansion sits high upon a hill, just above the Missouri River. After going through security, they park car and an official greets them.

"Good day, Miss Glenn, welcome," he says.

The young man leads them through the lush gardens to the veranda.

"Only a privileged few meet with Governor Dixon in a more casual setting. Tea is waiting for you outdoors on this lovely Missouri summer day. Enjoy," he says, leaving them.

White linen and antique china are tastefully set upon the table where the Governor sits. In marked contrast to the formality wearing a Panama hat and sunglasses, the governor rises and extends his hand.

"Welcome to our home. I am sorry the first lady couldn't be here, Miss Glenn. I am Governor Dixon."

"The pleasure is mine. I am Tracie Glenn and this is my friend, Ace Kennedy, who is a reporter for the Kansas City Star. Thank you for allowing me to bring a guest."

"I am pleased to meet you both. Won't you join me for some tea? Why not take advantage of the incredible weather we are having this summer? The office air can be stagnant."

A servant pours tea for the three of them.

The Governor says, "This is my opportunity to thank those of you who went over and beyond the call of duty to support our campaign. Your efforts helped put me here and I never want to forget those who did. Would you care for a cookie?" He passes a plate to her.

Tracie Glenn chooses one. She takes a sip of her tea savoring this mountaintop experience.

"You are an ambitious and successful woman; your reputation precedes you. What good work you are doing in Kansas City!" the Governor exclaims.

"Why thank you for those kind words. I wasn't aware you knew me at all," she says modestly.

"Are you kidding? You are being much too humble," he says.

"Rubbing shoulders and employing effective strategy go hand and hand, do you agree, Governor?" she says with a wink.

"Oh yes. We must understand where we want to go and bring others up with us. We do not arrive alone. Please call me Jay," he says smiling.

"Oh sir, how grand of you… I mean, Ray." Tracie Glenn says looking star-struck and finishing her tea.

"Miss Glenn . . . "

"Please call me Tracie," she says in a whisper.

"Alright… Tracie. I am pleased you came all the way up here today, to give me a chance to show my gratitude. I would like to present you with this plaque and perhaps Ace could take our photo? On behalf of the entire state of Missouri, I want to thank you for your support," Governor Dixon says. He shakes her hand and Ace snaps a couple of pictures.

The server offers to fill their empty tea cups, but they decline.

"Now what is happening in Kansas City? What are the issues you care about? This is your chance to make your voice heard. I cannot promise I will aid your cause, but being aware of what is going on is half the battle. How is the streetcar project coming along?" he asks.

"Quite good, next year is the target date of completion. A two mile rail will connect the River Market area to Union Station. It will be a boost to tourism and make our city more accessible," she says.

"See, there is an example. Roadblocks to the light rail proposal.... one must have the muscle on their side. It's imperative for progress," says Dixon.

"I couldn't agree more…Ray," she says.

"Our appointment is the last on my schedule. This time of the day,

I enjoy a sociable cocktail. Would you be offended if we allow them to take the tea away and bring us something a little more appropriate for the hour?" he asks. "Of course you may need to get on your way. I know how busy you are, and your absence must be felt in your office," he says.

"Well, Ray, I can't think of anything I would enjoy more," she says, then smiles and winks in the direction of Ace.

Soon the server comes with a new tray and takes the tea away.

Governor Dixon says, "What will it be my friend? Missouri white wine, red wine or . . ."

"Long Island Iced Tea, Ray. That is what I like," she says confidently.

"Superb, I like a lady who is not shy when it comes to the spirits. And for you kind sir?" he asks.

"I would like a Boulevard, if you have one," he says shyly.

"If I didn't keep Boulevard stocked in the Governor's Mansion, I wouldn't be a true patriot, now would I? Please bring what the people want. I will join our friend Tracie with a Long Island Iced Tea," he says.

Within minutes the server arrives with a tray of bottles and ice. He serves the beer to Ace and mixes the specified drinks.

The Governor and his two guests sip and talk. After the Kansas City Royals, the St. Louis Cardinals and Kansas City barbeque are discussed the Governor extends his hospitality further.

"Would you like a little tour of the garden? With help of the mansion staff and the state facilities manager the First Lady put in the first vegetable and herb garden the mansion has ever had. It is coming along nicely. We are quite proud of it," he says.

"We would adore a tour!" Tracie says, answering for her silent partner and hiding her jubilant look from the Governor.

They follow the Governor, listening in earnest as he points out details. Summer raindrops surprise them all. The stroll is over and they scurry to the shelter of the covered verandah. The early evening shower turns into a complete downpour.

"Looks like you are going to be here until this lets up. Shall we have a short one?" the Governor asks, his cheeks now slightly rosy. A relaxed Tracie Glenn agrees to the idea. The three observe the server's professional ease at mixing the drinks for an audience.

"Do you know what I like most about you, Ray? You seem to really like me!" Tracie says, giggling at her own forward assumption. "Not everyone likes me, and I don't know why. I am a likeable person."

"I quite agree!" Ray responds.

"My math teacher from high school didn't like me. She never did warm up to me. I did well in her class, I didn't cause any problems, it was a mystery," Tracie says.

"I can't imagine you having trouble with anyone. You are attractive . . . I hope you don't mind me stating the obvious. You are intelligent and you are a goal setter. More women should be like you!" the Governor says.

"That may be the nicest compliment I've received," she replies, "A woman can never have enough kind compliments. Romulus Royce is another example of someone who doesn't like me. He has never been a supporter. I should consider myself vindicated now, now that we know what he really is," she says, making her point.

"What a cad!" the Governor says. "And to think I counted him among my friends! The story of the arrest and the homicide was terrible! He should be locked away for life," he says.

"Precisely what I intend to do," Tracie notes.

"Our civic duty is to protect the innocent. Men like him can be shifty," the governor responds, taking a long drink of his Long Island Iced Tea.

"I agree. When people are threatened, our responsibility dictates our actions," she adds.

"We will all rest easier with him safely put away," he says.

"The public will see his true colors!" Tracie adds with confidence.

"When the basic moral standards of this society are breeched, the wheels of justice need a little grease, if you know what I mean," Ray says with a wink.

Tracie says, "I am saving lives. The cost might be high but I am willing to pay. We are the kind that make the tough choices, are we not?"

"Yes, reminds me of a case I tried several years ago. It was a repeat offender, a dangerous threat to society. I may have cut a corner or two, but it was the right thing to do," he says.

"Oh, believe me, I understand. Romulus Royce would never be charged. I knew that," she said, taking another long drink.

The Governor says, "Courage is required to take the risks, ultimately protecting the innocents. A burden we bear, I'm afraid."

"That is exactly what happened in the Royce case. I couldn't let other women fall victim to his violence," Tracie says.

"I will never admit this in public, but we do what must be done. I'm not proud of some of those choices either, but I am relieved the worst of our society is locked up. Besides, you didn't fabricate anything. You witnessed the crime. I like you Tracie, I really like you!" he says as he lifts his glass.

"Thank you, Jay. No one can be sure what happened before Romulus actually shoved Miss McNeil, but obviously the evidence of his scratches and her torn gown paint the picture. Why let him lie his way out? With his sterling reputation, his shoddy story might be accepted as truth, and a killer would be free to kill again. When I divulged the conversation I overheard in the theater, the motive will be clear," she says with conviction.

"Talk about being in the right place at the right time!" he says.

Tracie says, "And its fortunate I can read lips because hearing was impossible in that large theater. Speech reading should be a prerequisite for law school!" And once more the laughter comes barreling out.

"You are a treasure, my dear Tracie. A real treasure. You must invite me over next time we are in Kansas City. Perhaps then we can celebrate justice, once Royce is locked away," he says, patting her hand.

"Indeed, Ray," she says.

The rain stops and the sun shines once more.

Governor Dixon says, "Thank you once again for all of your support. Please don't mention the casual nature of our meeting. You will make everyone jealous," he says, winking at her.

"Oh I think we understand each other quite well," she says. They shake hands and the Governor's assistant shows them the way out.

The two get in their car, Tracie giddy with satisfaction.

"I have a friend in the mansion. This could change everything," she says, completely pleased with herself.

"It looks that way to me," Ace says.

Chapter Twenty-Nine

The next morning, bright and early, Keefe emerges from an elevator with a Starbucks in hand, accompanied by his good friend, Giles Anderson.

"Giles, I won't need you for about five minutes," Keefe says.

Anderson takes a seat in the corridor.

Keefe opens the glass doors of the District Attorney's office and approaches the receptionist. After going round and round to help pound out Romulus's defense, he takes his chance.

"Tracie Glenn, please," Keefe says.

"Do you have an appointment?" she asks.

"I don't think I need one. Tell her that Keefe Remington is here."

Immediately her door swings wide open and Tracie Glenn emerges.

"Keefe Remington, it has been too long!" she says approaching him with a guarded smile and a handshake.

"What brings you over? I've got a full slate today-"

"I can help lessen that load. May I?" Keefe asks, pointing to her office.

"Why certainly," she says, leading him in and shutting the door. "Heartbreaking what is happening toRomulus Royce. I know you admired him."

"I greatly admire him. That is what brings me to your office this morning," Keefe says. He sits in one of the four large chairs facing her desk.

"Of course you are aware this office is not at liberty to discuss any details," she says, "and be clear, I am not the one who is bringing charges against Mr. Royce. That would be one of my assistant prosecutor's."

"Oh no, I'm aware," Keefe says. He pauses, allowing her to dangle in her thought process.

"What can I do for you?" she asks.

"Simply retract your statement to the authorities about what you overheard in the theater between Romulus and Sheena McNeil,"

Keefe says, smiling politely.

She picks up her phone and asks for her calls to be held. Tracie grimaces.

Tracie says, "How would you know anything about that? Damn office leak…hapless investigators….heads are going to roll!"

Immediately, she reaches for her desk phone. Keefe stands quickly, slamming his hand on the receiver to stop her.

She stands and leans in toward him. They stand face to face.

"I won't retract a conversation that I witnessed," she says, with her teeth gritted.

"You might have observed something, but you didn't actually hear a conversation, am I right about that?" Keefe asks.

Tracie stammers, "Of course I did! What on earth are you talking about? I think you need to leave!"

Tracie circles to the front of her desk.

Keefe meets her before she can get too far. Towering above her he says in a very soft and controlled voice, "I think you'd better sit down, Miss Glenn."

Tracie Glenn sits back in her chair. She crosses her legs with a huff.

"Isn't it true that you believe that lip reading should be a prerequisite for law school?" Keefe asks.

"What? What are you talking about?" Tracie says, dumbfounded.

Keefe takes a small voice recorder from his jacket and turns it on.

"I think lip reading should be a prerequisite for law school," she hears herself say, followed by laughter. And, as if she is jolted by her realization, she blurts out, "Ace recorded my meeting with the Governor? You can't . . ."

"Nope, Ace didn't do it," Keefe says. He finds some satisfaction in watching Tracie begin to lose her composure.

"The Governor recorded our conversation?" she asks, with complete dismay.

"This man did," Keefe says.

His friend walks through the door in his Panama hat and sunglasses.

Tracie stands up from behind her desk.

"May I introduce my buddy, Giles Anderson? He is the groundskeeper at the mansion," says Keefe.

"Good day, Miss," Giles Anderson says with a tip of his hat.

"What in God's name are you saying . . . it was you?" Tracie asks, looking back to Keefe. "This man impersonated the Governor in his own home?"

"Excuse me, Miss, but I'm directly responsible for everything that happens outside the threshold of the mansion's doors as head groundskeeper. I don't generally go inside the Governor's home," he says casually.

"But the servant, the assistant who led us out to the veranda?" Tracie says, nearly spitting with anger.

"I thought they did a mighty fine job of mixing those Long Island Iced Teas, don't you agree?" Giles asks.

Tracie Glenn's angry face is flushed. She begins pointing fingers.

"I was coerced! He nearly poured cocktails down my throat," she argues.

"There was no alcohol in those bottles but there were plenty of these," Keefe says, placing a small bottle on her desk.

"What's this?" she stammers and scoops up the tiny bottle.

"That's alcohol flavoring; it's gaining in popularity. Just a couple of drops taste like a good stiff one, which is something you'd probably like about now," Keefe says.

"I was called by the Governor's office, my visit was all arranged!"

"We called your office and made the arrangements. The Governor was out of the state for most of last week. Giles had the run of the whole place. You are exposed, Tracie Glenn!" says Keefe.

Tracie points her finger at Keefe, her hand shaking in anger.

"This proves nothing! I witnessed Royce strong-arming Miss McNeil, and the threats he leveled against her," she says in a last ditch attempt to regain her composure.

"Let's clarify. You didn't hear anything, as you admitted on the recording. If you want to gamble your increasingly unstable public image on what remains of your flimsy statement about what you saw, be my guest. But add this incriminating recording, admitting you bend the rules to convict those you deem are guilty, and I think you might start looking for a soup line, Miss Glenn."

"What are you going to do?" Tracie Glenn asks, already knowing the answer.

"I am taking you with me right now to the police station. You are going to tell them the truth. You never saw Romulus act in a physical way with Sheena McNeil, and you did not overhear any conversations between the two of them. Then you will resign from your position and public office. I don't ever want to see you in a position of power again," says Keefe.

"I won't cut my own throat and proceed defenseless!" Tracie says hysterically.

Keefe pushes the recorder on again. They all three listen when she refers to greasing the wheels of justice, manipulation and playing judge before those charged are given their due process.

"Miss Glenn, calm yourself. You will do what I ask or I will turn the recording over to the authorities, after which you will not only be suffering the consequences of your lies in the McNeil case, but you will be responsible for a multitude of cases in which you bent the rules or enhanced the facts to serve yourself. I am afraid those hungry for justice will keep you tied up in legal ramifications for years. And we can only pray you aren't prosecuted by a wheel greaser. Are we clear?" Keefe asks. "Get your purse, Miss Glenn."

Chapter Thirty

Dodging fire and those frantically fighting it makes traveling through London nearly impossible. The ravenous flames jump several houses at once. The feeble attempts at creating firebreaks are not quick or significant enough. The blaze is being fed, gaining strength and getting dangerously close to Riverside Warehouse where timber, coal, oil and tar are stored.

People are backed up waiting for passage out of the city, their wagons full of what they can save from their dwellings. Refugees fill the hills surrounding London. Vigilantes hunt down foreigners and Catholics, believing they are responsible for the fire. Quinn, Pony, Chamous, Cashton and the professor arrive at Apothecary's Hall and Phillip Culpeper's office. The door is unlocked and ajar. They enter cautiously, not knowing who or what might be on the other side, but their concerns are unfounded, the room is empty.

"Where in this chaotic city are we going to find this Culpeper?" Pony asks, sounding defeated.

The professor goes directly to the open door at the rear of the room.

"We observed the lantern hanging next to the door, lit and resting on the table, a tray with dishes. Keefe and I both suspected someone was in the space behind the door. Culpeper claimed he worked alone," the professor tells them.

Pony rushes around them and speeds down the cellar stairs, stepping over broken boards.

Chamous lingers, examining damage to the cellar door.

"The lock is busted," Chamous says.

"Sapphire!" Pony calls. "She's not here. We need to find this doctor!" Pony turns on his heels and dashes past the group on his way back up.

"Wait, Pony, if Sapphire was here, we may find some answers," Cashton says.

"This bed is in pieces," Quinn says.

Chamous rolls the wood at the bottom of the landing with his foot.

"This was used to ram the door," he says.

"Someone was being cared for," Quinn says, examining a tray with empty dishes.

With hands in his pockets Pony paces, but something on the wall stops him- a faint scratching of words in the stones of the cellar wall.

"Wait!" Pony says, directing their attention towards it. "Letters scratched in the stone; it's a message from Sapphire!"

"Beware of Annabeth!!! Going to save Culpeper's daughter- Sapphire."

"She escaped!" Pony says.

"Save Culpeper's daughter, from what?" Quinn asks.

"She is most likely sick, like scores of others," Cashton says.

"I've made a discovery," the professor calls from upstairs.

"The counters were neat and orderly last time we were here. The same can't be said for this time. Looks like a big project, look at this mess. Some bottles even tipped, a project done in haste?"

Cashton finds notations.

Pony peers from behind his shoulder.

"Her handwriting!" Pony exclaims.

"These are simple compounds," Cashton says, reading the list.

"What knowledge would Sapphire have of those things?" Chamous asks.

Cashton says, "Never underestimate someone like Sapphire."

"A clever girl from the twenty-first century could lead another to assume she had some superior knowledge about these compounds. Part of a plan of escape, perhaps?" the professor speculates.

Pony adds, "Sapphire could be helping. Her message referred to saving Culpeper's daughter!"

"She wouldn't know what the actual compounds in medicines are, right?" Chamous asks.

"Whether she does or doesn't, her freedom might rest on Culpeper's belief that Sapphire has knowledge he doesn't have," Quinn reasons.

"Why is Culpeper holding Sapphire against her will and why is he helping Annabeth?" the professor asks.

"The word I would use in connection to Finnegan and Albert and even Sheena McNeil is frightening. They changed from regular people to something else, from normal to bizarre," says Pony.

Quinn says, "Spiritual warfare between two spirits for one body is called possession. That is one tool that Petulah, alias Annabeth, uses--possession."

"Do you think this Culpeper is possessed too?" Pony asks.

"He seemed of sound mind and body when we questioned him." the professor says.

"Culpeper would be a supplier of important items Petulah needs to carry out her destructive plans. She wouldn't want to risk injury to him," Cashton says.

"Why would Culpeper hold Sapphire, unless he is evil like Petulah? If he's not on her side why would he agree?" Pony asks.

"Remember, those suspected of the spreading sickness are best quarantined, a guise used to convince the doctor to keep Sapphire under lock and key, perhaps," the professor suggests.

Cashton says, "If Sapphire finds that Culpeper is a victim too, she may try to help him."

"Let's find Culpeper. When we do, we might find her," Quinn says, leading them out.

Chamous stops a passerby.

"Where is the residence of Phillip Culpeper?" he asks.

"He lives at the end of the lane, but he left with his family for the countryside, like the others," the stranger says adding, "A good doctor, a fine fellow."

Although the stranger's comments are reassuring, Sapphire remains missing. They ride to Gresham College, the only central place available to figure out their next move.

The sun is rising when they find nourishment and refreshment. Men on horseback approach the college.

"Is that Keefe?" Chamous says.

Quinn recognizes Keefe immediately. The man riding next to him is unfamiliar to her and blocks the other riders.

Cashton and Pony lead the way out the door while Quinn, Chamous and the Professor follow.

"Father is with him!" Cashton says.

"Tera too!" Quinn exclaims.

Quinn's heart leaps, and relief washes away days of tension. Those she loves in plain view are the miracle she prayed for.

Romulus dismounts and enthusiastically embraces his son.

"It's about time you joined us, Father!" Cashton says.

Chamous helps Tera down from her horse and into his embrace.

Keefe talks to the footman who takes the horses, giving Quinn time to greet her father first.

The relief Romulus feels is evident in his expression. Quinn throws both arms around her father.

"How did this happen? I am more than relieved," she says.

Romulus says, "My release came quite suddenly. Let's just say ego blinds even the cleverest among us. Tracie Glenn fell victim to her own ambition and Keefe found a way to expose her. He works fast. He'll fill you in, and it's an extraordinary story."

Quinn's gratitude overwhelms her.

Romulus says, "May I present an old friend, Archbishop of Westminster Thomas Tobler? He is the real reason we are on this Quest. This is my daughter Quinn, Polaris."

"I am pleased to meet you," Quinn says with a bow of reverence.

Thomas Tobler returns the respect by nodding to her.

"I am more than grateful you are here," Tobler says.

The lively conversation continues as they walk towards the college.

Anxiously, Quinn looks to Keefe, who removes his saddlebag and passes his reins to a handler.

She hurries to him, and his arms circle the whole of her. She is overcome with joy, so thankful for what Keefe has done for her father and sinks to her knee, head lowered. She places her hands over her heart.

Quinn says, "My Lord, thank you. Thank you." Her tears flow with abandon.

"Quinn," Keefe says. He grasps her hands and guides her to her feet, uncomfortable with the reverence she pays him.

"I don't know how you did it. I love you," she says.

Keefe brushes Quinn's hair away from her face. His tender kiss communicates what they both are feeling. The joy of reunion is sweet.

She lays her face against his chest. The beating of his heart is the only words she needs to hear. Everything is going to be alright.

Chapter Thirty-One

The Guardians have much information to share with one another. Jexis explains what's been accomplished so far, but even she needed updating since the visit to Dr. Culpeper's offices. Quinn recounts the experiences at St. Paul's Cathedral. She is not looking forward to sharing the devastating news with Romulus about Petulah.

"In the Black Witches' den, we found a most unlikely and unexpected development. Beef was there," Quinn says.

Romulus says, "Beef? What on earth do you mean?" His stunned expression matched the others who had not yet heard.

Cashton says, "As unbelievable as it sounds, Beef held some sort of… affection for our mother! His grieving upon her grave hours after the battle that ended her life . . . resurrected her, Father!"

"Resurrected? What are you saying…impossible!" Romulus says in utter disbelief.

"The poem from the book . . . fear the lover's tears at dawn. Sapphire and I discovered it in one of the books in the tower room," Quinn adds.

Cashton says, "She would remain in the ground unless a pure soul possessed genuine love for her, despite her black heart. That someone was Beef. His tears were shed upon the soil of her resting place and set her free. Now she seeks revenge. She's manipulated all of it, even the fact we are here."

"You mean the Annabeth, who fashions chocolates of poison, and who is spreading the plague, is the same person as Petulah?" Keefe asks with dismay.

"She would never be able to carry out her plan in Nadellawick, so she brought us here!" Romulus says aloud to himself, as the pieces fall into place. He rises in frustration, his chair nearly toppling. "Wounds remain fresh from her deceit! Please Lord, have mercy on us. She stabs the same wound again and again!"

He approaches the head of the long table and places his large hands on the smooth wood. With his head lowered and his voice shaking with anger he says, "I ended her life, she melted into the ground! She has murdered those I love. She is responsible for sending possessed spirits! She took another innocent life, and now our baby. Damn her! Damn her!"

"We know Sapphire was held by Culpeper but it appears he too may be a victim. Sapphire left a message in Culpeper's office. We found evidence she used her advanced knowledge to help him prepare a …treatment for his daughter," Chamous explains.

"We went to his home, but were told he fled to the country with his family. From what we know he means no harm to her," Quinn says.

"Sapphire is not with us, therefore she is vulnerable to PETULAH! She IS in mortal danger!" Romulus yells out, slamming his fists to the table in frustration. "Amidst this chaos, we must find the witch!"

"Maybe not Father," Jexis says quietly.

"What do you mean, Jexis?" Romulus asks.

Jexis says, "Why not get her to come to us?"

"How are we going to do that?" Keefe asks.

"What does Petulah want more than anything in the universe?" she asks.

"Power and revenge!" Cashton answers.

"Exactly," says Jexis. "Let's give her what she wants!"

"Executing a plan amid this catastrophe is not going to be easy. We must get ahead of this fire or London will be lost and multitudes will lose their lives. There is no place left for the people to go. The gates out of the city are already bottlenecked. Soon it will be like an incinerator!" Keefe says.

Thomas Tobler says, "Romulus wanted me to be here for this very reason, my plan to stop the fire... a stockpile of gunpowder sits in the Tower of London. I am not certain exactly how many barrels but thousands. An explosion of that magnitude would block the fire from being carried by the east winds. This would save the rest of the city and many lives."

"The firebreaks have not been effective," the professor mentions.

"The explosions are too small. With this amount of gunpowder, that would be different. That is the only thing I can come up with... and prayer. This wind, we don't need this wind!" worries the bishop.

"Best idea yet, but how do we go about executing it?" Quinn asks.

"We will need the cooperation of his majesty's Royal Army. Two or three hours will be needed to make the arrangements. If we leave for Whitehall Palace, we can begin the process," Archbishop Tobler tells them.

"Quinn, during this time I will set another plan in motion. If I can manage this, the explosion will end more than the fire," Jexis says.

"Jexis, explain," says Romulus.

"Father, there is no time, trust me. The detonation of the gunpowder must be from inside the tower at exactly midnight. Leave that up to me. The Royal Army may stand ready to use cannons if I am unsuccessful," Jexis says.

"I will be helping her with her part of the plan," Cashton says.

Romulus embraces them both.

"Godspeed," Romulus says.

"In two hours then," Jexis says, nodding to the others.

Cashton joins her and they ride away from Gresham College.

"Do you trust me brother?" Jexis asks.

"You know I do," he says.

"The plan is two-fold: Channel a couple of spirits and rally the troops," she says, "and the last thing . . . at impact, shift to dove."

Chapter Thirty-Two

Romulus, Keefe, Chamous and Pony leave for Whitehall Palace. Professor Enderlee shakes hands with a few of the gentlemen arriving for an emergency meeting of the Royal Society. Once the door to their gathering is closed the professor joins Quinn and Tera so they can all leave for the Tower of London.

"This is staggering. I just shook hands with some of the most influential minds of the seventeenth century!" exclaims the professor. The first gentleman to come through the door was Robert Boyle, known to us as the father of chemistry. Robert Hook followed him. He will eventually be given the title of England's Leonardo Da Vinci. He will later be credited with identifying and coining the word cell, the basic biological unit of all known living organisms! Sir Isaac Newton followed after the other two, the most significant scientist of all time, perhaps. The last man is Theodore Monroe. He will actually be canonized as a saint one day. Historians, mathematicians, chemists, poets, bishops, and inventors meeting inside this room!" the professor says. The distinguished renaissance man of the future shakes his head in awe and takes a seat near the two women.

"And a plague like the one two hundred years ago could put an end to these lives, preventing their significant contributions to the world," Tera says with astonishment.

"The ripple effect of this Quest reaches all the way to the twenty-first century. The consequences are staggering," the professor adds. He packs his pipe with tobacco.

"We accept the responsibility of a Quest with a faithful heart, and little else. Faith makes things possible, not easy. I pray the Archbishop is correct in his assumption the approval from the King and the assistance of his Army come without obstacles," Quinn says.

Professor Enderlee lights the tobacco in the pipe and puffs until it smolders.

"The meaning of Archbishop Tobler's reoccurring dream, it is clear to me now. He wanted to discount its importance, but he couldn't, and he wasn't sure why. I believe his dream is why we are here," says the professor.

"A dream, Professor?" Quinn asks.

"A raven waits collecting a toll to enter his magical valley, where all afflictions are cured when fruit is eaten from the only tree standing. The desperate are warned about avoiding a swift flowing river eager to sweep them over a treacherous waterfall and to certain death. When they count their coins for payment, the raven laughs and explains the steep price. The toll is the loss of their eyesight, a steep price, but the afflicted choose life. When they step foot on the grass of the valley their ability to see is gone. It is a

difficult task to find the tree with no vision. As soon as they feel the water, they heed the raven's warning about certain death. They wander and eventually die, never finding the tree. The tree lies full of fruit just beyond a tiny brook only a stones' throw wide. The water stopped them, and without their vision they couldn't see the brook presented no obstacle. The raven deceived every hopeful soul," the professor says.

"Horrible." Tera comments.

"The loss of vision in the dream is symbolic of the loss of faith. Those who lose their faith are unable to recognize the very thing that will sustain them, cure them and ultimately save their soul. Petulah is the raven. She spread sickness and carefully chose those leaders whose deaths would significantly impact the already fragile faith of these frightened Londoners. That is why Thomas Tobler could not dismiss the dream. That is why we are here and why Petulah must be stopped," the professor says.

"Your insight is why you are one of the chosen Guardians for this quest, Professor. Blessed is the day you came into our lives," Quinn says.

Tera puts her hand on top of the professor's and smiles with equal gratitude.

Quinn says, "I want both of you to take a deep breath. What we may experience tonight will be like nothing else. When the Apalacid was placed on my finger as Polaris, visions for my eyes only revealed to me all I would need to know about our history as Guardians. Profoundly spiritual, the visions changed me in a way that could never be explained. The angelic realm is a mystical world like places created in the minds of storytellers, but this fantasy is our reality. And this realm is where the battle will commence. Prepare yourselves and pray Jexis and Cashton can do their part."

They mount their horses for the journey to the Tower of London.

The three struggle to keep their horses calm as they ride through the dark and fire-filled streets on their way to meet with the others. Pandemonium is at an all-time high as the blaze burns out of control. With most Londoner's trying to flee, some remain fighting to save their homes, and others on the lookout for Catholics, the scapegoat for the crisis. When the trio comes upon a crowded mob, they dismount and lead their horses on foot. The chaos becomes clear, as innocent lives are being threatened. Voices shout loudly over the mayhem.

"Lynch them!"

"They started the fires! They are responsible!"

"Get the ropes!"

Four people struggle while men tie their hands. Three men and a woman cry for help, each with terror-filled eyes. Quinn takes action, with Tera and the professor close behind.

"Release these innocents!" Quinn shouts.

"Get out of our way, leave us or stand guilty yourselves!" a tall man says, as he puts a noose around the neck of the first victim.

"We've committed no crime!" the woman cries.

Professor Enderlee advances, shoving the tall man with unusual force.

In retaliation, he charges back at the professor and takes a swing.

The professor has become strength-fortified and flings the tall man like a rag doll. The crowd is silent and Quinn and Tera are stunned at the incredible show of power.

Instantly, two dark-robed spirits hidden in the fullness of the trees swoop down, knocking the professor to the ground. They scoop him up and carry him away, soaring through the smoke-filled night sky.

The sight terrifies the mob and they disband, leaving the victims tied.

"Go Quinn, go to the professor. I will take care of these people," Tera urges.

Quinn runs into the dark forest, desperate to save the professor.

Her speed increases as trees flash past in her pursuit. She shifts into a mighty dove and soars into the night sky. Quinn catches a glimpse of the professor, his body being pulled through the night air by the dark spirits. Quinn lands near a large valley and conceals herself behind thick trees.

The ground begins to vibrate before a jagged bolt of lightning strikes near the professor. Electrically charged coils spring out in all directions as the Black Witch Petulah appears within them.

Motionless, she waits in skin tight garments and a flowing scarlet cape. Finally, she raises one arm high and legions of black robed guards descend from surrounding trees and stand unified. Petulah's silky black tresses hang long over her shoulders. She looks knowingly to where Quinn lingers.

"Is this what you want Polaris Quinn? You want to save his feeble soul? He is valuable to you?" she asks.

Just as Quinn prepares for battle, another lightning bolt strikes with an ear-deafening crash and marks the spot where two more figures materialize. Quinn recognizes the innocent woman that was to be lynched, and Tera.

Tera struggles to free herself from the chokehold of the woman. Petulah moves from the professor and grabs a handful of Tera's hair.

"Or, is this more what you had in mind? Yes, you are right. I staged that whole pathetic scene with the mob and the lynching and the Catholics! The Circle of Sun is so easily deceived!" Petulah says and laughs, exposing her dozens of tiny, razor-sharp teeth.

From behind the tree line, Quinn studies the unfolding urgency. The eastern sky is flooded with multitudes of birds in service to the Black Witch. They flap their wings in a forward thrust as they land in formation behind her. As soon as their claws touch the ground, they're transformed to headless sword bearing soldiers wearing flowing and shredded robes of ebony. Their shadowy essence is hidden by large hoods. With new threats in both the southern and western skies, Quinn reacts.

"Cheveyo, White Wolf of Light, your time has come!" Quinn shouts.

With one simple command to the night sky, white clouds begin to move, revealing the strong and agile legs of a mighty white wolf. Cheveyo races through the night to Quinn, and is joined by dozens of other wolves, creating a powerful fighting pack to aid her. All bow before her, waiting for her command.

Quinn says, "Cheveyo, send a messenger without delay to our Knights. Our Guardian forces must unite."

One wolf is dispatched to deliver the message for Quinn. He crouches close to the ground and leaps forward, taking flight, the wind blowing through his brilliant, silvery-white coat.

A sea of black birds from the south transforms in midair to broad-winged gargoyles. With contorted, bat-like faces, pointed ears and razor sharp claws, they land on the battlefield and perch within the rocky hills to the south, guarding the place where Tera has been taken.

The western skies become filled with black birds so dense, no space can be seen between them. Thunder fills the battleground as they touch down and transform to their skeleton shapes. Spiked armor outlines their shoulders and guards with spikes are strapped on their fleshless legs. Gloved hands bear swords rusty with the blood of their last enemy. The round shield in the other hand raises to glorify their Black Witch, as they cry out to her from opened jaws.

With the seemingly uneven odds, Quinn breathes a sigh of relief when the howling of the fierce white wolves echoes across the valley, signaling their return. Brilliant doves follow, then transform into her Knights, taking their places beside her. Romulus, Keefe, Pony and Chamous have arrived. Simultaneously, the western sky swarms with white doves, followed by an ocean more to the south and east. The Circle of Sun stands united.

From a peak of the rocky hills, Petulah forms her strategy against the growing threat.

Quinn commands, "Keefe, lead the Guardian forces from the west."

Promptly Keefe mounts the strong back of a White Wolf who delivers him to his post. He stands awestruck observing white doves transforming on contact into winged warriors. Each warrior has two sets of massive wings, one set white, and the other gold. Their protective armor of hammered silver is adorned with pearls and jewels. Chain mail gauntlets protect their arms.

With battle-ready expressions, they draw mystical swords, shimmering yet lethal, prepared to fight the ground enemy.

Other white doves transform and hover over the battlefield. Feminine warriors in trailing gowns of buttery gold appear, their long hair blowing gently against wings of silver. With their heads cocked and aiming, their bows are loaded with their first fiery arrows prepared to battle the airborne enemy.

"Chamous and Pony we need you to lead the Guardian forces in the west," Quinn commands.

Chamous and Pony transform to brilliant white doves and soar through the skies before descending and transforming back when they reach their posts. White winged stallions breathing fire prance anxiously as they wait for the cry of battle.

As if nature foresees the impending clash, wind gusts become loud and wailing.

"Cheveyo, join Pony and Chamous to the west. The Black Witch holds Tera and the professor captive in the southern hills. We must eliminate the enemy that blocks access to those hills. There is no time to waste!"

Quinn stands on the highest northern hill and addresses the Circle of Sun.

"Once more Archangel Michael calls us to defend and conquer. Courage and strength flows from our creator. Charge your enemies and send them back to hell, where they belong!"

From the rocky hilltop, Petulah summons her Gargoyles to the north to destroy Quinn and Romulus first. They take flight and soar towards them; White Wolves bare their teeth, ready to rip them apart. Hissing and roaring, the Gargoyles spew red fire at the wolves as Quinn and Romulus charge them, their swords drawn. The clash is fierce as the white wolves tear at the Gargoyles attack. Rearing upon their hind legs, the mighty wolves overpower many of the Gargoyles, sending them reeling backward. Once on the ground the white wolves waste no time ripping at the throat of the first casualty. White Wolves go after their next victim, red covering their white coats. Promptly upon death, each dark spirit vanishes in a vaporous puff and melts into the soil, returning to the underworld.

A White Wolf howls out in pain, burned by a Gargoyle who spews blistering fire from the air. As the gallant warrior whimpers and dies, his spirit takes the form of a single white feather that floats heavenward.

Quinn raises her sword to the Gargoyle, using her shield to prevent his fiery weapon from penetrating. She thrusts her shield violently against his snout, knocking him back. Wielding her weapon, she slices his throat and the now lifeless creature dissipates in a puff of vapor.

Romulus rides high on the back of a White Wolf. He comes under attack by two Gargoyles at one time. With his shield staving off the fiery advance of one, he uses his boot to kick the other Gargoyle, breaking his jaw. Hungry wolves below snatch at its legs, pulling the Gargoyle down to death. Romulus flings his shield like a saucer out to the Gargoyles, destroying a whole line of them. He puts his palms out, powerfully deflecting other attacks of fire and sending it right back, incinerating a band of enemies.

Quinn's sword renders injury to multitudes of Gargoyles and the White Wolves finish them off, yet dozens of white feathers rise from the ground on their way to eternity.

Chamous and Pony deliver powerful volts of electricity from their swords as they fly on the backs of winged stallions. The armored skeletons are no match for them. With one strike of their sword, many of skeletons fall, defeated. Each pile of bones is hastily pounced upon by the wolves before they vaporize.

The Guardian forces are advancing on the battlefield, getting closer to Tera and the professor.

Pony takes his opportunity to act. Signaling to Chamous, he points towards the rocky hills, where Petulah dispatches a small contingency to join the fight. Pony and Chamous wait in the wooded area.

The dark soldiers creep along the jagged hills, on their way to bolster the numbers on the battlefield.

In a surprise attack from the back of a mighty winged stallion, Pony delivers a volt from his sword, searing a fiery path and cutting the forces off at the knees.

Chamous joins against this small band, and the Knights have

broken the threat. They have created access to the hills, a way to reach Tera and the professor.

Meanwhile Keefe and the Guardians wage a mighty effort in the eastern valley.

The ghost-like opponents, with swords drawn, charge the winged soldiers of light. Many perish on the battle ground.

The feminine warriors send arrows of fire across the horizon as the lightening from Keefe's sword sends a destructive voltage of death. Brilliant flashes ignite the night sky, and Londoners will assume a lightning storm, and never know what is truly happening.

With the headless soldiers gaining ground against them, Keefe climbs on the back of one of the white wolves. With powerful beams of destruction sent from them, Keefe winces from a blow. This only firms his resolve as he leaps from the back of the wolf mid-air and spins around, sending volts from his sword in all directions and causing deep casualties among the darkness. Keefe and the Guardians advance very close to the rocky hills now.

The Black Witch recognizes no chance for a victory on this field for now.

"Retreat!" the Black Witch Petulah screeches to her forces, the command piercing throughout the vast valley. The battlefield is murky with the vaporous remains of dark warriors.

Petulah retaliates. "Execute the captured immediately and then join me in London!"

Petulah takes most of the remaining troops with her, anticipating her date with destiny.

Crouching below the bushes, Pony and Chamous sneak ever closer to the captives.

Pony is ready. With as much courage as he can muster, he rushes the camp with his rising sword.

Chamous follows. He delivers a voltage thrust, knocking three Gargoyles to the ground, and his companions and fellow wolves finish them off.

One of the Gargoyles attacks Pony and before he can raise his weapon he is knocked down. The Gargoyle spews a deadly line of fire right for his face. He rolls like a shot out of the path of destruction, jumps to his feet and swings his sword around, slicing the Gargoyle's neck.

Chamous slays the first aggressive creature who charges at him, now becoming the aggressor.

Pony leaps upon a boulder and directs his volt towards two more who surround the captives and Chamous kills two more. All but two of them fall and the wolves, growing in number, attack those remaining.

Running to Tera, Chamous cuts the binds and sets her free.

Pony does the same for the relieved professor and the three transform to Dove and soar to the Knights, who stand victorious on the battlefield.

They land and are joined by the Quinn, Romulus, and Keefe.

"Are you ok?" Romulus says rushing to them.

"Pony and Chamous saved us! They battled most impressively," the professor says lightly.

"They were magnificent," Tera says.

Quinn tends to Keefe's injury.

Quinn says, "We have little time to waste. We have to get to the tower."

Chapter Thirty-Three

Within the dungeons deep beneath London Bridge the black robed guards aimlessly roam. These spirits are devoid of purpose and honor only the darkness, souls forever imprisoned in the underworld. Although hundreds escaped when offered their due judgment, thousands still remain. Webs of spiders and residue from rodents darken the stone floor with the stain of regret and lost hope, an appropriate place for a duo to return to their glory.

Guards part a path for the darkest of royalty to proceed.

The female speaks and echoes her hate and heinous morality. Her gown, once white in life, is gray and soiled, and her face, once beautiful, is hollow and ugly. Multitudes of snakes make up her head of hair. With each step, her skirt billows out revealing serpents clinging to her legs.

"Is the chamber prepared for the return of the great god Hades? Is its splendor befitting Hades, the one from whom all blackness comes?" Medusa says, speaking with authority.

In a childlike voice a guard replies.

"Readied hundreds of years ago, awaiting this hour."

Guards open towering doors, welcoming Medusa and Hades to elevated honor where they take their places on their thrones of entitlement.

The thunderous alto voice of the Hades commands respect.

"Gather all. Mark this day in our victorious history, as we prepare for the coronation of the Black Witch Petulah! The reign of terror bringing London down demonstrates her power. Petulah escaped the grip of death! There is only one final task remaining to secure her position as my Queen. Bring her to us," Hades commands.

The room is silent except for the snapping sounds from the snakes on Medusa's head. After a few minutes, Petulah walks through the doors, her black silky hair glistening in the candlelit room. Her voice sounds guttural as she addresses the royalty.

"Who," she begins.

Medusa cuts her off and aims her scepter in Petulah's direction, sending a powerful beam of pain and rendering her immobile.

"Do not address the King of the Underworld," Medusa commands. "Come and kneel in submission, you simple witch."

Petulah, now able to move again, rises and approaches the royalty. She kneels and keeps her head lowered.

Hades says, "I am the god of death and the god of regret. I claim sovereignty over the realm of the underworld. Your black heart beating inside earns favor in our realm. The cries of sickness and despair filling the air are the melody my soul longs to hear. You may rule beside me in the underworld if you are able to conclude your quest of revenge."

"I will complete my revenge and I will rule by your side," says Petulah, her head lowered.

Medusa says, "Hades offers purpose to the dark souls roaming these catacombs. They are to accompany you to the Tower, where you may find your final revenge!" The snakes on her head snap and roam. Medusa's laughter fills the room, attracting the attention of every spirit. "There is much to celebrate. They are captured! Those you despise most are captured! The Royces are responsible for setting fire in a bake house. They hang in the Tower of London at dawn!" Medusa throws back her snake-filled head and from deep in her belly the booming laughter impacts Hades and he, too, laughs out loud. This news of the Circle of Sun's capture and death sentence brings a smile to the evil Petulah. Her joy is immeasurable. She joins in the jubilation, laughing too.

Medusa says, "But we steal their spoils!" Again her laughter echoes and fills the hall. "Tonight, when the moon is high and the sky glows blood red from consuming fire and innocent bloodshed, you will be the one to deliver them to death before all of London has their chance. If even one second of a new day passes, our time in this realm expires and so does your triumphant coronation. Complete your final revenge before the first sand grain of a new day and you will have the crown. If you fail, I will rule beside him."

"I am not a simple witch, for the hell raging in London is crafted from my hand. I see no remnants of your glory, Medusa," Petulah says mockingly.

"Silence!" Hades commands. "The corals of the Red Sea formed from her spilt blood and vipers of the Sahara from her blood droplets. Medusa's triumphs stand the test of time since the dawn of man. Silence, or rule without the use of your tongue!"

Hades turns his attention to the black robed guards.

"And to the rest of you, you shall be in homage to your soon-to-be queen. You may escort her to the tower for her revenge and then coronation," Hades bellows.

Immediately, her sanctified protectors surround her and lead her out.

In a triumphant finale, Hades and Medusa grasp hands and levitate upward, evaporating into the air.

With despair and death overrunning the streets of old London, Petulah enters the room royally. The entire army of black robed guards stands at her attention and parts a path for her to enter.

High above the room, Medusa perches on a floating throne to the right, and Hades on the same to her left. Between them are the victims, gagged and presented in traditional black hoods of death, each bound and their necks in nooses. On Hades' request, holes are cut so Petulah can view their horror.

Between the victims and the Black Witch sits an immense hourglass, its sand flowing out. Directly in the center and below the scaffolding is the lever of death. It sits in the center of a pentagram surrounded by candles. Illuminated by a chandelier laden with thousands of glowing candles above, Petulah takes her spotlight.

"The revenge you seek is at hand. Will you show mercy on the lives of the wretched before you?" the guard asks. He strikes each as they are identified, Romulus Royce, Quinn Clarke Royce, Cashton Royce, Jexis Royce and Sapphire Royce!

"No mercy!" she says, giddy with delight.

Hades says, "Then, you know what to do next…before the last grain of sand falls from the hourglass the glory will be yours."

Petulah shouts passionately, "I want to see their faces, remove their hoods!"

Medusa says, "Look! The last grain of sand approaches! She wants me to rule, the crown will be mine after all!" Medusa throws her head back and her laugh fills the tower with her jubilation.

With not a second to spare, Petulah grabs the lever with both hands. With the power of ten men she moves the lever all the way over. But the lever does not drop the victims to their death. Instead, the floor beneath her moves. Suddenly, the pentagram she stands on buckles from under her. Simultaneously, the chandelier above her falls. The flames from two thousand candles stand ready to ignite the kegs of waiting gunpowder below.

Medusa and Hades rip the hoods from the victims, exposing their true identity as guards and not Petulah's arch enemies. In less than a second the explosion with, a magnitude never before seen, ignites instantly, incinerating every dark soul in the tower. And above the exploding inferno, two magnificent white doves soar majestically and triumphantly, ahead of the danger.

Chapter Thirty-Four

Cheers erupt from the Royal Army and the crowds gathered to observe this last ditch effort to stop the great fire of London.

Shielding her face from the magnificent light created by the blast, Quinn quickly searches the skies, anxious for signs of her siblings. With all eyes on the explosion, she sees them safely land and shift to their human selves. She runs towards them. Romulus and the others follow.

With weakened bodies but joyous souls, they embrace Quinn and, soon after, their father. All are grateful on this night that no harm came to them.

"PETULAH IS DEAD, THEY ARE ALL DEAD!" Jexis announces.

"She is right Father, it is over!" Cashton says.

The east wind now subsides and, without fuel to further its destruction, the flames die their own death.

Cheers erupt from the crowds in celebration. The firebreak stopped the spreading fire. Goodwill and good fortune are celebrated.

Feeling the sting of an empty victory, Pony breaks away from the group. His young heart not able to wait any longer, Pony searches the crowd. He runs as fast as his feet can carry him. With tears clouding his vision, he wipes them away often, searching for her face among the thousands of people in the streets. Then, at almost the exact same time, their eyes meet. He recognizes the emerald eyes of his beautiful Sapphire, and he races in her direction.

Sapphire yells, "Pony? Stop the wagon, please Phillip!"

She gently hands a child over and runs to him. Under the clouded and smoky sky, Pony and Sapphire reunite.

With his arms around her, he lifts her, twirling her around.

Sapphire's eyes overflow with tears of joy and she accepts his tender kiss.

The rest of them join in the reunion.

Sapphire embraces her father. His strong arms encircle her, so strong, so safe.

Romulus says, “Sapphire, are you alright? Are you hurt?”

“No Father, I am fine. Dr. Culpeper made sure of that! But wait… what are you all doing here?” Sapphire asks.

“We are all here to find you!” Quinn says, her eyes misty with emotion, along with the others.

“And you did,” she said, her tears flowing freely down her cheeks. Her smile turns somber. “Annabeth did this!”

“Annabeth was Petulah, and may I put the emphasis on WAS!” Pony says with a smile as he holds Sapphire again.

“Your sister incinerated her in the tower! It was bloody brilliant,” Cashton says.

“You made a convincing Hades!” Jexis says, laughing.

“Me? You were a triumphant Medusa!” Cashton replies. “Unbelievable… pure magic, your plan to lure her by offering her final revenge against us, and with promise of a crown! How could she refuse?”

“Greater is He who lives in me, than he who lives in the world,” Jexis says.

“What exactly are you two referring to?” Romulus asks, his interest piqued.

“Father, Cashton and I will fill you in on the details. Until then let’s go home,” Jexis says.

“But, I’m confused… Annabeth was Petulah?” Sapphire asks, trying to make sense of it all.

“You will love this story!” Pony says.

Quinn says, “Sapphire, what Pony has done is extraordinary. He found your ring at the base of the dark transit, and courageously took the transit, bringing him here. We followed him, leading us here too.”

Pony takes the ring from his pocket and slips it back on her finger. He kisses her on the forehead.

“I knew you would find the ring, and find me,” Sapphire says.

“Pony and Chamous saved the professor and me from the clutches of the Black Witch,” Tera tells her.

“Our battle was victorious, although there was loss of life. Keefe, Chamous, Pony and our father fought bravely. But wait, our Quest is not complete!” Quinn says.

"She is right," Sapphire says. "Hold on, I want to introduce you to a family."

She motions to Phillip Culpeper and he drives the wagon over to them.

"This is Phillip Culpeper. He saved my life. This is his wife and their two children, Martha and Millicent. Millicent was quite sick, but she is much better now."

The fair haired little girl is wrapped in white blankets, her cheeks rosy again.

"May I hold her once more?" Sapphire asks, reaching her arms to Mrs. Culpeper, who gladly allows her to hold Millicent again.

Dr. Culpeper touches Sapphire's cheek.

"Sapphire is our angel, our miracle--Sapphire, the merciful," Dr. Culpeper says.

Quinn beams with love and pride for the confident young woman with infinite abilities.

"Sapphire has made many sacrifices to complete her Quest. Some of us are here because of her. Many lives have been saved today from poison, illness or fire. Some will contribute to our world in extraordinary ways. We are only beginning to grasp the importance of this Quest," says Quinn.

"Quinn, look," Sapphire says, looking to the child. She gently unfolds the child's blankets. Glowing from within the blanket, safely tucked next to Millicent, lies a brilliant, miraculous Fidesorb.

Quinn gasps, along with everyone in the group.

"Your merciful heart guided us all here, Sapphire! One sick little girl hundreds of years ago brought us to this place and time," Quinn says, looking to each of them.

"The Lion Malachi prepared me for this with the pomander, knowing it would save little Millicent, and even what Petulah had planned for us," Sapphire says. Their Quest was finally becoming clear to her.

"Malachi knew Petulah would be capable of anything to get her revenge. He already had the plan in place," Romulus says.

"Even with the best laid plan, Guardians would need great faith to accept the Quest and the courage to see it through. And because we acted in faith, in spite of our doubt, we've recovered another Fidesorb," Quinn says with gratitude.

Romulus offers the Circle of Sun shield to Quinn to lay the Fidesorb upon. Chamous and Tera, the professor and Keefe, Pony and Sapphire observe the glowing orb representing the light of the world. Each of them grasps the round shield firmly and offers it up to the heavens. The orb rises slowly from the shield. It levitates in the smoky air before moving up through to the clear night sky, dotted with thousands of twinkling stars. When they can no longer see it, they look to one another with gratitude and love. No words would serve this moment. Each continues to grip the shield, not wanting to let it go; nor the power they feel as guardians of the Circle of Sun.

The End

AUTHOR KIM LUKE

Author Kim Luke once had to help a customer at her family Christmas tree farm chop down a fresh tree in a business suit and heels. She was comfortable in that attire, the "uniform" of her marketing profession. She was not as comfortable as a Christmas tree farmer, but she's learned to be supportive in this family endeavor. The tree farm is located in Missouri, the setting for both of Kim's two novels in her Circle of Sun series.

A literature major in college, Luke has always enjoyed a good story and loves using her imagination. Of her many passions, writing has been with her the longest. She finds it pure joy, like eating a delicious piece of cheesecake. The cornerstones in her life are her faith and family.

Kim and husband Bob are blessed with three children, incredible in-laws and three grandchildren. The Lukes live with their two Alaskan Malamute dogs on a beautiful 20 acre farm, where they indulge in a love of books, coffee, wine and positive thinkers.

You can connect with Kim at www.kimlukeauthor.com, on Facebook at Circle of Sun or on Twitter, @kimluke. She is also a Goodreads author.

Glossary for Black Inferno

Apalacid- (a pal' a sid)- Ring worn by the Polaris of the Circle of Sun.

Fidesorb- (fied' us orb)- Orb of light representing faith on earth.

Madowent- (mad' o went)- Sacred cave of the Circle of Sun in Nadellawick.

Regions or seasons in Circle of Sun:
Aderlucia (Add er loo' sha)
Fezalopia (Fez a low' pia)
Hudovistan (Hu do' vis tan)
Moriah (Mo ri' a)
Nadellawick (Na dell' a wik)
Ranaconda (ran a con' da)
Sigartoff (sig' er toff)

Circle of Sun Hierarchy

Archangel Michael

Knights

Pathfinders

Sleepers

41142403R00126

Made in the USA
Lexington, KY
30 April 2015